SOFT LAUNCH

SOFT LAUNCH

A Coming-of-Adulthood Novel

SARAH VACCHIANO

Little a

This is a work of fiction. Names, characters, organizations, places, events, and incidents are either products of the author's imagination or are used fictitiously. Otherwise, any resemblance to actual persons, living or dead, is purely coincidental.

Published by Little A, New York

www.apub.com

EU product safety contact:
Amazon Media EU S. à r.l.
38, avenue John F. Kennedy, L-1855 Luxembourg
amazonpublishing-gpsr@amazon.com

ISBN-13: 9781662536908 (hardcover)
ISBN-13: 9781662536885 (paperback)
ISBN-13: 9781662536892 (digital)

Cover illustration and design by Philip Pascuzzo

Printed in the United States of America
First edition

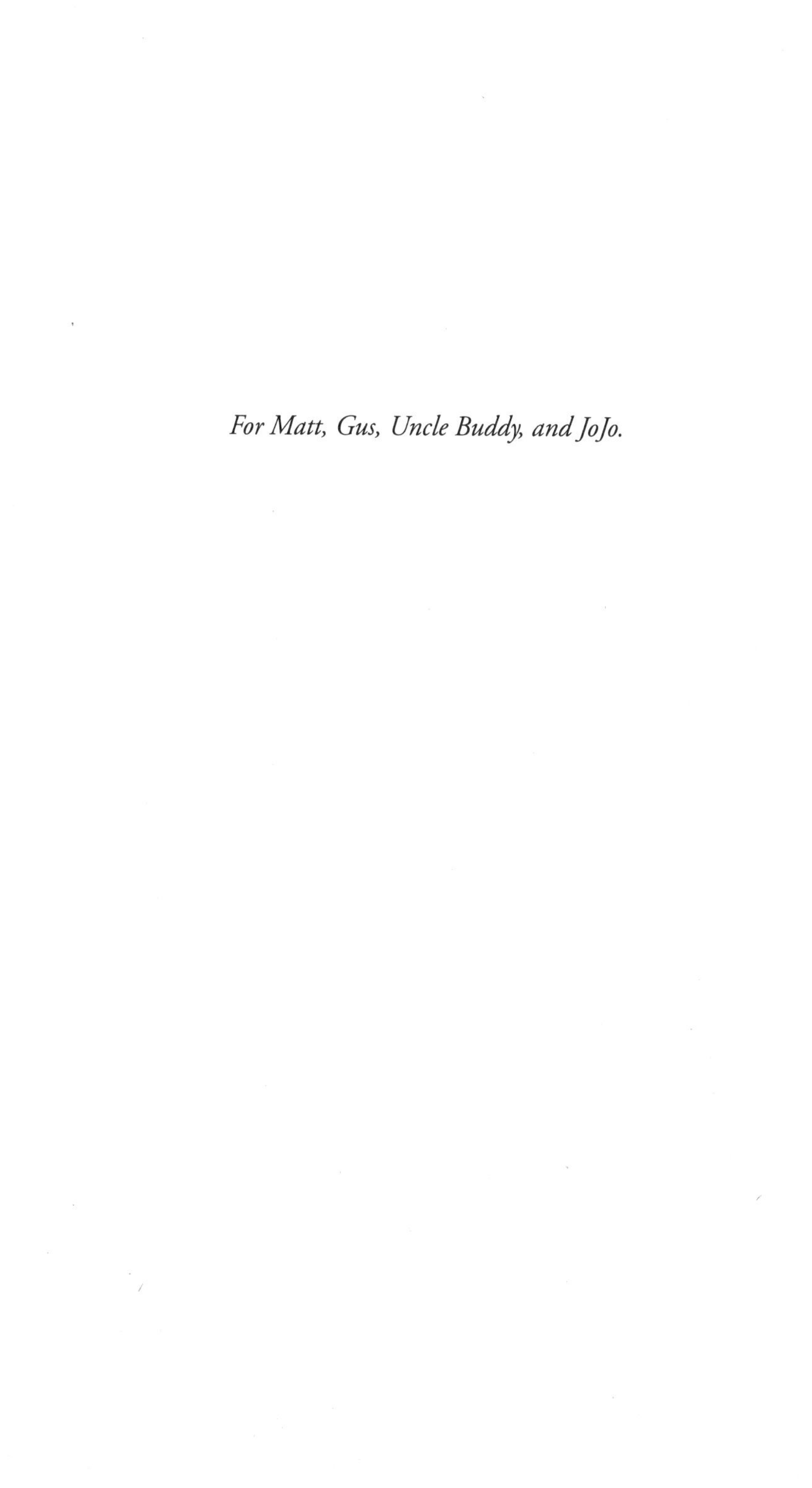

For Matt, Gus, Uncle Buddy, and JoJo.

Chapter One

I'd never been inside a courthouse—not during three years of law school, not until that day. At first, I barely gave it a second thought. With two weeks until the bar exam, I was surviving on turkey sandwiches and Red Bull, studying twelve hours a day. I didn't bother with makeup or even a second glance in the mirror. This was nothing more than a quick errand.

The clerk finalized everything in under a minute, handing me the papers Ben and I would need to sign. I stepped back into the July heat, my mind already back to studying. And then I saw it: *Samantha DeFiore, Plaintiff, v. Benjamin Walker, Defendant.*

I got in my car, rolled down the window, and breathed out hot, humid air.

The voice in my head repeated, *You can't send that to him. You can't send that to him.*

I couldn't read that word again.

Defendant.

I spun the AC to full blast and bent forward, taking shallow breaths. I needed to get my shit together.

I got out of the car and walked unsteadily across the street to Vin Rouge, a wine bar I knew well from late nights at Georgetown Law but somehow never realized was next to the courthouse.

The ambience was different in the afternoon. It was barely three o'clock, and I was the only patron.

I ordered a bottle of rosé on special, maniacally flipping through last week's issue of *The Hollywood Reporter*, waiting for the numbness I was chasing to kick in. Wishing the wine weren't so sweet.

At some point, I noticed the bottle was less than a glass away from empty, and my buzz weakened.

The words *I choose you* echoed in my head, the inscription on the white gold wedding band I'd custom-ordered from his parents' jeweler. I had meant every word of it. There was a time when I had chosen Ben.

I felt my face flush as I noticed Matt, the bartender, drying chalice-size glasses behind the bar.

It had been a month since I'd come in for a late-night "study break" and closed down the bar listening to him talk about twentieth-century American poetry and telling him all about the bright future waiting for me in New York.

I've finally lost the thread, I thought. *Divorcing my husband, drunk at four o'clock when I should be studying for the only exam that could make or break my career.*

I didn't know how other twenty-nine-year-olds handled getting divorced, but this no longer felt graceful.

"Hey there. What're we drinking?"

I turned the label of the bottle to face him. He squinted. "White zinfandel?"

I forced a smile. "Yeah. The new guy upsold me . . . or downsold, I guess. Said it was his favorite rosé. Half price."

He nodded, feigning approval. "Looks like you've been here for a little bit. You got the pre–happy hour, happy hour special." He winked. "Want me to switch it out? Something French? I'll do it for the same price. Just for you."

Just for you.

I let the words float in the air for a moment, then shook my head. I hadn't earned this kindness.

"No, it's okay. I chose it. Sometimes a girl has to stick it out."

I immediately wished I didn't sound so cynical.

It had been a year since I'd told Ben I didn't want to spend my life with him anymore. It was the hardest decision I'd ever made, and it took years to make it.

When I finally knew it was the right choice, the internal script I wrote for myself felt airtight: I'd married too young, before I understood how much life waited on the other side of that choice—a life that didn't match the one Ben wanted. Staying would only end up hurting him more. He'd be happy again. All of this would fade to a slight blemish in his otherwise beautiful life. He'd find someone else, and our starter marriage would be an accessory detail in *her* love story. I imagined her gushing to her girlfriends, *He was married once in his twenties, but it didn't work out.* They wouldn't believe someone could have left him, the perfect man. And for her, he would be. Just like he had once been for me.

I watched Matt uncork a bottle that was a lighter shade of pink. He poured a sip into a new glass, resting it gingerly in front of me.

"Come on, Sam. No one should be forced to drink wine they don't like."

I smiled. "My brewing hangover thanks you."

"Everything okay? Is this the two-weeks-before-the-bar meltdown? I see it every summer, and I promise you: They all pass. Far as I know, at least. But I guess you never hear from the ones who don't."

I patted the top of the bar-prep book and took a sip. "Multitasking. And thanks, this one doesn't taste like a cupcake."

He laughed. "You're not really worried about passing, are you? It'll be done before you know it. One and done."

Kind of like my marriage. I flinched at the thought.

He leaned over and picked up the book. "Seriously, though. If it's a bottle-of-wine-at-three-p.m. kind of day, let it be that kind of day. Don't force it. Besides, look at how much ground you've covered."

He flipped through and landed on the divorce papers.

I couldn't tell if he had seen them, but he quickly shut the book and set it back down.

"Just give yourself a break, ya know?"

By this point I was too buzzed to be embarrassed.

I felt my phone vibrate, and we both looked grateful for the distraction.

"Hey," I answered sheepishly as a familiar British accent barreled through the phone.

"Where are you? You're more than twenty minutes late."

Fuck. I completely blanked on our standing 4:30 p.m. run.

"Em, I'm . . . shit. Sorry."

"You're not coming? Did something happen?" She paused. "Did everything go okay at the courthouse?"

I bit my lip. "It was fine . . . I mean, it's pretty much done."

I searched for the right way to say what had really happened, how seeing the word *defendant* next to Ben's name had triggered an avalanche of guilt.

"I filed the papers and freaked out. I'm at Vin Rouge. I've been here for a while."

I heard Emilie sigh, imagined her looking down at her sports watch, jogging in place, her long brown hair tied tightly in a high ponytail, weighing whether to quickly run the trail or come meet me. Emilie's baseline was a combination of irritation and exaggerated apathy. Only a few of us knew how hard she worked to cultivate effortless perfection, or how much she actually loved being a dead ringer for Zoe Saldaña. Her dream was to be a Supreme Court justice by forty, and no one doubted she would do it.

"I'll be there in twenty."

Unsure if that was what I really wanted but too tipsy to decide, I took a dramatic sip of Matt's charity wine and rubbed my right temple. I could feel dehydration overtaking both sides of my brain. I asked for a glass of water and forced myself to sip it until she arrived. I slipped a pair of sunglasses on my face and tried not to cry.

I met Emilie in law school, just after Ben moved out. I'd told him I was leaving a few weeks before, and the air in our spacious DC townhouse had become so heavy it felt like we were swimming.

I'd started pulling late nights in the library just to have an excuse to be out. One night I looked over and saw Emilie sitting with another guy in our class. Neither of them studying. I envied them. I felt worn down from the weight of robbing someone of a marriage. I remember thinking that Emilie and the Scottish international student I would learn was named Connor couldn't possibly coexist in my emotionally fraught sphere. He waved me over, and the three of us became fast friends. Emilie was from London and Connor was from Edinburgh, and both seemed to have a European fascination with the idea of a starter marriage.

Matt reappeared as Emilie slipped wordlessly into the seat next to me.

"Glass of wine?"

She gave him an exasperated look as we sat in silence for a few seconds.

"I'm still not sure what happened. You got upset because you filed? You've been totally antiseptic about this entire thing until now."

She motioned to the bottle of wine next to the prep book. "And now this? Come on, Sam, you look just a little bit silly wearing those in here."

I took the sunglasses off in wordless compliance.

She flinched. "Okay, put them back on." She waved over to Matt. "We're going to grab that corner table in the back. Can I just carry this stuff over?"

He nodded, purposefully avoiding my eyes.

She took the water glass in one hand and the study book in the other. "I know the library is getting stale, but this really isn't the time to fall apart."

I rolled my eyes. "Is there ever a good time?"

We sat down, and she set the water in front of me. "Are you going to tell me what happened? Or should I have just gone for a run?"

I felt tears coming and readjusted the sunglasses.

"I can't really explain it. I got to the courthouse, and everything was fine. And then they gave me the papers, and then I left . . . and then I *saw* the papers. And honestly, I don't think I can live with myself." My voice broke.

"You 'saw' the papers? Aren't they just standard divorce papers?"

"I mean, I guess . . . This is my first divorce, you know."

I put my head in my hands. "Not that it's a huge surprise. Both my parents have been married twice."

"A lot of parents are divorced. That doesn't mean anything."

"But theirs was ugly. A total legal marathon."

She looked around the empty bar. "You can feel better then. This is as ugly as yours gets."

I pulled out the papers and pointed to the caption. "I have to send *this* to Ben."

I searched her face for validation, but she was unmoved.

"What am I looking for?"

I felt irrationally frustrated. "How can I file a *legal* document that calls Ben the same fucking thing as someone accused of murder?"

Emilie looked closer, lip-reading the caption. "Oh. Defendant."

I covered my eyes. "Once was enough."

She impatiently slid the papers back into the book. "I wasn't going to repeat it."

I rested my head on top of my forearm, the wooden table cool against my skin. I could feel her impatience radiating across me.

"*You* left *him*. So you're the plaintiff."

"That's not the point."

"What is the point then? It's barely five p.m., and you're drowning in wine. I'm not saying that this isn't traumatic, but you haven't even batted an eye until today. I haven't seen you cry once over this."

"Right. I don't think that's normal. I don't think I let myself process how bad I feel. I've been in denial about ruining someone else's life."

She shot me an irritated look. "Listen. It's not that I don't think you have a good reason to feel miserable. You're divorced, you're pushing thirty, and you're two weeks away from taking the bar, which might be the worst part if you keep this up. Do I think you could have timed everything better? Yes. I think this whole thing should have taken a back seat to everything else in your life right now. But now you have to be a big girl, send the papers to Ben, and move on. You made the right choice *for you*. You can unpack these emotions after you pass the bar."

I nodded, or at least I think I did. The words blurred in my head—*divorced, pushing thirty, move on*. She wasn't wrong. But it suddenly felt like I'd been emotionally stripped bare, as if every nerve in my body had been dragged to the surface.

Chapter Two

Three weeks later, the Amtrak train lurched to a stop as the person in the window seat shoved past me. I instinctively reached for my handbag, then scanned the overhead compartment for the two suitcases that held everything from my old life.

I waded through Penn Station toward the escalator up to Eighth Avenue, the August air hitting like a wet sponge.

I had a week to find an apartment before starting as a first-year associate at Abramson & Klein. Jessica, my college roommate who traveled weekly to Copenhagen for work, offered her pullout couch in Brooklyn until I found a place. Emilie and Connor were separately spending time in Europe before starting their jobs in New York, and the city felt more solitary than I expected.

After a few long days of schlepping from building to building and collapsing onto Jessica's couch each night, I was convinced I'd never find a place to live. I cycled through four different brokers in five days, each with apartments more underwhelming than the last. I hadn't planned to live in Brooklyn, but out of desperation I almost settled for a studio in Jessica's building where every window faced a brick wall.

Once I started working, I wouldn't have any time to hunt for an apartment. With less than forty-eight hours until I started at the firm, I started desperately trolling Craigslist. It was impossible to tell which postings were legitimate. I kept thinking about the comfort of the fully renovated, cookie-cutter townhouse Ben and I had shared in the quiet suburbs of DC.

On the sixth day of sweating profusely between showings, I collapsed onto a hot bench in Madison Square Park and pulled up Facebook Marketplace on my phone to see if there were any viable rentals.

Free for a drink tonight babe?

There was so much condensation on the screen, I almost didn't see the text come in. I exhaled warm air. I hadn't even started working, and the city was kicking the shit out of me.

I met Caroline the first summer I interned in the city through a mutual friend I went to college with at the University of Virginia.

Caroline grew up in Iowa and was recruited by Goldman Sachs out of Yale. Now barely thirty and a senior vice president in the risk management division, she was everything people imagine about women in New York: elegant, independent, fiercely ambitious, and always dating the wrong guy.

We made a plan to meet at Wilfie & Nell in the West Village.

"Try the spicy agave margarita," she said as I fanned myself with the menu. "We need to get you used to real cocktails."

"I'm going to need more than one to shake off this week. I'm going to be homeless soon."

"What's your budget?"

I never wanted to be asked that again.

"I'm only looking for a studio. I was hoping to keep it under $2,000, but I could go up to $2,500."

I could never tell my parents how much I'd be paying to rent an apartment in New York. I wasn't raised to spend money like that. They still had no idea how much I'd borrowed for law school.

Caroline clicked her tongue as she scrolled through her phone. "So, my neighbor in 5E just got engaged and is moving to San Francisco. It's the same layout as my studio. Let me text her."

I'd pretty much lost all hope, but this was starting to feel like it could turn into one of those magic New York stories. The rumored *only* way to find an amazing apartment: have a friend like Caroline.

"Do you know how much she pays?" I was already mentally reshuffling my finances to make it work.

"No, but I pay $2,500."

I held my breath as she texted her neighbor. Between the tequila and the prospect of finding an apartment *in the West Village*, I barely heard anything else until her phone buzzed.

"Okay—she says we can come by tomorrow, and she'll put in a good word with the landlord."

"Holy shit."

"How're you feeling about the rest of it?"

"I honestly feel like being a lawyer is going to be cake compared to finding a place to live." I dabbed the last beads of sweat off my upper lip. "I still have to get my hair trimmed. And buy an entire lawyer wardrobe. You know, the small stuff."

"I'll text you the number for my hair salon on Thompson Street. And for the rest, Theory is all you need."

"Is that a school of thought or a clothing store?"

"It's J.Crew for former versions of ourselves."

~

I left Jessica's apartment the next morning and mapped the closest subway line to the Meatpacking District. Half an hour later, I found Theory's flagship store on the corner of Greenwich and Gansevoort.

The air-conditioning hit me like an IV. A stylishly dressed male holding a mini Evian took one look at me and clicked his tongue.

"Oh, honey. The world is literally burning to the ground, and we're all just walking around trying to make it out alive." He handed me the water. "But I'm here to hydrate you. What are we looking for today?"

"Thanks—I start a new job on Monday, and I just need a few things. Basics."

He nodded knowingly. "You came to the right place. What kind of job? Smart casual? Bit stuffier?"

"A law firm."

He nodded knowingly as he gave a long once-over. "Right. Let's see . . . You're probably an extra small on top, and I'm thinking a four for slacks. Maybe a six, depending on the cut. Curves are a blessing and a curse. Size 2 in a dress. Hold tight and just sip that water, sweetie. We'll get this done."

I pressed my palms together appreciatively.

I pulled out a navy blazer from the closest display, absentmindedly flipping the tag. I instinctually blinked. I wasn't in J.Crew anymore.

Is it crazy to spend $600 on a blazer? I texted Emilie.

I could see her immediately typing.

You're about to make $200,000 a year. Time to transition the Georgetown Law t-shirts to pajamas.

I knew my credit card bill would keep skyrocketing until I got my first paycheck. Even with my split from selling the townhome I owned with Ben, I was going to be one of those people who used their year-end bonus to pay off at least one maxed-out card.

I charged $2,000 at Theory, deeply unsettled when everything fit into two light bags.

Caroline's building was a short seven blocks away. I balanced the bags on one arm, iPhone in hand, and headed down the iconic cobblestone streets, past the trendy weekend brunch crowd and private brownstone driveways. In my loose-fitting white shorts and oversized tank top, I felt like the worst-dressed extra in *Sex and the City*.

Five minutes later, I walked up to an elegant café with a few tables nestled under an awning. Caroline emerged ten seconds later, pulling me in for a hug.

"That's my building," she pointed across the street, grabbing the Theory bags. "Oh, you did good! Let's drop this stuff, and we can pop over to 5E."

It was the most charming corner in the city.

All week I'd been running around ragged, a girl from the middle of Virginia, hoping to shed my identity as a suburban DC housewife. Never in a million years had I believed there was a chance of finding an apartment here.

My heart was racing as Caroline unlocked the building. She pointed behind us to a group of tourists taking pictures of a brownstone across the street.

"That was Carrie Bradshaw's apartment."

As soon as we walked into apartment 5E, I knew I'd do anything to make it mine. Even in its imperfections, it was everything I'd dreamed about. Tiny but cozy, with a galley kitchen that had just enough room to open the refrigerator. It was tastefully outdated in that classic prewar style, with original wainscoting and two oversized windows that looked out over treetops and brownstone rooftops.

Caroline sent a personal reference letter to the landlord that afternoon, and I signed the lease the next day.

I felt dangerously lucky. If karma was really a thing, leaving Ben for a new life should have meant luck wasn't in the cards. But the apartment was mine. I'd be able to move in the weekend after I started working. Luckily, Jessica was in Europe for the week, so we wouldn't be on top of each other.

Sunday night, I pulled out the navy Theory dress I'd chosen and draped it over the back of a chair, then rummaged through the closet for the handheld steamer Jessica swore was back there somewhere. I felt overwhelmed by how much had happened in the last few weeks. If leaving Ben meant trading in his happiness for mine, I had to get it right this time.

Chapter Three

I decided to become a lawyer when I was in fourth grade. I read *To Kill a Mockingbird* and felt a kinship with Scout and a deep admiration for Atticus Finch. I was a pleaser, and it seemed like being a lawyer meant always doing the right thing.

That same year, I was cast as Orphan Annie in a school production. The experience was like a drug. I started auditioning for anything I could. My entire identity became entangled in fictional characters from plays and musicals. When I was ten, I went all out for the role of Maria in the town production of *West Side Story*. I wanted it so badly that I believed my love for the role transcended age (the casting director disagreed).

Performing made me feel closer to the world I wanted to be part of, far from a small town and an unhappy homelife. My parents separated for the first time when I was thirteen, then flip-flopped for the next five years, meaning my brother Artie and I spent middle and high school bouncing between them.

The instability at home drove me deeper into theater. I was devastated when my parents only let me apply to state schools. I ended up at the University of Virginia with a plan: If I could hack college theater, I would secretly apply for drama scholarships in New York. I was one of two freshmen cast as nonspeaking fairies in the campus production of *A Midsummer Night's Dream*. My dorm was covered in application materials for the American Academy of Dramatic Arts. My essays were spell-checked, reference letters were written, scholarship applications were done.

At the end of spring semester, my parents' marathon divorce finally came to a head, and life changed dramatically. Litigating a divorce for half a decade had drained their financial resources. Neither one was happy with the outcome. It was the end of "supported" life as I knew it. I'd taken on moderate student loans my freshman year, but my living expenses and a large part of my in-state tuition had been covered.

I needed a job to support myself if I wanted to stay in school. I went from wide-eyed college student to pragmatic survivalist. I withdrew my drama school application and switched my major to political science. I found a full-time summer job as a nanny, and when the fall semester started, I condensed my course schedule to two days a week so I could nanny the other three. I waitressed in between.

The toxicity from my parents' divorce felt boundless. Everything had become muted. Colors. Emotions. Motivation. Even my ambition.

Then, I met Ben.

Ben was friends with my freshman roommate's older brother, who had just graduated from MIT and moved back to DC. We met when I tagged along to her family's house over fall break. He got my number, and before long, we were talking on the phone a few nights a week. I was nineteen, and he was twenty-four. I wasn't very worldly, and he felt decades older.

I quickly grew attached to our conversations. He was working as a data analyst for the International Monetary Fund, which made him a big fish compared to the microscopic world I came from. He read David Foster Wallace and knew everything about history and politics. He'd traveled to Egypt and Iceland and New Zealand. I'd barely been outside of Virginia.

Our first date was at an Ethiopian restaurant close to campus. It felt very culturally sophisticated. And after all the time spent on the phone, the conversation seemed effortless.

"You've never even been on a *small* plane? Not even one of those regional ones that flies out of airports with one landing strip?"

I shook my head. "And now the thought of flying terrifies me," I said, eyeing the platter of fermented flatbread.

"Do you have a passport?"

"Not yet," I said, my nose tingling from the unexpected taste of vinegar. "But I'd like to get one," I added quickly.

He leaned back and took me in, like I was a tabula rasa in the form of a girl who needed someone to make her world bigger.

"Well then, let's book your first flight."

There was a kindness—and a calmness—to Ben that I responded to. Despite our different upbringings, he seemed to get me. His intellectual curiosity notwithstanding, he had a profound appreciation for the simple things. He came from a tight-knit family. I had grown up with a dysfunction that made a happy family life feel just out of reach. Ben gave me the chance to build a life with someone who would quickly become the antidote to the instability I'd grown up with.

By the end of that semester, even though we were separated by distance, Ben and I were seeing each other seriously. He would drive the two hours down to UVA, and we'd spend our weekends visiting nearby wineries or camping in the Blue Ridge Mountains. I took a full course load during the summers so I could graduate a semester early, even though Ben wanted me to take an internship in DC to be closer to him. I was focused on the long game, still driven by the urgency that I'd felt since childhood to make something of my life.

I finished my last exam on a Friday and started a job the following Monday at a nondescript marketing agency in Arlington. We moved in together, and our lives fell into a comfortable routine. I'd found a partner.

Being with Ben grounded me in a way I'd never felt before. A year later, I told him I wanted to get married. I was so resolute, no one second-guessed me.

Chapter Four

I woke up Monday morning jittery with excitement. I'd slept with the window open, and it felt like fall inside Jessica's fifth-floor apartment.

I threw on gym clothes and sneakers and walked to the corner bodega for coffee before walking west to the Brooklyn Heights Promenade. I reached the water and stood very still, absorbing the shape of Manhattan, the only way to really take it all in, with a river in between. In a matter of hours, I'd be another person in the city, rushing to the office, on my way to making it all happen. I felt a million years away from the first time I wondered if my marriage would survive law school.

In fairness, the person Ben married hadn't known she was actually going to law school. But the more content he became, the more restless I felt. I started to wonder what I would be doing with my life if I hadn't gotten married when I was twenty-two.

We bought a suburban, open-concept townhouse and quickly settled into day-to-day life just outside of DC. We had our routine, our favorite restaurants, all of it. Ben made more money than me, but we were building a comfortable life. Only, the more our lives "improved," the unhappier I felt. I didn't have anything in common with our circle of friends, most of whom were Ben's friends on the cusp of parenthood. I couldn't stop thinking that I'd deserted the person I could have become.

A few years after we got married, a small art-house theater popped up close by. I started going to the movies alone while Ben watched sports. Most of the time, I was the only person there. It became a total guilty pleasure. He joked that if he didn't know better, he'd think I was having an affair.

I'd grown up obsessed with musicals and old movies, but I discovered a new love for independent film. It was bittersweet at first because I missed acting. I even looked up auditions for local theater productions but couldn't bring myself to go. That ship had sailed.

Still, I felt like I'd left something on the table.

I was disarmed by the honesty and ambition of filmmakers like Richard Linklater and Lisa Cholodenko. In between dodging Ben's TV shows and cleaning up dinner, I tucked myself away in our bedroom, researching ways to break into the film industry. I read reviews for every movie that premiered at Cannes and Sundance. I daydreamed about becoming someone who could champion emerging talent. I pored over bios of Hollywood's most powerful agents and executives, struck by how many had gone to law school.

That was how I discovered entertainment law. For the first time since my pivot away from acting, I knew what I wanted to do with my life.

A few weeks later, I came home with an LSAT prep book. I set it on the kitchen table and tried to gauge Ben's reaction.

"What's all this?" he asked, setting place mats down in the same spots we ate dinner every night.

"I've been thinking about law school," I said, grabbing plates.

"Huh," he responded. "Where?"

"Somewhere close by," I answered quickly. "George Washington, or maybe Georgetown, if I do well on the LSAT."

His face relaxed slightly.

It took six months and two tries, but I did well enough to apply to Georgetown. I was wait-listed before I got the much-anticipated admissions email three weeks before the fall semester started.

Ben and I took a trip to Lake Anna to celebrate. We'd been married for almost three years by then, and Ben had warmed to the idea of having a lawyer for a wife.

"Maybe I can finally be a stay-at-home dad," he said as he dipped a tortilla chip in salsa verde. We'd gone to a Mexican restaurant for lunch that Ben heard was good, and wouldn't it be fun to do tequila flights for lunch? But neither of us was a heavy drinker. I could count on one hand the number of times I had gotten drunk during our marriage, and our wedding wasn't even one of them.

I washed the second tequila shot down with sparkling water. "I totally get that women don't like when men feel threatened by their success and all that, but I'm still just not sure how I feel about the whole stay-at-home-dad thing," I admitted.

He told me about a coworker whose wife recently graduated from law school. They decided to start a family during her last year. It made good sense, he reported: She'd have the baby, take the bar exam, then start working when the baby was old enough to go to day care. At first I thought it was the tequila talking, but I quickly realized Ben was seriously floating the idea.

Our dissonant realities hit me like a punch in the nose.

All the nights I'd spent tucked away in our home office studying for the LSAT, falling more and more in love with the idea of becoming an entertainment lawyer, mulling over the pros and cons of living in New York versus LA—none of that mattered to Ben so long as I went to law school and started a family before I'd even started practicing.

The all-consuming intensity of law school kicked in overnight. I commuted to Georgetown and spent every waking minute studying. The nagging feeling about being unfulfilled in my marriage receded. Finding my footing as a law student required me to kick everything else to the back burner. Instead of torturing myself about my future with Ben, I forged ahead with my plan to excel academically and find every chance I could to break into entertainment law. I'd figure out the rest later.

Halfway through my first year, I brought up the idea of working in New York when I cautiously told Ben I wanted to spend the summer interning in the city.

"You mean we'd spend two months apart?" he asked.

"It's pretty routine to go away for summer internships," I explained nervously. "It would be with a top independent film company."

He finally looked up from the TV. "Are you saying you already have an offer?"

"A Georgetown alum is their general counsel. He came down a couple of months ago to talk to the Entertainment Law Society about what he does. I got his card and kept in touch. I had a phone interview last week, and he emailed me this morning."

He looked proud and distressed. "Wow . . . okay. What happened to that DC trademarks firm my friend told us about? It'd be way closer. You sure you want to go all the way to New York?"

"Trademarks and entertainment law aren't the same thing."

He looked sullen. I flopped down next to him on the couch and kissed his cheek. "We'll visit each other a lot. It'll fly by."

Ben only came to New York once to visit. By the time he visited, his presence felt like an intrusion. The internship was immersing me in a life I never could have imagined when I was shopping for cold cuts to pack his lunch. I was only responsible for myself. I rented a small room on the Lower East Side. Celebrities routinely came into the office for meetings. I was getting a preview of what life could be like. My world was becoming bigger.

I came back to DC as a second-year law student with an even clearer sense of what I wanted and what I didn't. I was already a different person from when I started.

That year, I felt confident enough academically to survey the social landscape and go to the Barrister's Ball—the law school prom—with a few friends. I'd asked Ben to come, but he wasn't in the mood, so I went solo. Some of the guys from class asked where my husband was. I was surprised they even knew I was married.

I had a blast that night. I drank sugary cocktails, danced with a guy from my Trademarks class, and—for the first time in a long while—felt young and untethered.

When I got home, Ben was in bed watching TV.

"You have fun?" he asked, too distracted by a *Seinfeld* rerun to look over in my direction.

I tipsily tried to make him jealous. "So much fun. Everyone wanted to dance and buy me drinks all night."

He chuckled. "That's all right. I know who you're coming home to." Something about the way he said it made me feel unsettled in a way I couldn't shake.

After four years of marriage, we were both guilty of letting romance fade. When we first bought our townhouse, we'd camp on the back patio and have sex to Dave Matthews. He would read aloud from his favorite books. Every experience felt new and exciting, because my world was just beginning. Now, we'd settled into a comfortable companionship.

I knew we were a ticking time bomb.

When I said I wanted to end our marriage just over a year later, he couldn't make sense of it. He thought we were happy. But what is happiness when you're in your twenties and you've barely experienced the world? Having someone to crawl into bed with and watch the same TV shows night after night? It was impossible to ignore that our visions of happily ever after didn't match up.

Chapter Five

I finished my coffee and walked back to Jessica's apartment, wanting to give myself enough time to figure out the subway from Brooklyn to the office. I showered and put on the Theory dress, then packed black pumps, my new employee paperwork, and a bottle of water into my Longchamp tote. I slid into the stylish pair of Tod's loafers Jessica told me to borrow for the commute and did a final once-over in the mirror. I still felt like Ben's wife pretending to be a New York lawyer.

The subway was overrun with men and women in suits. I finally found a seat after the train emptied at Wall Street, reading orientation emails until the train reached Forty-Second Street.

Abramson & Klein occupied floors forty-five to fifty of the MetLife Building, a glass-and-steel monument towering above Grand Central. The firm mainly hired from Harvard, Stanford, and Columbia, with a few recruits from less elite but still-prestigious schools who somehow made the cut. I was one of the lucky few. I'd cold emailed a partner who was a prominent Georgetown Law alum and was granted a courtesy interview. It was pure hustle; I had no connections.

Among the usual suspects of "white-shoe" law firms, A&K had a distinctive reputation for taking on high-profile cases with newsworthy clients, most of whom were titans of industry, from studio heads to college dropouts turned app inventors. The corporate lawyers closed deals that single-handedly moved Wall Street. I'd been warned by more than a few of my professors that even though it was one of the strongest choices in terms of reputation, the culture was cutthroat, and the hours were brutal.

The elevator opened to a receptionist who saw me coming a mile away. I stepped into the firm lobby, which was starkly decorated with splashes of expensive artwork and framed accolades.

"Samantha?"

Susan Klein, the firm's head of HR, was nearly six feet tall in heels, with short hair styled the way Demi Moore made famous in *Ghost*. Height aside, she had the presence of a woman who'd spent decades watching associates come and go or rise to partnership. She started her career overseeing the secretarial pool and was running HR twenty years later.

"Welcome. I'll show you to your office," she said crisply, guiding me back to the elevator. She put on tortoiseshell readers and looked down at the folder in her hand.

"Your employment file from last summer lists you as Samantha Walker." She glanced at me as the elevator door opened. "Congratulations, then."

I swallowed my pride and stepped confidently into the elevator. "Thank you."

I was prepared for everything except explaining my new last name.

We stopped in front of a door at the end of a long hallway. She paused to knock lightly, which confused me until I saw that the office had been converted into a shared space with two desks and a small partition in between.

"Charlie Bronstein, Samantha DeFiore. She starts today."

Susan pointed to my side of the office as she explained the firm had recently poached sixty partners and associates from a competing firm, and now first-year associates needed to double up.

He jumped up and shook my hand. "I heard you were starting today," he said with an approachable smile.

"Charlie was with us as a paralegal during law school and is one of the few to be offered an associate position. So I'm sure he'll be helpful in getting you up to speed."

She handed me a sealed manila envelope. "Here's the orientation schedule for your first week. If you have questions, you can set a time with my office."

She closed the door behind her. I was still clutching my Longchamp, floating uncomfortably in the middle of the room. My eyes landed on a sealed MacBook box sitting on my desk.

"First things first, I guess?" I said, trying to look like I wasn't surprised to be sharing an office.

"Oh yeah. Set that thing up first. It'll take all morning to get through the security prompts," he said.

"I knew I should have taken that cybersecurity class at Georgetown," I said half jokingly.

"Ah, a DC draft pick. That's refreshing."

I lifted the silver laptop out of the box. "What about you?"

"Fordham, but originally from outside Boston. Still not sure how I ended up here," he said good-naturedly. His dad was a history teacher, and his mom was a nurse. Most of his friends had gone to community college, but he went to Boston College. On a whim, he took the LSAT with his girlfriend their junior year. She got a 164, and he got a near-perfect 177.

"I actually got into Yale and Columbia, but Fordham gave me a partial scholarship," he said. "Less debt and law school in the city seemed like a no-brainer."

He moonlighted as a paralegal for A&K during his second and third years to cover living expenses, and the firm promised him a job if he passed the bar. Somehow, we'd landed in the same place, only I had a quarter million in student loans.

Charlie had started a week before me. "I know they like me, but I just want them to see me as an actual associate now, instead of a paralegal, you know?"

I nodded along, grateful to have an officemate. It somehow made everything feel less intimidating.

"We have tech training at 10:30, but after that I can take you down to the cafeteria and show you what's safe to eat. Almost everyone takes lunch back to their office. It's a real scene. Associates running into each other, too busy looking down at their BlackBerrys so they can race upstairs the second they get an important email. Luckily the food is decent, and the service is fast."

He clicked his pen. "What else can I tell you . . . oh. Make sure you take the billing tutorial sooner rather than later. They just started docking pay if you're late entering your time."

"Have you been put on any interesting cases yet?" I asked.

Charlie took off his glasses and I noticed one eye was greener than the other.

"So far, just one of the cases I worked on as a paralegal. It's been going for eight years. But I'm keeping an eye out for new ones. If you hear of anything . . ." He winked.

"Is the firm as competitive as everyone says? Is anyone trustworthy?"

Charlie shook his head. "Not even me."

"That's tough, given we're sharing an office."

He pointed to his monitor. "Tricks of the trade. Screen protector. I could be playing blackjack all day, and you'd never know. Even though we sit three feet away from each other."

"If you're playing blackjack all day, at least I won't have to worry about competing with you for cool cases."

He grinned. "All they told me was your name was Sam, and we'd spend every waking minute together for the next two years. I guess this is a bad time to tell you I don't know how to talk quietly on the phone."

A calendar alarm went off on Charlie's laptop.

"Tech training," he announced. "To be continued."

~

The first week at the firm was a blur of learning how to track and enter time, reserve a conference room for clients, and navigate the unspoken rules of office life. We were being given the tools to succeed, but it was up to us to find enough work to meet the lofty requirement of twenty-five hundred billable hours a year, which meant billing at least ten hours of actual work Monday through Friday and multiple hours most weekends.

"It's like the best and worst system," Charlie said Thursday afternoon at Hatsuhana, the sushi bar around the corner from the office. After three days of orientation lunches catered by the firm, I was ready to be outside in the middle of the day. "No one is going to come in and make sure we're billing enough time. You have to be focused and direct. Know what type of work you're interested in, and go find it. You want to defend finance guys when the SEC is on their ass? Figure out which partners bring in those clients. Like Rich Kepler. Represent producers who are getting sued, Eddie Kaufman. But the Eddies and the Riches of the firm are literally being stalked by associates all day long. So you have to be tactically aggressive."

"Eddie Kaufman is the reason I'm here," I admitted, feeling self-conscious. Charlie had probably watched dozens of associates try to get on Eddie's radar in his paralegal days.

"Get ready to cut in on a very long line. It can be done, but you have to get in there."

"I know. Even if it doesn't happen right away, I can be patient. I've read every single article about him, going back to his prosecutor days."

Eddie Kaufman was a Greenwich Village kid whose later life looked nothing like the early years working in his parents' drugstore on Mott Street. He'd gotten a full ride to Harvard, studied political science, then worked full-time to support himself through Columbia Law. He was one of the only graduates recruited to join the US Attorney's Office as a prosecutor right out of law school. A chance meeting with the great poet Bob Dylan early in his career prompted a pivot to music, and thirty years later, he was New York's most high-powered entertainment lawyer.

I patiently waited while Charlie finished chewing the handroll he had taken in one bite.

"When did you know you wanted to be a lawyer?"

I bit the tip of my chopstick. "Don't laugh. After I read *To Kill a Mockingbird*. When I was nine."

"I hope you put that in your cover letters."

"And all my application essays."

"Obviously."

"What about you?"

"You can't laugh either."

"I swear."

"Josh Lyman."

"From *The West Wing*?"

"Oh yeah."

"Does that mean you want to go into politics eventually?"

"Social justice work. Maybe immigration or prison reform."

"Oh, the easy stuff."

"Yup. I'm just putting in a few years in Big Law so I can pay off my student loans. Then I'll burden myself again with poverty-level wages."

"Seems like a solid game plan."

He checked his watch, then waved for the check.

"Okay. I have an insider tip, but I'm *only* giving it to you because I think the movie business is a dying industry, which means we're not competing for work. Seriously. Anyone who sinks millions into a terrible business model shouldn't be bailed out."

"Hit me."

He leaned in. "Every Thursday, the paralegals get a list of new clients and the partners who brought them in. There's usually a one-line description of what the matters are about too. Lena leaves it in my mailbox. She's the supervising paralegal. It's only supposed to be for them, so if I share it with you, you gotta keep it confidential. But we can look at it together in our office if you want."

He half jokingly looked over his shoulder. "It's not like we're *really* gaming the system—you still have to fish out which senior associates are doing the heavy lifting for partners in terms of how they staff the case, that kinda thing . . . but it just gives you a little lead time to get there first. We can see what looks good and come up with a game plan."

"Why are you being so nice to me? Even if you're not competing with me for entertainment stuff—what's your angle?"

He shrugged. "I worked with a lot of associates when I was a paralegal, and you seem different. You admitted *To Kill a Mockingbird* made you want to be a lawyer. It takes balls to be that cliché."

"Okay, Aaron Sorkin."

He grinned. "Everyone needs a partner in crime, especially in this place. Officemates unite, or something cheesy like that."

~

We called them Thank You Thursdays. Lena put the list in Charlie's mailbox at 9 a.m. We'd meet at Joe's Coffee in Grand Central on the way in, then swing by the mail room before heading to our office to divide and conquer.

The first few lists had more matters Charlie was interested in than I was. While I kept plotting a way to get on Eddie Kaufman's radar, I tried to set meetings with senior associates who worked with him. It was even harder than I thought. He either worked with one or two associates on most cases or handled them solo. He also spent a lot of time in Los Angeles, which made it more difficult because when he needed to staff a matter, he only needed LA people. It was starting to feel like I needed to cast a wider net and find work outside of the entertainment practice. Luckily, the firm gave new associates six weeks to ramp up before the billable-hour requirement kicked in, but the end of the grace period was hurtling toward me. I couldn't keep spinning my wheels.

On the fourth Thank You Thursday, I complained to Charlie as we walked back from Joe's.

"I'm thinking of reaching out to the Intellectual Property group to get on some copyright cases. At least that wouldn't feel like a total failure. Copyright is kind of in the realm, right?"

He shook his head. "Nope. Maybe take on a copyright case just to get some hours in, but it's way too soon to give up."

He pushed the elevator button and grinned. "Besides, we got the list. Something is bound to turn up on there. You just need one little break, and you'll be golden."

Charlie closed the office door behind us. "Damn, there's six pages this week! Here, take the first four. I have a good feeling about those."

"Here goes," I said hopefully.

There were four new Eddie Kaufman matters on the first and second pages alone.

"This is interesting," I said cautiously. "It's a pro bono matter for Film at Lincoln Center. I didn't even know someone like Eddie did pro bono."

Charlie smirked. "He probably has associates do it all. Could be cool, though. Work with Eddie *and* do something good for the world. Besides, not a lot of associates want to do pro bono because the firm only lets you bill half your time. So you might actually have a shot. Maybe you should email Patricia."

He explained Patricia was Eddie's longtime assistant who notoriously scheduled his entire life.

"And say, 'Hey, I'm dying to work with Eddie and willing to only bill half my time to do it'?"

"We can do a little recon on the Lincoln Center thing. I'm sure it's some kind of relationship, and he's doing it for optics or whatever."

I couldn't have dreamed up a more perfect opportunity. "Film at Lincoln Center puts on the New York Film Festival," I explained. "The biggest filmmakers in the world screen their movies there. Everyone from Ingmar Bergman to the Coen brothers . . . Godard, Truffaut, Kurosawa, Tarantino. Absolutely insane."

Charlie nodded. "I've heard of at least two of those names."

Through a combination of Google and Charlie's paralegal moles, we learned that Eddie had recently become a board member of Film at Lincoln Center. Beyond that, no one seemed to know what the case was about. I just needed an in so I could prove myself.

Chapter Six

Later, I met Emilie and Connor at a martini bar downtown. Emilie had just started at a boutique litigation firm that was ranked the top appeals firm in the country. Connor ditched law entirely and was working for a private equity firm known for buying distressed companies.

"What can I say. I'm just really good at finding diamonds in the rough," Connor responded when we asked him how it was going, his Scottish accent in full force from having just been home.

Emilie gave him a playful punch. "Does that also apply to dating?"

Connor raised his glass. "Time will tell, ladies. Even the cringiest chat-up lines roll off with an accent," he said as we toasted for the fourth time in ten minutes. I was so happy they were finally in New York.

Connor was living in Williamsburg with two other friends from Edinburgh.

"Just come for the view. It's insane. Really. It's worth the stench of beer and sweat. Honestly, you won't regret it."

Emilie made a face. "I need a couple of months before I can psych myself up for a Brooklyn frat house."

"Have you even left Manhattan since we got here?" I asked.

She gave me a look. "This is the first time I've left the West Side. So, no."

"Right. When do we get to see mum and dad's little slice of America?" he asked.

Emilie shrugged. "When I've finally had a chance to unpack my boxes. I moved back on a Saturday, started work that Monday, and it's been nonstop since. I got staffed on two DC Circuit appeals my first day and haven't seen anything other than the inside of my apartment, my office, or a cab for the last two weeks."

Connor tsked disapprovingly. "*That* is why I am not at a law firm right now, girls. I like being able to tell hookups I went to law school but never practiced. They love that for some reason."

"I'm ignoring you," Emilie said with feigned disgust.

"You can judge me all you want. But the phrase is 'work hard, play hard,' not 'work hard, *work harder*.' You need a little balance. If you start that shit now, you're going to be miserable before you know it."

I held up my hand. "Okay, wow. No one is going to end up miserable. Except maybe your date from Saturday night."

Connor winked. "That's not what she said on Sunday morning."

Emilie raised an eyebrow. "She spent the *night* with you? After your roommates date bombed you at the bar?"

"That's what sealed the deal. I never looked better. They're a laugh, but I'm the funniest. She was smitten. Still is, I'd bet."

I took a sip of my wine. "But you wouldn't know because you still haven't texted her."

Connor shook his head. "It's only Thursday. We just saw each other on Sunday. And we saw a lot of each other. I even took her to Barry's. Where *Drew* had reserved the treadmill next to me. So it was a bit awkward."

I forked a croquette. "Is Drew the guy you hooked up with when you were here over spring break last year?"

He nodded proudly. "And he looked better than ever, ladies."

Emilie groaned. "Seriously, the whole population is fair game to you, and the world is still too small. Does she know you're an equal opportunity offender?"

Connor looked wounded. "Doesn't matter. I made her part of my Sunday routine. I liked her enough to invite her to work out with me. She's a cool girl, girls. She's a pan. Why are you roasting me?"

Emilie rolled her eyes. "She's a cool girl that you haven't texted since Sunday."

I held up my hand. "Wait. She's a 'pan'? And did she *want* to go to Barry's Bootcamp? What did she even wear? It seems a little . . . sadistic."

"I'll text her tomorrow. Putting someone else on the hot seat now, please. I know at least one person at this table whose love life is more exciting than mine."

Emilie scoffed. "I know you're not referring to me."

Connor patted Emilie's arm. "Not you, Miranda. You're not making it into the book at this point. I'm talking about the pretty divorcée to your right."

"Hey guys, it's old news now. Except I completely let HR think I was a newlywed my first day at the firm."

Emilie looked disgusted. "Why would you do that?"

"Name change confusion."

Connor grinned. "I still remember when Emilie told me you were going through a divorce. I couldn't decide if it made me sad or turned on. Sometimes I still jerk off to the memory."

Emilie reached over and pretended to cover Connor's mouth with her hand. "Seriously, that is so fucked up. She's *divorced* for Christ's sake."

Emilie and Connor had drunkenly hooked up once right after they met in law school. Even though they became close friends after, her tolerance for him fluctuated.

"It's fine. I'm great, work is great. A little closer to thirty, still divorced." I held up my glass. "Really, I'm feeling okay about it."

Connor shot Emilie a *get off my back* look. "Have you been dating? Or chained to your desk like our feisty little friend here?"

"All my energy is going into work. And figuring out ways to meet Eddie Kaufman without looking like a stalker."

Emilie's eyes widened. "He's the guy who reps all the actors and producers, right?"

"Basically anyone and everyone in entertainment. Which makes him almost impossible to work with."

Connor raised his beer glass. "Make a big impression, Sam. Tell him you're a divorcée."

Emilie squeezed my hand. "Ignore him."

The waiter arrived with more food, and I was grateful for the reprieve. I didn't want to admit it, but I couldn't shake off Connor's implication that being divorced was going to become my defining factor. If anything, it felt like a reason to be taken less seriously.

After dinner, Emilie and I walked west across Bleecker Street toward her parents' massive pied-à-terre just off the Gold Coast, that stretch of lower Fifth Avenue above Washington Square Park where stylish, silver-haired couples strolled out of their doorman buildings and over to the Strip House on East Twelfth Street for martinis, oysters, and steak. Even though it was just one neighborhood over from mine, it felt worlds apart.

Her parents' apartment was like stepping into *The Bonfire of the Vanities*. The windows were heavily draped, and the parquet hardwood floors covered with imported rugs. Ornate wallpaper in every room.

Emilie hadn't lived at home since her family spent her freshman and sophomore years in Manhattan. Her dad was a British diplomat, and her mom was the daughter of a renowned novelist in the pantheon of great American crime fiction writers. They were living in their country home in the Cotswolds, and Emilie had the apartment to herself.

"Doesn't Connor's total ambivalence over everything annoy you?" she asked as we paused to sit on a bench in Washington Square.

"He's not really ambivalent over everything, is he? He seems pretty serious about dating. And making money."

Emilie sighed. "I love him, but since I got to the city, I keep feeling this pull toward something more purposeful. Maybe more meaningful relationships. Not friends who make jokes about you getting divorced. At some point he's going to have to grow up."

"Sure, at some point. But we don't love him because he's mature. We love him because he's been there for us, and deep down I know if my world was falling apart, he'd be there for me in his own way, just as much as you would."

Emilie snorted. "In his own way."

She took a deep breath and stared at the fountain. I was temporarily distracted by a young couple passionately groping each other on the bench to our right.

"Just don't forget how hard you worked to get here. If it had been up to Ben, you'd be filing trademark applications at some stuffy DC firm. And that doesn't make him bad, it just wasn't *you*. You have just as much of a shot as anyone at doing what you want to do."

She reached into her bag and took out a cigarette, something I rarely saw her do.

"I guess Connor's jokes are funny sometimes, but tonight they just fell flat for me because I know what you sacrificed to be here."

Emilie's sincerity was making me emotionally unbalanced.

"I know it's weird, but sometimes I have this overwhelming urge to call Ben and tell him what's happening. Or ask for advice. I know it's probably the narcissist in me, but there's just some part of me that wishes he could be proud of me."

"I get that. He's a part of your journey in a way that no one else will be, probably for a while." She patted my leg. "So long as you know that you don't need his approval to be proud of yourself. Because he *definitely* hates your guts."

We laughed, but the ache lingered.

Later that night, too tired to even brush my teeth, I climbed into bed and pulled the duvet over my head. Just as I was drifting off, the soft glow of my phone lit up the windowsill. I tossed off the covers and grabbed it, thinking it might be work.

If you get this before tmrw am—our spot at 9? (caffeine pregame).

I smiled down at the screen.

See ya then.

Chapter Seven

I spotted Charlie in Grand Central leaning against the wall next to Joe's, reading a book.

"Hey, early bird," I said lamely.

He looked up and grinned. "Got here early. You're never going to believe what I have for you. I literally couldn't sleep."

I laughed as I turned to order, pulling out the Amex that was creeping closer to my credit limit every day. "I'm almost scared to ask."

He held up his wallet. "My treat. When you get on that case and save the movies and every celebrity from here to LA, I can say I bought you a latte when."

"I should be buying you a latte for masterminding Thank You Thursdays."

"That was all Lena. I just brought you into the fold. Anyway, save your money for celebratory cocktails."

"You're really keeping me in suspense."

"The film gods are feeling surprisingly generous right now. Did you know the New York Film Festival just happens to be at the end of the month?"

I nodded. "Of course."

"Nerd. Guess what's happening Thursday night."

"I have no idea."

"The firm bought a table at the Film at Lincoln Center gala. It's a fundraiser for this retrospective they're doing on first-time filmmakers."

"The firm 'bought a table'? What does that mean?"

"One of the biggest perks of the job. The *big* part of Big Law." He handed me a latte. "Seat fillers."

"As in we get to go to these fundraisers?"

"If the firm needs to fill seats. Can't have empty tables."

"Will Eddie be there?"

"Probably not, but it's a hell of a boondoggle way to mastermind your way into working with him on the pro bono stuff."

"Wow. How do I get on the list to be a seat filler?"

He grinned. "We're already in."

~

On Sunday afternoon, I met Caroline for brunch at Buvette on Grove Street. I told her everything between bites of tomato and whipped goat cheese tartine, from the meeting with Eddie to the cocktail dress I'd found at Bloomingdale's.

"Where does Lincoln Center do their galas?" Caroline asked.

"This one's at Cipriani's downtown."

She smiled. "It's pronounced *Chip*-riani's."

"Very glad I figured that out before Thursday."

The waiter brought over a second French press.

"Do you have any idea what the pro bono case would be about?" Caroline asked, refilling my coffee mug.

I leaned in to be more discreet. Buvette was your typical West Village bistro, with tables so close to each other, it felt more like communal seating.

"Eddie just got on the board a couple months ago," I explained.

"And he's sending you in to charm them."

I made a face. "Hardly. But it's an awesome opportunity to meet people connected to the New York Film Festival and show initiative when I do finally get face time."

I buttered a flaky croissant. "I'm actually really glad Charlie's going. He's so easygoing and can talk to anyone. Even if we're at a table with ten other people who can't make small talk, he'll bring it out of all of them."

Caroline leaned in. "So, what does he look like?"

I raised an eyebrow. "Average height, graying hair, apparently runs the New York Marathon every year, so he's in pretty good shape. Otherwise looks like your typical partner, I guess."

She laughed. "I meant Charlie."

I took a sip of the mimosa, already feeling the effects of the pitcher that Caroline had ordered before I got there.

"Charlie's nice looking. I don't know. Glasses, a little scruffy. Not what you would think of as an associate at a big firm, but honestly, he's so smart and funny. And he's somehow always upbeat. It's weirdly hard to have a bad day when he's sitting five feet away," I said, swirling the champagne flute to blend the orange juice that had floated above the prosecco.

"Anything there?"

I chuckled. "Absolutely not. Just an all-around nice guy."

"Who you also just described as cute, smart, and funny."

"Who is also my officemate," I reminded her. "And even if he wasn't, I'm not even close to being there. I didn't leave Ben to meet someone else. I'm here to become someone."

"Got it. So you have to become someone else before you meet someone special."

"Right." Every day I reminded myself that it took upending someone else's life to finally have a chance at my own. Being single was my own form of penance. I needed to do this next part all on my own, without the distraction of someone holding me back.

"Okay, so you kick ass on this film festival thing, Eddie keeps putting you on cool stuff . . . What's next? Making partner?"

I gingerly poked a grape tomato. "Oh, you know . . . make those Top 35 Under 35 lists . . . be in the know about all the trendiest restaurants . . . get invited to a client's movie premiere . . . that kind of stuff."

"What about just having some fun? Dip your toe in the dating theme park that is New York City?"

I shook my head. "No time."

Caroline grinned. "That's the perfect mindset for Tinder Social."

I stacked an empty plate under another. "The last thing I want to do on a Friday night is explain to someone what happened in my 'last serious relationship.'"

"When was the last time you were single?"

I squeezed one eye. "Eighteen?"

"Seriously?"

"Nineteen."

She raised her mimosa. "Okay, babe, you're gonna have to trust me on this. You have to learn how to be single in New York. Are you free Friday night?"

I cleared my throat. "I'll probably be working late."

"Let me see your phone."

"Seriously?"

She nodded. "I will make this *painless*."

I sighed, figuring I could play along now and get out of it later. I reluctantly unlocked my iPhone and handed it across the table. I leaned back and finished the mimosa as she took over my phone with comical intensity.

"Okay, I downloaded the app and made a skeleton profile, but you're going to have to zhuzh it up later."

"Sure."

Caroline squealed. "There's more to life than work. You'll see."

"If you say so."

"The most fun thing you have lined up is a charity gala with a bunch of stiffs."

"And Charlie!"

She smiled. "We'll get you out there."

Her phone dinged with a calendar alert. "Oh shit. I forgot I signed up for hot yoga."

"You do hot yoga after mimosas?"

She shrugged. "You either do or you don't. I've rolled the hot yoga dice so many times I've lost count."

"I don't think I know what that means, but brunch is on me. I never even got you a thank you gift for finding me an apartment."

"I don't need you to pay for brunch. Go on a Tinder Social date with me instead."

I groaned. "No promises."

Caroline was distractedly looking at her phone. "I'm obsessed with this yoga studio, by the way. It's on Greenwich Street, like five minutes from our building." She leaned back in her chair. "I don't know what it is, but I always get *so* turned on when I go to hot yoga. It's so sensual. Maybe it's just me."

She signaled for the check. "This is going to sound like a weird segue, but you should totally come with me."

We both burst out laughing. "I guess I can roll the hot yoga dice with you."

Chapter Eight

Thursday night, Charlie and I took our seats at a table reserved for Lincoln Center's most prominent benefactors because someone had clearly expected Eddie and his guest to fill the seats. Instead, we were getting our first real Big Law perk: a charity gala where the guests could have paid off our student loans at the snap of a finger.

"Listen to this," I overheard someone say across the table. "My wife and I wrote one check about twenty-five years ago, and then someone—presumably our accountant, because it sure as hell wasn't me—just kept writing that check every year, and now our nineteen-year-old goes to school with her last name etched on the college gymnasium."

I had never been in a room with so many influential people. Half the conversation was fluff, but the air buzzed with possibility. Everyone looked like their life was more fascinating than the next. I secretly wished that someday I'd have a real reason to be there.

If anyone could appreciate the people watching more than me, it was Charlie.

"Kind of makes you want to just become an observer of human behavior," he said as he bit off a huge chunk of a breadstick. "It's why I majored in anthropology."

We didn't know anyone else at the table, but it was clear they weren't there to fill seats. The woman on the other side of me was Pamela Klaflin, a journalist turned film producer whose documentary was premiering in a few weeks at the New York Film Festival. Charlie was seated next to a veteran film composer who had worked with Jerome Robbins and Leonard Bernstein. We explained that we were associates who worked at Eddie Kaufman's law firm.

"I see," Pamela said. "Have you met Alan Fox? He recruited Eddie to the board."

I shook my head. "I just joined the firm. We're here representing A&K," I explained. "What's it like to have a film premiering at the festival?"

"It never gets old seeing people watch your work. I've had films at festivals all over the world, but screening at my home festival is still a thrill."

I nodded. "It's really a dream just to be here. I love so many movies that came out of the festival."

"What's one of your favorites?" she asked.

"*The Diving Bell and the Butterfly*," I answered quickly. "I had never seen a French film before. But I went to see it in theaters after the New York Film Festival reviewed it, and I fell in love."

She folded her napkin and smiled triumphantly. "Come with me."

We walked to a table at the front of the room where she tapped a man on the shoulder. "Alan, this is Samantha. She works with Eddie Kaufman, and she's a huge fan of Julian's."

I reached out to shake his hand, hoping I looked more at ease than I felt. I could feel my nerves beneath the wine buzz. "I just joined the firm a few weeks ago," I added.

"Julian Schnabel? I think he's here somewhere. Julian loves a fan."

"I loved *The Diving Bell and the Butterfly*. It would have been magical to see it screened here."

"Well it's nice to meet you, Samantha. We're all Eddie Kaufman fans here. The festival is lucky to have him in our corner. Especially with the red tape we're dealing with fighting the city."

"The pro bono matter, right?" I asked quickly, hoping it seemed like I had some idea of what he was talking about.

He nodded. "Are you working on 'festival-gate' too?"

I shook my head. "Not yet. But if there's an opportunity for me to pitch in, I'd love to help any way I can," I added.

"We're going to need all the muscle the firm can give. The kickoff meeting is next Tuesday. Do you have a card?"

I was so grateful I hadn't left my Longchamp behind. "Absolutely," I said, digging into my bag.

Pamela looked satisfied with having made the connection. "Shall we head back to our seats?"

"Very nice meeting you, Sam. Give Eddie my regards," he said enthusiastically. My brain was firing in all directions. I knew I'd be checking my email obsessively between now and Tuesday.

Charlie was reading an email on his phone when I got back to the table. I leaned over as soon as Pamela started talking to the person next to her.

"You'll never believe who I just met."

"Robert De Niro."

"Close. I met the guy who convinced Eddie to join the board."

"No way! What did he say?"

"I think he's going to email me. He mentioned something that I'm pretty sure relates to the pro bono matter Eddie's working with them on."

"Sick."

I laughed. "When I wake up tomorrow, is any of this actually going to be real?"

"You mean, my genius plan is working."

The gala ended promptly at nine o'clock.

"Nightcap?" he asked.

"Did you learn that word from *Mad Men*?" I asked.

"Yes, and I'm bringing it back."

I laughed. I felt like I was on a networking high. "Okay, sure. Maybe somewhere between here and the West Village?"

Charlie smiled. "I'm sure we can stumble into something."

I stood up slowly, willing my heels to get me to whatever bar we stumbled into.

Charlie quickly hailed a cab outside Cipriani's. "Moore and Greenwich Street?"

The driver shot up the West Side Highway, making such impressive time that before I knew it, we were being dropped off at Smith & Mills, an unassuming bar in an old carriage house across from the Greenwich Hotel.

We found two corner seats, and Charlie ordered a Montauk Ale.

"I think I just need a second," I said to the bartender, who nodded and went to get Charlie's beer while I looked over the cocktail list, trying to decipher ingredients that might as well have been written in French.

"Do you think they can just do a vodka soda?" I asked.

Charlie leaned over the bar. "A Ketel and soda, please."

I feigned offense. "I can order my own drink, you know."

He looked genuinely embarrassed.

"Hey," I said, lightly punching his shoulder. "I'm like two months into swimming in a man's world. I have to joke about this stuff when I can."

He peeled off the label of the beer.

"Was tonight everything you never expected when you imagined yourself at an outrageous charitable event?"

I reached for the vodka soda.

"I think I have one of those in me for every billable quarter."

He laughed. "At least you're picking up the nerdy lawyer jokes."

I toasted my tumbler against his beer bottle. "Fake it till you make it?"

"Exactly." He folded and refolded the beer label. "So, I wasn't planning to bring this up—at least, I wasn't sure if I was going to . . . but I went for beers with some of the guys from your summer class, and they mentioned you were married when you interned at the firm last summer. But you never mentioned it, and I didn't want to be nosy. But I mean, we basically spend all our time together, and I guess at the end of the day I'm just a tipsy, nosy schmuck," he said, looking embarrassed again.

I felt myself sit up straighter. It wasn't that I'd intentionally kept Ben from Charlie—I just figured it would come up at some point. At least now that it had, I could blame the unlimited wine and a vodka soda for pretending I wasn't as self-conscious about it as I was.

I told Charlie about meeting Ben in college, then getting married soon after I graduated. Deciding to go to law school. Long days of class and long nights of studying and making lunches and dinners in between. Interning in New York. Growing apart. Wanting more from life.

"Law school changed me so much. Sometimes I didn't even recognize myself. I could *feel* myself evolving past our life together, and as much as I tried to ignore it at first, I was just so unhappy. When I told him I was leaving, I thought he knew it was coming. But he didn't. At least, he said he didn't. He expected me to finish school and go back to the life we had before. But everything had changed."

Charlie leaned forward, resting his forearms on the table. He didn't say anything right away.

"You're a cool girl. I'm sure it sucked for him to lose you. But at the end of the day, you deserve to do what makes you happy, and he deserves to be with someone who's happy with him. He'll find his person. You can't feel bad for outgrowing someone. Now that you're here, just give it everything you've got, and make it worth the growing pains."

I nodded, a quiet sense of relief loosening in my chest. "I'm actually glad you asked."

"Tough having secrets when you share an office."

I looked down at my watch. "And—we have to be at work in about seven hours," I said, mentally calculating the glasses of water I needed to drink before I let myself fall asleep so I wouldn't wake up a total zombie.

"Yeah, we should head out. But seriously—anytime you want to talk about stuff, I'm here. Literally, I'm here, twelve hours a day, five days a week, right next to you."

"Forced proximity therapy. I'm very into the efficiency of that," I said as I felt around to slip my feet back into my heels.

"I'll walk you home and then hop in a cab," Charlie offered.

I shook my head. "I should just get a cab. It's a twenty-minute walk for me, and these heels aren't going to make it."

He hailed a cab and opened the door for me.

"Hey. I think your story is going to work out just the way you want it to. Whatever that is." He smiled. "Thanks for a fun night."

I felt just south of drunk. "Thanks . . . Okay, I need to get in the cab," I said, laughing at my inability to form an eloquent response to one of the most hopeful things anyone had said to me in a while.

He stood there while I got into the cab and then knocked on the driver's window.

"Get her home safely, please."

Chapter Nine

Not nearly enough hours later, my left eye squinted open. I thought I heard my cell phone ringing but had no idea where I'd put it.

I glanced at the clock. 7:30 a.m.

No one called at that hour in New York, especially not on a Friday. The 10 a.m. start to the workday is sacred for Manhattan lawyers.

But it was *definitely* my phone. I cursed into my pillow, feeling drunker than when I got in the cab and said bye to Charlie. I threw the covers off the bed, spotting my phone on the floor less than a second after my voicemail kicked in.

I hit play immediately. "Samantha. Eddie Kaufman . . ."

Fuck.

I couldn't make any sense of why Eddie Kaufman would be calling me at all, let alone this early in the morning. Before I finished the message, my phone rang again.

Fuck, fuck, fuck. I didn't have the brain capacity to screen a second call.

"Hello, this is Samantha," I said, trying to sound as if I'd woken up restfully, or was at least caffeinated.

I pressed my palm anxiously against my forehead.

"Samantha, morning. Look, I'm sorry for the early call, but I got the nicest message last night from Alan Fox saying he met you at the fundraiser and that you struck him as a particularly mature and capable young associate. I just took on a new client late yesterday and I need someone junior on it immediately. I realize that I'm technically supposed to ask what your workload is, so just assume I'm asking you—but before you answer, let me just say I hope you have the right answer for me."

I sank down on the edge of the bed, wishing I could take a pill to defrost my brain. Was I still drunk? How was this happening? Not even Charlie would believe the plan had worked this fast.

"Of course, I would love to help," I said, trying to muster all the enthusiasm I felt but couldn't articulate in my altered state.

I could tell he had switched to speaker and was typing emails as he talked.

"Okay, good. Listen, there's a lot of sensitivity surrounding this client. She's being arraigned downtown in the Southern District later this morning. She's not a household name, but most of the people she's associated with are, so there are going to be cameras. She flew in on the red-eye from LA, and she's coming back to the office afterward so we can get the full download on whether any of the allegations hold water. I'm confident that this is a matter any associate would kill to be staffed on, but I'm nervous about the sensitivities. I only spoke to her for ten minutes yesterday, and she's very focused on this not becoming a media circus because of the big names involved and celebrity factor. Given the sensitivity, I need a first-year who is mature enough to deadpan the meeting."

There was no way this could be the Film at Lincoln Center pro bono matter. My brain couldn't connect the dots.

"Do me a favor and reserve a conference room for later this morning. We should be back from court around eleven a.m."

It was definitely not the same thing.

The fog momentarily lifted, and the training from my first week at the firm kicked in.

"Of course. I'll email you the conference room number and put the client's name on the visitor list. I just need her name, and we'll be set for eleven a.m."

Eddie paused again, clearly distracted by something else. "Just google 'Andie Reese, Poker Princess.' There's a *New York Post* article online that will give you about as much of the background as I have right now, which is scary given I'm about to appear in court on her behalf in an hour."

Eddie hung up as I silently cursed myself for overdoing it last night. *Of course today's the day all my dreams come true,* I thought to myself, willing the pulsing in both temples to go away.

I got up and stood in front of the bathroom mirror for a few seconds, mentally creating a checklist of everything that needed to happen before I could go out in public.

Forty-five minutes later, I took stock of my reflection. Black pantsuit, mascara, heavy concealer, hair combed, teeth brushed. The irony of being hungover from a night that was curated to get me to *this exact moment* was staring me in the face. I felt like the opposite of a mature and capable young associate. If I pulled this off, I seriously needed to get my shit together.

I glanced at the clock and weighed taking the subway or an Uber. I needed time to read the *New York Post* article on the way to the office. I punched the Uber app on my phone as I threw on flats.

I had just enough time to run downstairs and grab a coffee at the corner deli. I ordered an extra-large black coffee and spotted the car waiting in front of my building. Juggling my laptop bag and coffee, I swung open the back door of the Toyota Camry and threw my bag across the back seat.

"I'm so sorry if you were waiting. I always think I have enough time, but then you guys are so quick!" I exclaimed, short of breath.

A bewildered face turned around, and I immediately realized I had jumped into someone's actual car.

"Oh my God, I wasn't even paying attention to which—"

I saw a driver across from the car I'd aggressively trespassed honking and waving at me. I apologized again and hurled myself into the right car, barely hearing the driver say how many times he'd seen people get into the wrong Uber. I shoved my coffee in the cup holder and googled "Andie Reese, Poker Princess."

~

The arraignment lasted an hour longer than expected. I waited in the conference room, alternating between feeling overly caffeinated and mentally drained. I tried answering emails. I googled to find out more about Andie Reese, but there was nothing beyond the recent *New York Post* article. She didn't seem to have any social media presence.

Just after twelve o'clock, Eddie emailed to say he'd left Andie in the lobby with directions to the conference room and would join us as soon as he handled another client emergency.

A minute later, the door swung open, and a petite brunette wearing black pants, a cropped pink blazer, and matching magenta heels walked in. She stopped short when she saw me.

"Eddie Kaufman's assistant sent me to 50B. Am I in the right place?"

I'd been sitting at the opposite end of the room. The walk to shake her hand felt like an eternity. "I'm Samantha. I work with Eddie. He should be back soon." I motioned to the Olympic-size conference table. "Feel free to sit wherever," I said.

She forced a smile and took a seat on the other side of the table, dropping her black Céline bag heavily on the table.

I had never done an introductory client meeting. Was I supposed to make small talk? What could we even talk about without Eddie there?

I squinted in the direction of the beverage cart that catering had brought in when I got there an hour earlier.

"Do you need anything? We have coffee, tea, juice. He should be back soon," I repeated.

She didn't look up from scrolling. "Sorry, what was your name again?"

I cleared my throat. "Samantha. Sam."

She nodded, still not making eye contact.

It was clear she didn't want to chat, and I still hadn't decided if small talk with a new client was even kosher, so I opened my laptop to reread the article.

According to the *Post*, Andie Reese had gone from small-town girl to bona fide poker madam, winning over the respect of Hollywood and Wall Street elites and becoming an indispensable player outside of the poker table. I didn't know anything about poker, but the article alleged she had built a million-dollar business organizing private games with buy-ins that were multiples of the buy-in of a typical friendly game. The last game she had run was raided by the FBI. A week later, federal agents showed up at her door with a warrant and a thirty-page indictment with her name on the cover, accusing her of illegally running poker games in violation of US Criminal Code Section 1955.

The article left off where Eddie picked up. The day before, she flew to New York accompanied by two federal agents, and following her arraignment that morning in Manhattan federal court, she was sitting in a conference room in a midtown high-rise. With me.

The *Post* article made it sound like we had our work cut out for us.

I typed "US Criminal Code 1955." The full name of the federal statute came up as "Prohibition of illegal gambling businesses."

I shifted uncomfortably in the chair, reading through the dense statutory text.

I emailed the firm's copy center and requested three printed copies of Section 1955. Five minutes later, a mail room courier knocked lightly and handed me a sealed envelope. I weighed whether to give Andie a copy but decided to wait.

After what seemed like an eternity, Eddie finally appeared.

"My apologies to you both. Someone filed an injunction against the release of a client's movie, and we had to file an objection before one p.m."

Andie nodded expressionlessly.

"Have you two discussed anything yet?"

I shook my head. "I wanted to wait until you were here." I really hoped he hadn't expected me to start without him.

"Good. Let's jump into it. Here's what I'm thinking, Andie. You are the only woman in a thirty-three-person indictment. The prosecutors assigned to the case are white men. Regretfully, so am I. Depending on what you tell us today and over the course of the next few weeks, we will assess the merits of your case and decide whether you should plead out early or negotiate for a deferred prosecution. In any event, the short term is going to be filled with uncertainty. Samantha is a very competent young associate who will be in every meeting with us, both here and with the prosecutors. It's likely to get bumpy, because from the indictment and the arraignment, it looks to me like the US Attorney's Office wants to make an example out of you. Their endgame here is so numbingly transparent, it makes me wish there was a mechanism to file sanctions. But it's the government against you, and we have to play ball."

Andie was stoic. The *New York Post* article said she was facing up to five years in prison.

"Are you aware of Section 1955 of the US Criminal Code?" he asked.

She shook her head. "I wasn't until yesterday."

He nodded. "All three of us are going to need to get intimately acquainted with it. Samantha, can you pull it?"

I reached for the envelope and pulled out the papers. "I printed three copies," I said, hoping that I'd at least gotten something right.

Eddie handed a copy to Andie and kept one for himself. "Great. We'll go through this next. But before we do that, I want to be straightforward here."

He took off his readers and looked directly at Andie. "I've agreed to represent you, but I can't guarantee what the outcome will be. It's important that you understand that. Depending on the facts that we learn, I'll decide if it's worth trying to negotiate with the government. But I need one thing from you right now, and that is complete honesty and transparency. Under no circumstances can you cherry-pick facts or the questions you answer truthfully. I can't do my job if you're dishonest with me. Samantha and I are bound by attorney-client privilege, which means nothing that you tell us leaves this room unless we collectively agree to disclose it to the government."

He tapped the readers on the table. "Can I count on you to tell us everything we need to know?"

She looked unconvinced. "Yes, but I also need to be able to trust you. I've been burned over the past couple of years, and getting slapped with an indictment by the government takes the cake. Defending myself could mean ruining other people's lives. I'm not willing to do that," she said, her voice heavy.

Eddie inhaled sharply as he tapped his pen on the conference table. "I understand that. But it's kill or be killed when the government gets involved, and whoever these people are, I guarantee you that when push comes to shove, they'd give you up in a second to save themselves. We're not going to name any names you don't want to, but my job is to tell you when I think you need to talk in order to help your case. If you don't want to take my advice, that will be your choice."

Andie met my eyes for the first time in the meeting. "I never want to hear any of these names repeated outside of this room," she said coldly.

I nodded. "Of course. That's my job."

"Andie, Samantha is a professional. She's at this firm for a reason. I know we don't trust each other yet, but I never want you to walk into a room—whether it's here or at the US Attorney's Office—and be the only woman in that room. If there are things you're not comfortable talking to me about, you can tell Samantha, and she'll find a tactful way to get me the information. I'm not trying to make this about gender, but in my opinion, that's what the government wants to do—and so I'm doing what I can to counteract that with your defense team."

"I'm used to dealing with men. I get along better with them. I always have," she said sharply.

I looked down at my legal pad, trying not to look as uneasy as I felt.

"But Eddie—I trust your instincts. I hired you because you're the best, and you're used to the absurdity of the world I come from. So to answer your question, yes. I can promise honesty and transparency. Can we get started now?"

The rest of the meeting played out like a who's who of Oscar-winning celebrities, politicians, and Wall Street elites. No one was left out. I deadpanned each name drop and salacious detail.

Four hours later, Andie left for her hotel, and Eddie rubbed his temples.

"Jesus, that was long. Thanks for stepping up today. Do me a favor and get those notes into a concise memo, then start researching recent Second Circuit cases with the antigambling statute. We'll pick this up tomorrow."

I couldn't wait to tell Charlie everything.

Chapter Ten

I sank into a chair as soon as they left, sure that I'd been partially holding my breath since Eddie called at 7:30 a.m. I hadn't even texted Charlie to let him know where I was all morning and saw he'd sent multiple texts. *Was I sick or just hungover? Had something happened?*

I gathered my laptop and thirty-plus pages of handwritten notes. With the adrenaline slowly subsiding, my left hand felt numb from gripping the pen so tightly. I needed food and a gallon of water.

Last minute client meeting. Grabbing food then coming up, I responded as I rode the elevator down to the lobby. I grabbed a premade salad and Smartwater and sprinted back to the forty-eighth floor. I excitedly swung open the door to an empty office.

I dumped everything onto my desk and fished out my iPhone. Back in the office, where are you?

He responded immediately. Ran down to SDNY for last min filing. But glad you're alive (also wtf??!)

I chugged the bottle of water. Crazy morning. Thankful I didn't die in my sleep from alcohol poisoning.

He typed a question mark, and I reminded myself not to put anything in writing. Text me when you're on the train back, can meet you at Joe's on your way up, I wrote back.

I sat at my desk, looking at the view of uptown Manhattan for what felt like an eternity. I spent the next ten minutes reading through my notes from the meeting. I was struck by how fascinating it all was on a second read. *This* was the reason I had gone to law school. The reason I wanted to work with Eddie.

It was clear Andie was a force of nature. For four hours, she'd told us everything, starting at the very beginning, when she first moved to Los Angeles and found a job as a personal assistant to a high-net-worth entrepreneur who liked to have other high-net-worth friends over for a weekly poker game. One day, she was making music playlists and charcuterie trays. Soon after, she was running an empire. Celebrities, titans of industry, studio heads all wanted to get into *her* game. The price of admission was in the hundreds of thousands. Players either won or lost way more than that. She didn't even know how to play poker, but she knew the mind of a poker player inside and out.

I couldn't believe I was part of her defense team.

Charlie looked exhausted as he waited outside Joe's a couple of hours later.

"Late night?" I winked.

He groaned. "I already had my wild days as a paralegal. My body can't tolerate that little sleep."

I filled him in as we walked back to the elevator bank, careful not to repeat any names.

"I just want to nail this memo. It feels more make or break than anything."

He grinned. "Nah, you're in the circle now. All you have to do is stay in the circle."

I crossed my fingers. "Can we talk about how ridiculous some of those people were last night?"

"Oh, yeah. I figured I'd let you form your own opinion, but those events are garbage. There's a reason the firm opens them up to seat fillers, and it's not because they're generous."

"If they all end with getting staffed on cases like this, I'll fill a seat anywhere they need me."

Charlie rolled his eyes. "Okay fine, I'll be your plus-one, but only for the free booze and titillating conversation. And I'm not even talking about ours."

I rubbed my temples as we sat down at our desks. "I might have to crawl under the desk and nap before I can turn these notes into any sort of coherent memo."

Charlie peered over the desk divider at the stack of pages, which I promptly grabbed and put on the side of my desk.

"*Highly* confidential!" I exclaimed, yawning simultaneously.

"You nap, I'll flip through them."

"I'm serious. Can I trust you to leave them alone if I just put my head down right here for five minutes?"

"Not a chance. You know what I just went down to court for? Some real estate investor got an eviction notice from a commercial building in Midtown, and we had to file a temporary restraining order. I'm desperate to read anything that doesn't mention REITs."

"Don't make me ask."

"Real estate investment trust."

"You're better than that."

"I'm not Hollywood material. Too nerdy."

"And I'm an Italian girl from Virginia. Probably the last person who belonged in that meeting."

Charlie grinned. "You'll belong wherever you decide you want to belong. Not sure if high-stakes poker is really your scene, though."

I took a deep breath and glanced warily at the stack of notes. "No napping. I need this memo to be the best thing Eddie ever read."

I harnessed a second wind and started summarizing recent rulings of Second Circuit cases where the antigambling statute was front and center. I was struck by how judges could write such dry opinions about gambling.

"Is poker easy to learn?" I asked a few minutes later.

"I've got a game going right now on my phone." He grinned. "I can give you a quick tutorial, if you want."

I hesitated. "I don't really have time. I have to keep going on this memo."

He shook his head. "A good lawyer becomes an expert in whatever their clients are into. Otherwise, you're a half-baked advocate."

He swiveled his chair toward my side of the desk. "Here. I'll show you the basics."

The "basics" were all I needed to realize poker was complicated.

"It's honestly fucked that the government lumps poker in with all the other games where you clearly have no control over the outcome. It's a game of skill, not chance," Charlie said.

"Kind of tooting your own horn there."

"Think about it. You have just as much of a chance winning roulette or the lottery as anyone else. But if we sat down and played a game of poker right now, I'd crush you."

I frowned. "This article says the antigambling laws were enacted to crack down on racketeering."

"Uh, yeah. We've all watched *The Sopranos*. The government figured out a long time ago that gambling and organized crime go hand in hand."

I made notes to draft a section pointing out Andie's lack of connection to organized crime. And learn poker and watch *The Sopranos*.

Charlie was on calls for the rest of the afternoon. His phone voice filled every square inch of the office. It was the auditory equivalent of manspreading. I tried putting in AirPods, but it was impossible to concentrate.

Two hours later, Charlie got off another call, and I was starting to feel desperate. The hours were slipping by. I needed to focus.

"I reserved the small conference room down the hall. Just need to bang this out," I said. I hadn't figured out how to diplomatically say *there are two of us working in here, please shut the fuck up*.

"Shit, am I too loud? I swear I talk louder when I'm working," he said apologetically.

I mimicked an understanding smile. "I don't think I'd even hear you if I weren't so focused on nailing this."

I unplugged my laptop from my monitor and slipped out to the small conference room at the end of the hall.

~

The clock in the upper-right corner of my monitor read 12:13 a.m. I'd relocated back to our office around 9 p.m. after Charlie texted he was finally heading home. Without looking, I took a distracted bite of the half-eaten protein bar beside me and chased it with cold coffee.

"My first all-nighter," I muttered, the office feeling still and small. Outside the window, Park Avenue was a clear runway with barely a headlight all the way uptown.

I wanted Eddie to have the memo in his inbox by morning.

I'd spent countless hours reading dozens of New York and federal cases to get a sense of how courts ruled whether something was an "illegal gambling operation." Everything hinged on whether Andie's poker games would be considered an illegal gambling business that would put her within the crosshairs of Section 1955. If convicted, she was facing up to five years in prison. I'd made pages and pages of notes, but somehow only drafted a few coherent lines for the memo.

MEMORANDUM

ATTORNEY WORK PRODUCT

PRIVILEGED & CONFIDENTIAL

To: Eddie Kaufman

From: Samantha DeFiore

Re: The Federal Illegal Gambling Business Act (18 U.S. Code § 1955)

A gambling business is illegal under § 1955 if it satisfies the following three criteria:

(i) is a violation of state law in which it is conducted;

(ii) involves five or more persons who conduct, manage, supervise, direct, or own all or part of such business; and

(iii) has been or remains in substantially continuous operation for a period in excess of thirty days or has a gross revenue of $2,000 in any single day . . .

Charlie's words about poker being a game of "skill" kept replaying in my head. I typed "poker: game of chance or game of skill?" into Google. There was a recent news story about a case that centered on that exact question. The court had declared Texas Hold'em, a popular form of poker, a game of skill and therefore *not* an illegal gambling business. The ruling was on appeal, and if the higher court upheld the lower court's decision, we'd have a compelling argument that Andie's poker game wasn't an illegal gambling business either. I ended the memo referencing the Texas Hold'em case. It wasn't a slam dunk by any means, but it was something.

My phone screen lit up in the reflection of the window. I rubbed my eyes to readjust my contact lenses as I saw Ben's name.

Hey.

Short, simple, confusing. My mind raced. It was late. Was he drinking? Had he meant to text me?

My palms felt sweaty.

Since I'd been in New York, I had narcissistically tried to focus on everything *but* Ben. Partly it was survival. If I thought too deeply about how much I'd hurt him or how our marriage had failed, I was afraid I wouldn't be able to channel the forward motion I needed to succeed.

I stared at the phone long after his name disappeared, then moved it to the opposite side of my desk. I leaned back in my chair, a knot forming in my stomach. Who said avoidance was bad? Facing my past seemed worse.

I jumped as my office phone emitted a high-pitched ring.

"This is Sam," I answered shakily.

"Oh my god. It's after midnight. *Go home*!"

I exhaled an unsteady breath.

"Christ, Charlie. You suck. Let me work," I said, trying to steady my voice.

"Okay fine, but we were out till three a.m. last night! You need sleep. Hope you're winding down."

"Night. Bet I'll still be up before you in the morning."

He chuckled. "You already are. Get some sleep."

I hung up and decided to put off responding to Ben until I finished the memo. My mind felt like a sieve.

I was pure OCD as a junior attorney. Four hours later, I had spell-checked the memo eight times, read the cover email aloud three times to make sure it flowed, and deleted and retyped Eddie's email in the "to" line too many times. Finally, I squeezed my left eye shut and hit send.

I ordered an Uber as I leaned against the cool metal wall of the elevator, willing myself to stay awake until I got home.

As I settled into the Uber, I checked my Gmail and saw an email from Ben with everything the text hadn't said.

He was coming to New York next week for a conference at the Federal Reserve. He had work dinners every night but was free Wednesday. Did I want to have dinner?

Chapter Eleven

I didn't know how to feel about Ben coming to New York. It felt too soon after the wreckage of the last time we'd seen each other, three weeks before I flew to Rochester to take the bar exam. A week before I spiraled at Vin Rouge.

I'd been packing up my off-campus apartment when the doorbell rang. A FedEx driver handed me an envelope with the divorce papers I'd mailed to Ben with a note stuck to the front, asking him to sign and send them back promptly so I could finalize everything before I took the bar.

Relief washed over me. Even with something like this, he was still reliable, and I was grateful for it. I opened the envelope and pulled out the papers, marked with a "sign here" tab on each of the three pages that required Ben's signature.

He'd signed the first two.

The last page was blank.

I felt exhausted and frustrated. I'd spent the entire summer doing nothing but studying for the bar, and I needed to be able to file the papers before I moved to New York.

He picked up the first ring.

"Hey, it's Sam. The papers just arrived. There were three signature tabs, but you missed the third one."

The line was silent for a second, but I could hear his breath close to the phone.

"Sorry. It's been a rough week. Mail 'em back to me, I'll sign the one I missed."

I'd already done the unthinkable by leaving him. But I'd allowed myself to go on autopilot so I could just get through to the other side, and my anxiety had overtaken my guilt. "I can't wait that long. I'm driving them back to you now. Please be home."

I pulled in an hour later, rattled from stress. He had sold our townhouse and moved closer to his family, into an apartment complex that was reminiscent of the place he'd lived in when we met in college. Not seeing Ben for months had made it easier to ignore the emotional fallout from ending our marriage. I climbed a worn wooden staircase to the second-floor apartment, my eyes locking on what looked like a waste stabilization pond behind the building. Everything was a visual reminder of the impact my choices had had on his life.

I knocked and waited. I knocked again a few seconds later, then jiggled the doorknob and realized it was unlocked. The door opened to a plastic linoleum foyer that led to a carpeted living room. Ben was sitting on a couch I recognized from his parents' basement. There was a metal floor lamp bright enough to illuminate only half of the couch. From what I could see of his face, he looked tired. The circles under his eyes hurt to look at.

I set the papers down on the coffee table next to an ashtray brimming with cigarette butts.

"You're *smoking*?"

Ben hadn't smoked a day in his life. Not in college or in high school. Not even when he was drunk at a party. "You're smoking in your *apartment*?"

"Is there a law against smoking in your own apartment?"

I stared at him, unable to look away. I'd never seen anyone look so angry and sad at the same time. It was like a punch in the stomach. This was what my choices had cost him.

I slid the ashtray over to the opposite end of the coffee table. "Since when do you smoke?"

"Since when do you care? Are you going to take it all back if I promise to quit?"

A million tiny punches. The subpar apartment, when he certainly could have afforded a better place. His parents' old couch. The cigarettes. This was what I had done to him. It had been my decision to drive the papers over, but maybe that's what he hoped would happen by not signing the third page. Mailing them would have been less painful for both of us.

He sighed. "Where's the page?"

Somewhere between the linoleum and the cigarette smoke, I'd almost forgotten. "It's right here. I'm sure I have a pen somewhere . . ."

He grabbed a pen on the coffee table. "Don't worry, Sam. I'm ready for you."

Ben never did sarcasm and couldn't deadpan to save his life. Until now. He flipped to the signature page, signed, and handed it back to me.

"Sorry you had to come all the way over," he said flatly.

I stood there trying to figure out if it would be best to just take the papers and leave or try to talk honestly to the man who had been my husband. Neither choice was going to change anything. I couldn't flip a switch and feel less guilty, and he wasn't going to be less heartbroken. There was nothing I could say or do to fix it.

He pushed his laptop aside without looking up. "Do you need something else?"

I fumbled around for words. "No . . . thank you for signing. I'm sorry."

"Okay."

When he'd moved out a year earlier, he'd asked for space. We'd barely been in touch, save a few emails and texts here and there about bank accounts. Not seeing him had made it easier to convince myself that he was fine.

"Has it been okay living here?" I asked cautiously.

"Are you really making small talk?"

I flinched. "I guess I was trying."

Ben turned to face the window. "Really wish I'd just signed on all the dotted lines the first time like any jackass would've."

He turned back to his laptop, typing as we sat in silence. "Yeah, it's been fine living here. I'm writing a book. I've got six chapters down."

"A book? I don't know what that means."

"A book, Sam. With words and pages and shit."

I laughed despite myself. He reached into a small drawer on the side of the coffee table and pulled out a pack of cigarettes.

"I didn't know you liked to write. What's it about?" The question immediately felt intrusive. "If I can ask," I added.

He reached over and cracked the sliding door. "Sure, you can ask. It's called *Surviving a Baby Divorce*."

I felt like I'd stepped into a postmarriage twilight zone, where my ex-husband was a chain smoker writing self-help books.

"A what? What is a 'baby divorce'? It sounds like I got knocked up and you left me."

He dropped the cigarette in the ashtray and turned to face me. "No, Sam. *We* are babies. Babies shouldn't be getting divorced. I'm too young for this."

I looked over at the screen, but all I could make out was jumbled text.

"Babies shouldn't be getting married. We've been through this. And you're thirty-three. You're not a baby anymore," I said, sounding more exasperated than was fair.

He took a slow drag of the cigarette. "I thought I'd be having kids by now, not starting over. But that's the choice you forced on me."

I took a deep breath, unsure if this was a productive conversation. I knew I wasn't the right person for him to talk to, but I also wasn't sure it was better for him to be putting it all down in some cynical book.

"I'm sorry, Ben. I really am. But imagine waking up in twenty years, resenting each other, and having to face *that* reality in our fifties."

"Your parents did it."

"There you go."

He turned and stared out of the window. "Is there something else you need? Because it seems to me that you got everything you wanted."

I couldn't deny it. He was right. My own happiness had cost him his.

"I just want to make sure you're okay."

"I'm not *okay*, Sam. But I think you know that."

I had another split-second internal debate about rationalizing with him, then bit the bullet and took my shot. Like an idiot.

"Look, Ben . . . we had a good marriage. We just grew in different ways. Why does it all have to be a failure because we didn't end up spending the rest of our lives together?"

He shut his laptop and shot me a look.

"It's an honest question," I said quietly.

"Jesus Christ, Sam. This idea that you keep trying to shove down my throat—that divorce doesn't mean we failed because *some* of our marriage was good—I don't buy it. I'll never buy it. You find one person, and you love them through everything. *That's* not failing. You're *taking* that away from me. I wanted to be with you for the rest of my life. Maybe that's old-fashioned. You're forcing me to throw it all away just because you decided you don't want the kind of life you think I want. But you used to. And that fucking sucks."

"*I* don't even know what I used to want, Ben. I was twenty-two when we got married. That was seven years ago. People change."

"Is that what your therapist told you to say?"

I frustratedly swallowed the lump in my throat. "I know it doesn't mean anything, but . . . I'm so sorry. I really am. For everything. I never meant to hurt you. I shouldn't have married you when I didn't even know who I was. It wasn't fair to either of us." I took a deep breath as I picked up the signed paper off the coffee table. "You don't deserve any of this."

He put his hand up. "I don't need you to keep telling me you're sorry. I need this nightmare to be over."

I drove back to campus feeling like I couldn't breathe in deeply enough. I was still barreling toward New York at warp speed, but something in the narrative I'd been telling myself had been punctured. Making the decision to leave had nothing to do with knowing how to move forward.

Chapter Twelve

Monday morning, I woke up to a note from Patricia saying Eddie wanted to take Andie to dinner before she headed back to LA and to meet them at the Palm at six o'clock.

I reread Ben's email on the subway to the office. I knew I needed to respond, but the memory of the last time we'd seen each other was still palpable. Ever since my wine bar unraveling after I filed the divorce papers, I couldn't trust that either of us was ready to see the other.

Charlie was downtown again for the day, and the hours crawled. I read through the memo again and again, refreshing my email dozens of times and anxiously wondering if Eddie had read it yet.

He still hadn't responded by the time I had to leave for dinner.

When I arrived at the Palm, I spotted Andie sitting alone at the corner of the mahogany bar and momentarily panicked at the thought of another uncomfortable one-on-one. She was engrossed in her phone and barely noticed me sit down.

"Nice to see you again," I said with so much forced enthusiasm there was no way she couldn't pick up on it.

"Hi. Eddie's running late again."

She must have seen every muscle in my face tense.

"Drink?" she asked, almost throwing me the menu.

I nodded a little too emphatically and caught the bartender's eye. "May I have a French pinot noir, please?"

"Nothing French by the glass. Just California reds."

I pursed my lips and looked in her direction. "What are you having?"

"1942."

I hesitated.

"Try it. You won't even know it's straight tequila."

I took a sip. It burned like hell.

"I'll do the same, please," I said.

Andie looked pleased. "Any word from Eddie?"

I quickly scanned my emails. "He said to order appetizers, and he'll be here in twenty."

"He's a busy guy. Pretty impressive."

I looked down at my glass and took another sip, trying not to cough.

"When did you finish law school?"

I smiled sheepishly. "I started at the firm last month."

"Holy hell, you're green." She sighed. "I always wanted to be a lawyer. I wish we could trade places."

I tried not to look surprised. "When did you change your mind?"

She laughed. "When I realized there was a faster way to take over the world, I guess."

She took a sip of tequila and paused. I wondered if she was done with small talk.

Then she asked, "Did you always want to be a lawyer?"

I shook my head. "I always thought I wanted to be an actress, but practicality got the best of me. I didn't even know entertainment law existed until I was in my twenties. It seemed like the perfect way to pragmatically do what I love."

She suddenly looked interested. "You know I have a lot of connections in Hollywood, right? You never know what direction life could take you," she said, looking pleased that she could potentially offer something. I couldn't tell if her intentions were genuine or if she wanted to motivate me to work my ass off, but it didn't matter. At least we were having a conversation.

By the time Eddie arrived and the hostess showed us to our table, it felt like Andie's iciness was beginning to melt. I wondered if Eddie had intentionally given us a head start.

He ordered a bottle of Saint-Émilion. We each ordered steak, and Andie chose three shareable sides for the table. Two hours later, we'd learned everything about Eddie's beginnings prosecuting Brooklyn mobsters.

I watched Andie's eyes harden. "And now you're defending accused white-collar criminals. Like me."

"Accused, not convicted," he reminded her. I felt a jolt deep in the pit of my stomach, wondering if he'd read the memo.

She softened. "Well, I'm personally glad you switched sides. If I'd had an Eddie Kaufman in my corner earlier, I might have made better choices." She smiled. "Maybe I'd even have ended up like my new friend Sam. Climbing the Big Law ladder."

Eddie smiled. "We're all on our own path, Andie. I don't doubt for a second you're going to be okay."

He settled the check, and we walked out together. As he hailed Andie a cab, she leaned over and gave me a warm hug. "Come to LA. I'll introduce you to some fun people."

"That would be great, thanks," I said quietly, not wanting Eddie to get the impression I was soliciting a client for networking connections.

Eddie told me to expense the Uber. As the driver cut across midtown to the West Side Highway, I rolled down the window and felt the rush of the Hudson River to my right and the energy of all of Manhattan to my left.

~

I groaned when my alarm went off at 6:30 the next morning to meet Emilie and Connor for hot yoga at Y7.

I stretched in the dark while I waited for Emilie and Connor to find the two mats I'd laid out next to me. My mind was still shuffling through possible reasons Ben might've reached out.

He definitely wasn't ready to move on.

Was he still writing a book?

I imagined Ben turning into a bestselling author with a combination tell-all, self-help masterpiece on surviving your ex-wife's emotional immaturity.

I moved to Savasana and squeezed my eyes shut.

I felt a rush of cold air as Emilie raced in and crouched on the mat next to me. "He brought that girl," she whispered between clenched teeth.

"What girl?"

"The one he took to Barry's."

I looked over and saw a petite Zoë Kravitz look-alike trailing behind Connor, carrying two yoga mats.

"Morning, ladies. This is Gillian," Connor announced loudly as the instructor signaled for us to keep it down. We politely waved in unison as I breathed in deeply, trying to meditate away Emilie's agitation and my own mental spiral about responding to Ben.

Part of me wanted to tell Emilie, and the other part knew what she'd say. Of course it wasn't a good idea to see him. I couldn't have my cake and eat it too. I could either be here in this new life, chasing my dreams, or back in DC married to Ben, about to start a family—but not both. I had chosen to start a new life and needed to see that decision through. Dinner would only make things messier.

I showered at the yoga studio, dried my hair, and walked toward the 1 train. As I reached for my MetroCard, a new text lit up my screen—Ben, asking if I was free for dinner on Wednesday.

Without giving myself time to hesitate, I replied that Wednesday worked and offered to make a reservation in a convenient neighborhood.

I chucked my phone into my Longchamp, debating if the yoga-induced adrenaline was making me decisive or shortsighted.

An hour later, I dropped my bags in the office and went to make coffee in the kitchenette. Charlie was at his desk by the time I got back.

"All right, I need the download. Does she take her steak rare? Is she a vampire? Does Eddie Kaufman hate California wine as much as you do?"

I took a slow sip of coffee. "I was introduced to a fine tequila and learned that Eddie has a thing for French red wine. And I *still* made it to yoga this morning. But I need more coffee before you pepper me with any more questions."

Charlie laughed. "'Pepper' you? No one told me I was sharing an office with my grandma in Florida."

As he launched into another question, Patricia's name appeared on the caller ID.

"Hi, Patricia," I responded, working to keep my voice steady. Every nerve felt exposed as I waited to find out if Eddie had read the memo.

She relayed that he was heading to the airport at the last minute and didn't have time to call, but he'd read the memo, and it was clear there were two key people who would be critical to building Andie's defense. We needed to interview them as soon as possible. Both were in LA, so he wanted Patricia to book me a flight out Thursday morning. He would be coming from a deposition in San Francisco. Patricia assumed that would work with my schedule.

"Yes, of course," I responded immediately. I wondered if she could tell from my voice how relieved I was. He had read it *and* wanted me to come to LA for the interviews. I felt a wave of pride for the work I'd put in, both in terms of the legal research and applying the facts we'd gotten from Andie to the research. *Maybe I can actually do this,* I thought. I was starting to feel like a lawyer.

"I assume he'll email you with more details when he has a second to breathe," she said, and she hung up.

Ten minutes later, I was booked business class on an 8 a.m. flight to LAX on Thursday, returning Friday evening. Eddie was copied on the itinerary. Within minutes, he responded that I should plan to get him draft interview outlines by midweek.

Not even two minutes later, he replied to his earlier email, this time copying Leo Hirschman, a partner from the firm's LA office.

> Leo, meet Samantha, one of my new associates. She'll be in Los Angeles next week and I think you two should connect while she's there. She wants to do entertainment (I tried to convince her otherwise).

I jumped up from my desk. "Oh my *god.* Charlie—Eddie just sent an email to Leo Hirschman saying we should meet when I'm in LA next week."

If there was anyone whose practice was more exciting than Eddie's, it was Leo Hirschman's. He was the only lawyer at the firm who had successfully established a bicoastal entertainment practice. About fifteen years younger than Eddie, he was both a litigator and dealmaker—rare, since most lawyers specialized in one or the other.

Charlie raised an eyebrow. "Damn, straight to the top. New York's too small for you now. I'm adding West Coast domination to your résumé."

I stared at the email. *One of Eddie's associates.* "This is . . . nuts."

Before Charlie could respond, my phone rang again. I recognized Andie's LA cell phone number.

"Hi Andie," I answered cheerfully.

"Eddie said you're coming to LA to talk to Amanda and Maureen?"

I nodded into the phone. "Yes, we're hoping they can meet on Thursday afternoon or Friday morning. Speaking of, do you have their phone numbers?"

"I gave them to Eddie's assistant. You should take a few other meetings while you're out there. When do you fly back?"

"Friday afternoon."

"That's dumb. LA is way more fun than New York on weekends. Stay till Sunday."

I chuckled nervously. "I don't think I can. Anyway, I'm just prepping interview outlines for Amanda and Maureen. Can I call you if I have questions?"

"Sure. Okay, I'm boarding. See you guys in La-La Land."

Building a strong defense would require talking to all the different people Andie had worked with, and these two women had been back-to-back personal assistants who could hopefully give us a picture of what it was like working with Andie. There was so much to go through, it was almost overwhelming. Most of their communications with her had been on text, which meant painstakingly reading thousands of messages and tagging what could be helpful to prove Andie wasn't guilty of operating an illegal gambling business.

I had never done anything like this in my life. Everything I'd learned in law school was abstract and theoretical compared to what I actually needed to do to succeed as a lawyer. It felt like her fate was in our hands. I had to get this right.

Chapter Thirteen

I spent the day combing through the documents we'd pulled from Andie's phones and laptops—thousands of emails, texts, and spreadsheets. Everything had been uploaded into a fully searchable online review tool. I'd asked IT for a second monitor and now felt like a Wall Street trader.

I couldn't believe I was getting paid to read years of private correspondence for someone like Andie. Her world was filled with celebrities I'd grown up watching in movies or on TV.

By Wednesday morning, I had written two interview outlines and tagged three dozen relevant emails.

It suddenly hit me that I still hadn't made a reservation for dinner that night. Ben had said he was staying close to Union Square, so I emailed the hostess at Union Square Cafe, where Connor was friends with the maître d', and asked for a table for two at 8 p.m.

The sun was just beginning to set as I walked down Fifth Avenue, past the New York Public Library toward Union Square. In my fantasy, we were having dinner but ten years in the future. We could make lighthearted jokes about the utility of a starter marriage. He was happily remarried with a family. I would be in a relationship with someone who wanted the same things from life. We'd each have our own happy ending.

The air outside was considerably cooler than when I left the office. I nervously chewed my lower lip as I crossed Thirty-Fourth Street. The closer I got to the restaurant, the more nervous I felt. I suddenly wished I'd made up an excuse. I could have said I was out of town. The last time we saw each other had been agonizing. He'd been brutally honest about how angry he was. Would this time be even worse?

I spotted him as soon as I walked in, reading a book at the bar. He must have sensed my presence—looming, unsure, radiating nerves—because he looked up and waved me over.

"Here we go," I said to myself.

Ben stood up and gave me a hug that felt both genuine and formal. Then he stood back with his hands on his hips.

"Damn, Sam. Can't believe it, but you're a city girl. Love this place too. Excellent old-fashioned," he said, nodding at the bartender.

"1942, please," I said as I eased into the seat next to Ben. I hadn't really known what to expect, but his upbeat, casual demeanor was throwing me off.

I suddenly wanted to confess how nervous I felt, to overexplain just how much I wasn't sure what was real and what was pretense. I couldn't figure out which note to land on.

"It's good to see you," I said honestly.

It was. He *looked* healthy. His olive skin was more tanned than when I'd seen him over the summer, and even though it had only been a couple of months, he was noticeably more muscular.

"Really, you look great. How are you?"

He smiled warmly. "I just got back from backpacking in Machu Picchu. Highly, highly recommend. It was the trip of a lifetime."

"Wow. That's so cool! Who did you go with?" I asked, immediately regretting the ambiguity of the question. It felt too personal. An unnecessary perforation in the effortless atmosphere he seemed committed to.

He read my face and gave a good-natured laugh. "Just me. I joined a group that was already going. It was awesome. Met some great people, took unreal pictures. You've got to go. I came back with perspective I never thought I'd have after everything that happened with us. I know now where I went wrong."

I shook my head. Was he talking about reconciliation?

"You didn't do anything wrong, Ben," I said cautiously.

He nodded. "I did. But we'll get into that later."

"How did you decide on Machu Picchu?" I asked.

He shrugged. "I needed something to take me completely out of the place I was in. Peru felt far enough to do that."

The bartender returned with the 1942. "Your table is ready. I'll transfer these over."

I nodded and reached for my bag, but Ben had already picked it up. "Jesus, what's in here? You carry this around all day long?"

"It's my laptop. I bring it home with me in case any emails come in that can't wait until the next day."

"That's a recipe for back trouble," he said with a genuine frown.

I chuckled like an old-timer who'd been hearing that all my life. "I'm definitely destined for sciatica or something like that."

As we sat down at the table, I realized I *was* happy to see him. I'd forgotten there was a time when we enjoyed spending time together, before I started to feel trapped and anxious that I'd never figure out how to disentangle my life from his. Could we really have made it to the other side this easily?

Ben ordered another old-fashioned and I sipped the 1942 while we caught up over small talk and oysters. He had so many questions about my life in New York: Was it difficult to find an apartment? Did I work all the time? Had I made new friends? Did I ever have time to see a show or go to a museum? I treaded lightly with every answer, careful not to come off as overly enthusiastic. After everything that had transpired, I couldn't tell if his attention was genuine.

He opened the wine menu.

"Think they have a good bottle of Oregon pinot?"

I felt a sense of apprehension but tried shaking it off. "Ah. I haven't had an Oregon wine in years," I said lightly.

"There's a pretty reasonable Willamette pinot on the list. What do you think?"

I wondered if the evening's emotional land mines were one sided. "Okay, let's do it."

He smiled triumphantly. "Remember how we always wanted to go to Oregon wine country? You were obsessed with it for a while."

Every nerve in my body felt on alert, looking for signals that his relaxed manner and nostalgic attention were genuine, when one of the last things he'd said to me was *it seems to me that you got everything you wanted.*

But the tequila was doing its thing. I wanted to know more about the perspective he gained in Peru. I also wanted to know if he was still writing the book, and I was just tipsy enough to ask. "Hope it's okay to ask, but are you still writing that book?"

He swirled his cocktail, and I couldn't tell if he wanted the question to hang out there uncomfortably or if he was stalling.

"Here and there," he said casually. "I took a break when I went to South America. Didn't seem like the right place to write a self-help book about your wife leaving you for the big city."

I cringed.

"Sorry. But to be fair, you brought it up," he said with a thin smile.

I held up my hands as a peace gesture. "No more book talk."

I told him about the insanity of finding a passable studio apartment and the hours spent working days, nights, and weekends. Getting to work with Eddie. He was wide-eyed over the ground I'd covered in only two months. We ordered another bottle of wine. The more we drank, the less I noticed land mines.

We finished the second bottle and ordered dessert and sambuca. Suddenly everything seemed hilarious. We switched to reminiscing about all the trips we took when I inevitably over-Xanaxed myself because of my fear of flying.

"I couldn't even relax on a twenty-hour flight to Sydney," he laughed. "I had to stay sober just in case you overdosed on benzos and wine and we needed to call for an emergency landing."

I tried to catch my breath from laughing so hard. "Do you remember the letters I would write when I was hallucinating at thirty-five thousand feet? Declaring how lucky I was to have you take care of me while I blacked out on every flight? I was never more nostalgic than when I was on Xanax and airplane wine."

He looked at me squarely. "Part of me wished you stayed like that after we landed."

I looked down at my plate. "I was a lot sweeter when I was drugged," I admitted.

He signaled the waiter. "Can we each do one more sambuca?"

The waiter looked at me to confirm I wanted another one, and I nodded. We needed to end on a positive note.

I insisted on picking up the tab and walking him to his hotel. The second sambuca landed hard, and I had to pull out my phone to calculate the tip, which Ben thought was adorable. As we left the restaurant, laughing our way toward Park Avenue, Ben went back to describing how life-changing his trip had been and saying he wished he'd been there with me. He turned toward me and looked so earnest and hopeful that I instinctively leaned in. The next thing I knew, Ben was kissing me, and I was kissing him back, with an intensity that seemed unfamiliar and surprising to both of us.

I hailed a cab. As we slid into the back seat, I mumbled, "Perry and West Fourth Street, please."

Chapter Fourteen

I couldn't remember finding my keys or unlocking the door or taking out my contact lenses.

I didn't recall setting my alarm for 4:45 a.m. so I could throw clothes into a suitcase and make it to the airport on time.

All I know is Ben was next to me when I woke up.

I jumped out of bed and immediately realized I was still drunk.

"I'm supposed to be on a flight to Los Angeles."

I looked over and saw Ben sitting up in bed, rubbing his right temple. "You have to go to Los Angeles? When?"

I hadn't realized I was talking out loud. There was no way I could miss my flight. How would I explain to Eddie that I overslept for an 8 a.m. flight?

I had no idea what had happened, or if we'd even used protection. Had he been safe over the year we'd been separated? Did I need to find a twenty-four-hour pharmacy and take Plan B before the flight? My thoughts were racing so loudly, I was sure Ben could hear them.

"My flight is in three hours. I haven't even taken my suitcase down from the top of my closet . . ."

I sat helplessly in the middle of the floor, struggling to make a mental checklist of everything that needed to happen to get myself to JFK. I pointed to the step stool next to the dresser and drew a line with my finger from the step stool to the closet door.

"I need that to go there so I can take that down," I muttered, pointing to the shelf above the closet.

Ben looked confused. "What time is it?"

I squinted at the clock on the stove and jumped up, totally panicked.

I didn't have time to spiral.

"It's almost five a.m. It takes an hour to get to JFK from here . . . oh my god, why didn't I tell Patricia to book me out of Newark?"

Ben threw back the covers and was by my side before I could blink.

"Sam, it's okay. Just take a later flight . . . say you got sick . . . but don't go. Not yet. We need to talk. Please."

I looked at him as if he had two heads.

"Are you crazy? Ben . . . whatever happened last night, we can talk about it when I'm back from LA. Or I can call you when I get there. But I have to make that flight."

Ben shook his head. "Last night was amazing. The conversation we had at the end of the night, after we got in the cab—we need to talk about it *now*. I can't wait for you to come back from LA. Stay here with me. I'm asking you, Sam. For us."

I felt a wave of intense nausea and stumbled to the bed. I dropped my head in my hands. The room was spinning.

I didn't remember saying anything in the cab.

I had to get to the airport on time.

"You're welcome to stay as late as you like. It's five a.m., for Christ's sake. Go back to sleep. There are clean towels on the shelf in the bathroom. Please just lock the bottom when you leave."

He stared at me, a stunned look on his face. "Goddammit, you really are selfish. Not that I should be surprised. Everyone but me seemed to figure it out. But even after you ripped the rug out from under me, I still didn't want to believe it."

I felt the hot sting of tears but kept my back turned and continued packing.

"You can't even look at me, because you know it's true. You needed me, and then when you thought you didn't, you left. When we met, I felt sorry for you. But I don't anymore."

There was no way I'd make it through the day without throwing up.

"You think you're being given some 'second chance' to live the life you always wanted? I've got news for you—you're still the same lost, insecure person you were with me. You take yourself wherever you go, Sam."

I went into the bathroom to brush my teeth. When I said goodbye, Ben was lying in bed, facing the window. He didn't turn around.

The moment I shut the door to the Uber, my whole body shook as I sobbed. What had I done? I had wanted so badly to convince myself that despite everything, he'd be okay, that maybe one day, we could even be part of each other's lives again.

If that had ever been a possibility, I'd just destroyed it.

~

I hobbled through the security line at JFK and collapsed into my seat with ten minutes to spare. I had six hours in the air with nothing to do but think about how I'd stepped knee deep in shit. It hadn't even been three months since I found him in his apartment, angrily writing a divorce memoir. What was the point of getting *that* drunk? To feel less nervous? It would have been better to have ghosted him entirely.

The flight was bumpy. In my hungover daze, I'd forgotten to pack the Xanax Ben and I had joked about less than twelve hours earlier. Despite the captain leaving the seat belt sign on throughout the flight, I threw up in the business class lavatory three times, feeling more remorseful each time I sank back into my seat.

I knew I had the emotional upper hand, and I had abused it. *I* was the one who left and broke his heart. *I* should have known better.

He was right: I was still the same lost person. Just with more expensive clothes, a Manhattan address, and a sixty-hour workweek.

Nine hours after I woke up next to Ben, I landed at LAX, physically and emotionally wrecked. I shuffled through the terminal and foggily scanned the drivers until I spotted my name. I dozed in the back of the car and woke up at the Peninsula Beverly Hills. It wasn't even 1 p.m. yet. I was supposed to meet Eddie in a conference room at the Century City office at 3:30 p.m. I checked into my room, showered, and shut my eyes for a few minutes, willing my hangover to disappear. Twenty minutes later, I woke with a start, feeling slightly less nauseated but still exhausted. I called an Uber at 2:45 and forced myself to review the interview outlines over the ten-minute ride.

The LA office overlooked all of Century City, the former Fox studio lot. The receptionist deposited me in an unoccupied visitor office. I sat down in the plush leather desk chair and rested my head against the back of it, trying to ignore my persistent nausea.

I jumped at a knock on the door.

"Samantha, right? Leo Hirschman. Eddie said we should meet while you're out here. Think we're grabbing a cocktail at the bar downstairs after your witness interview. See you then?"

He was taller than I expected and looked about ten years younger than his law firm bio.

The irony of it all was too much. It was as if half of me was crushing this new life, and the other half was stuck in the quicksand of my old life. Taking a deep breath, I tried to compartmentalize everything that was happening *here*, in Los Angeles, from the emotional bonfire waiting for me back in New York.

~

I could barely appreciate how well the interview went. I sensed from Eddie's reactions that the trip had been worth it from the first meeting alone. We needed support for the argument that the poker game wasn't an "illegal gambling business" because, among other things, Andie hadn't employed the required threshold of five "participants" to help run the business. The only people Andie had worked with consistently were two personal assistants whose "duties," she maintained, were of a personal nature and had nothing to do with poker. The first assistant we interviewed had even brought the hard-copy planner she used to schedule Andie's life, and there wasn't a single entry that referenced poker games.

"That was fantastic. They're not all like that. But *that* was a win for us. Let's call Andie tomorrow and debrief."

I made a note to ask Patricia to schedule the call.

"Leo Hirschman said he mentioned cocktails. I need to send a few emails first, but you should feel free to head down," Eddie said as he headed out the door.

All I wanted was a soft pillow in a dark hotel room. But skipping drinks with Eddie and Leo would be career suicide. I stopped by the visitor office to grab my things and tried to pull myself together.

Twenty minutes later, I found Leo in a back booth, martini in one hand and iPhone in the other. The sight of him kicked my nerves into overdrive.

Leo personified the confidence of a young partner whose client list and accolades topped most veteran partners'. He had aqua-blue eyes and dark-brown hair that was almost black, and he was tall, lean, and tanned. He could have been an actor. He reminded me of a throwback to the old-school studio executives: handsome, dynamic, hypermasculine. He probably spent all his free time on the tennis court.

"Eddie's been full of praise for you over the last few weeks," Leo said with a friendly smile.

I managed a humble grin. "It's an honor to meet you. I'm sure you know this, but you're a legend in the New York office."

"Tell me more." He smiled. "Wait. Before Eddie gets here—*what* is Andie Reese like? Is she difficult? He won't spill a word," he griped.

I took a breath. "She's intense. Whip-smart. I'm a little bit scared of her."

Leo laughed. "You'll get over that. As long as she's scared of Eddie, everything will be fine."

"I know she respects him. He breaks everything down in a way that I appreciate as much as she does, given I've been at this for about two months."

"I remember when I first started at the firm. Never had any plans to make partner. I thought I'd bang it out for a couple years, pay off my law school loans, then try to be an agent or manager. At the end of every year, I realized I was just happy enough not to leave. And then the longer I stayed, the more it became who I was. And now it's been fifteen years."

"I used to think I wanted to be an agent too. Would you ever make the jump?"

"Nah, can't teach an old dog new tricks. Plus, I'd miss the drama of this gig."

"There must be a special type of drama that goes along with representing talented people."

"Oh, yeah. Few clients can get into this level of deep shit without being brilliant."

"I guess I never thought of it that way. Andie strikes me as someone who was so smart, she outsmarted herself somewhere along the way."

"How so?" he asked, looking genuinely curious.

"She created something people wanted. And she made it so desirable, it got the attention of some not-so-great people, which is how she got on the government's radar."

"Do you think she's guilty?" he asked.

I shook my head. "I really don't. She may have had some questionable business practices. But so far, Eddie doesn't think anything she did warranted a criminal indictment."

He handed me the wine list. I skipped over the Willamette Valley pinot, trying to ignore the pit in my stomach.

"Are you originally from LA?" I asked.

Leo shook his head. "Just outside of Philadelphia. I went to college at Penn. When I got into UCLA Law, I chucked all my turtlenecks and never looked back. Life is good out here. When I graduated, entertainment work was exclusively on the West Coast. My parents wanted me to go into politics, but I chose this. I started out only doing litigation and then, somewhere along the way, my clients forced me onto the deal side, and now I'm about fifty-fifty. It's not common, but it works for me, and more importantly, it's what the clients want. They know when I'm putting a deal together, I'm keeping in mind all the ways past deals have fallen apart." He smiled ruefully. "And at the end of the day, I'm just an insecure asshole who likes to be needed."

"I wanted to start in litigation too. But I'm also really interested in doing transactional work at some point, and it always seemed to me like it would be harder to try to learn litigation later."

"That's a smart approach. Not a lot of junior lawyers have the foresight to realize that. I'll try to find some deals that you can dip your toe in. I can't totally steal you away from Eddie right now, but you never know what's coming down the pipe." He raised his martini. "To playing both sides," he said cheerfully, then checked his iPhone. "Eddie said he's running later than he thought . . . One more round so we can wait him out?"

The wine was draining what little energy I had left but also distracting me from thinking about Ben. I nodded, and he signaled the waiter for another.

"Okay Samantha," he said, leaning in. "Your turn. Where/what/who/why?"

"Let's see—I grew up on a horse farm in Virginia. Then I went to UVA and law school in Washington."

"Georgetown?" he interjected.

I nodded.

"Why entertainment?"

I took a deep breath. "I was a theater kid all the way through my first year of college. I thought I wanted to become an actor. I woke up one day and couldn't do it anymore. My family's financial situation changed, and I needed to either drop out or switch to something more pragmatic. But I always missed it. So eventually I thought maybe I'd become an agent, and then I discovered entertainment law. And law school seemed like a safe bet. When I read about your practice and Eddie's, I knew this was where I wanted to land."

I paused. Leo had a way of making me feel like he already knew everything about me.

"Pragmatism is hard at any age, but I imagine it's tough to have the rug pulled out from under you like that in college."

"It just meant I needed to find a job. Which honestly wasn't a terrible experience. Balancing a full-time course load with a full-time job was like boot camp. It made me a much more focused person when I eventually got to law school."

He smiled. "And the who? Is there someone special in your life?"

I shook my head slowly. "Not anymore. There was someone, but we ended it before I moved to New York," I said, carefully choosing my words. I couldn't imagine telling this sophisticated partner that I had been married. There was no way he would take me as seriously.

Leo nodded approvingly. "Fresh start."

"Do you think Eddie's actually coming?" I asked nonchalantly, hoping to maneuver back into more casual territory.

"Unless something more important has come up, yes. Anyway, just to go back to the LA-versus-New-York debate, every June I host a summer barbecue for the firm at our house in Montecito. You should plan to come out for that. I have a feeling if you spend more time in the LA office, you'll rethink New York."

Before I could answer, Eddie appeared and dropped his briefcase next to Leo's chair.

"Sorry. I've been playing inbox catch-up for the last two hours. Can I get you both a drink?"

I shook my head. "I'm okay with this one."

Leo checked his martini glass. "I'll stay and have one more with you. We should probably let Sam get back to the hotel soon. I've been dictating my memoir for the last hour, and I'm pretty sure she's second-guessing her life choices."

I laughed. "Not even close."

Leo slapped Eddie on the back. "Seriously though, we're old friends now. Bad idea to show up this late. You missed all the pleasantries; we're already onto invites to the summer barbecue."

Eddie nodded seriously. "Great. I figured you two would hit it off."

"*Actually*—and sorry for thinking out loud here, but this just occurred to me—I signed a new client this morning. A billionaire tech guy who invested $20 million in a slate of movies and lost every penny. He's based in New York. He hired us because he wants to file a lawsuit but wants someone to dissect the investment first. Probably makes sense to have a New York associate. I'm going to have to come out next week to get the whole download anyway."

It was impossible to hide just how cool that sounded. I was dying to take on more entertainment work that was directly related to film.

"When did that come in? I haven't seen it on the new matters list," Eddie asked.

"Just this morning."

Eddie mulled it over. "As long as you don't need someone on it full-time." He looked over at me. "If you're interested in taking it on, you have my blessing."

Chapter Fifteen

I woke up jet-lagged at 4 a.m. with a text from Andie.

> Staying in LA through the weekend?

I rubbed my eyes. My contacts were welded to them. It was Friday morning. We had one more witness interview before I was scheduled to fly back to New York.

I texted Andie back a few hours later with my schedule. She responded immediately.

> Push your flight. Come to this barbecue in Malibu tomorrow. Lots of industry people.

Eddie would probably kill me. I was just beginning to get a sense of Andie's social network from her poker days.

> Let me check with Eddie. He might be weird about that kind of thing. But if not, I'd love to go.

She responded with a devil emoji. Eddie's your boss at work, not when you're in LA for the weekend.

I instantly regretted saying I needed to run it by him. I quickly texted back.

Send me the details in case I can make it.

As Eddie and I packed up our things after the witness interview later that day, I told him about Andie's invitation.

"Are you going to go?" he asked, looking concerned.

"I'd like to. But if you're not okay with it, I won't."

"I'm fine if you want to go. But just be careful. Optics are everything. If people are taking drugs, you should leave."

"I'll scope out the scene and leave if I see anything sordid."

He looked satisfied. "I trust you'll do the right thing."

I emailed Lawyers Travel to reschedule my flight for Sunday morning.

The next morning, I woke up early and went over notes from the witness interviews by the hotel pool. At noon, I went back to the room, showered, and quickly changed into jeans and a blazer. I figured the basics would be passable. I'd never been out in the real world with Andie, but I could only imagine the glamour disparity between Andie's crowd and mine. Besides, I was going as Andie's defense lawyer. I wanted to be taken seriously. If anything, I was worried about coming off as uptight.

It took over an hour to get to Malibu. I could have been relaxing or taking in the coastline along the Pacific Coast Highway, but instead, my mind was two thousand miles away, reliving the regret of sleeping with Ben. It felt like my small studio apartment, once symbolic of the new person I wanted to be, was the scene of an emotional crime.

The Uber dropped me off in front of a dirt road, and I quickly texted Andie that I'd arrived. Less than a minute later, a four-wheeler appeared, driven by a woman in ripped jean shorts and a bikini top. She gave me a quick nod before taking me up a winding, wooded driveway.

The trees eventually parted to reveal a palatial glass beach house overlooking the Pacific. Andie was waiting outside.

"This is unreal," I said, before I could filter myself.

She looked amused. "Leah's mother-in-law is a famous clothing designer. I'll let you figure out which one."

Andie led us through the house to an outdoor bar with panoramic views of the Pacific next to an infinity pool that seemed to merge with the beach below.

"1942?" she asked.

I had no idea whose house this was or what the people would be like. I looked around and recognized several faces: an actor from *Entourage*, a Victoria's Secret model, and a few others I recognized but couldn't place.

Seemingly out of nowhere, the most beautiful woman I'd seen in real life approached Andie from behind, wrapping her long, graceful arms around her neck.

"You came!"

Andie turned around and squealed. "Of course I came. I wouldn't have missed it for anything."

She turned and grabbed my hand as if we were the oldest of friends.

"Leah, this is Sam. She's my defense attorney from New York. She's out here for work. She wants to work in the film business, so I told her she had to come meet people."

Leah took my other hand and held it in hers.

"Sam. I'm *so* glad you're here. We love this one so much. Promise me you'll defend her with your life."

Everything felt surreal.

I promised that between Eddie and me, Andie was in good hands.

Andie paraded me around for the next hour, introducing me to everyone as "Sam, my brilliant criminal defense lawyer," as if I was the party guest they all needed to meet. One of them asked if I thought she was going to jail.

"Nobody wants that less than me," I assured them. No one seemed to realize I'd been a lawyer for all of two months.

Leah's partner introduced himself as an "old-school" TV producer who had done a string of MTV shows in the early 2000s. He generously offered to make any introductions I wanted.

"Anything for the one who promises to keep Andie out of jail," he said with a confident smile.

After an hour of small talk, Andie nudged me. "There's one more person I want you to meet, then we can go."

I followed her inside. The interior of the house was straight out of *Architectural Digest*: twenty-foot ceilings with pristine white furniture, a 360-degree fireplace in the middle of the living room, and a dining table that looked like it would seat thirty people. She led us past an immaculately designed chef's kitchen with a walk-in wine fridge, an Equinox-level gym and sauna, and a private screening room. We continued upstairs and down a winding hallway lined with windows overlooking the beach. When we reached the last door on the right, Andie knocked softly.

"Arlo? It's me," she announced as she opened the door.

It was every little boy's dream room. Oversized bunk beds and a campsite set up with a huge tent and a pretend bonfire. An entire wall of shelves filled with children's books next to miniature armchairs sized for kids. LEGOs everywhere.

"I told your mom I couldn't leave until I got a hug," she said.

Arlo jumped up from the fire trucks he was playing with and threw his arms around Andie's legs.

"I want you to meet my friend Samantha. She's helping me with my case. The one I told you about."

Arlo waved but stayed attached to Andie.

"The one with the card games?" he asked.

She tousled his mop of blond hair. "Arlo's my godson. Since you're in charge of my fate, I wanted you guys to meet," she said with a half smile.

"What's *fate*?" Arlo asked.

"Fate means everything that happens to us in our lives. Your fate is to be the best boy with the biggest heart."

The absurdity of this little boy's life struck me in more ways than one. High-stakes poker was just the beginning of how different her world was from mine. But despite having loyal friends with tremendous privilege, her fate depended on proving to the government she wasn't a white-collar criminal.

Arlo showed us his LEGOs for a few minutes, then I called an Uber to take us back to LA. We rode in silence for about ten minutes as Andie checked her phone and I answered emails.

"You know—I lost most of my friends when the bottom fell out with the game," she finally said. "They either thought I couldn't offer them anything anymore, or they were worried about being associated with an accused felon. But Leah stood by me through everything. They're my family. It's important that you see me as more than someone accused of breaking the law."

There were a lot of words to describe the way I'd perceived Andie until that afternoon: empowered, fearless, whip-smart, every synonym for persistent. There was no denying she was badass. But I hadn't seen this other side to her. It was more than just humanity. I finally saw a softness and vulnerability that allowed me to relate to her.

"I'm glad I stayed the extra day. Thanks for letting me tag along. Arlo is the sweetest. You can tell he really sees you."

Andie turned to look out the window.

"What about you? Who are the people that you care about?" she asked.

I played with the sapphire ring on my right hand. I didn't know if it was because she'd let herself be vulnerable with me or because I wanted her to know that I appreciated how much she trusted me. But I found myself telling her everything.

"I've replayed it over and over. I think I ruined any chance of him ever being able to forgive me. And for what? I knew he hadn't moved on. All I did was pour salt in the wound."

I wondered if I was crossing some sort of attorney-client boundary, but it felt like we were both navigating parallel isolating experiences that made it feel like she wouldn't be quick to judge.

"Now I like you even more. You're not just a smart lawyer bot. You're a real person, Sam."

I leaned back against the headrest. "Being a smart lawyer bot doesn't sound terrible."

"Let me ask you something. If you could do it all over again—to be in the life you have now—would you?"

"All of it up to the point where I got drunk and slept with him this week," I said softly.

She gave me a knowing look. "Exactly. You're building the life you wanted. You have to leave the rest of it in the past. You messed up. But letting yourself be derailed by that isn't a price that you deserve to pay for making a mistake. You're what, thirty? You have your whole life ahead of you to make mistakes. Trust me. Some of them are ones you have to sit with, and others you leave in the past so you can move on. I guarantee you that your life is going to be bigger than the regret you're feeling right now. Think about where you're going. It's just the beginning."

We pulled up to Andie's apartment. She leaned over and gave me a hug. "Take that advice. Get some sleep. I'll see you in New York."

Chapter Sixteen

I landed in New York Sunday afternoon to an email from Leo's assistant with a secure file attachment for Sterling Solomon, Leo's new client. He would call to go over what he needed me to do.

Sterling's "files" consisted of emails he forwarded to Leo and text messages he screenshotted from his phone. That's how his $20 million investment was papered. I was more diligent when I rented a gym locker.

My cell phone rang Sunday night with an unknown number that I knew instinctively was Leo. I felt a wave of panic. I didn't know the first thing about film investments. What if he thought I did? What if he expected me to have a game plan?

He went into full partner mode the second I picked up. It sounded like he was dictating a message on his phone.

"Samantha. Hi. Hope you had a great trip back. Two things. We need to draft a breach-of-contract complaint, even though I hope to God we never have to use it. I'll send over a couple samples, but it's important that we position this as a straightforward breach of contract, as in you need to *downplay* the movie aspect. We don't want to point out the risky nature of the investment. Apparently, he never consulted a film finance lawyer, and that type of schmuck decision-making is exactly the information we don't want in front of a judge. Find some recent breach-of-contract case law and then get all the facts you need from him tomorrow. I'm coming to New York in a few weeks to meet him in person, but I don't want to lose time—so I need you to sit down with him at his office this week and get the full download so we can have a draft of the complaint ready to put in front of him when I get there."

I took furious notes as Leo continued speaking a mile a minute.

"Again. We need a coherent complaint to placate the client, but between us, I do *not* want this lawsuit getting filed. His only bet at recovering anything is us coming up with a creative strategy to force a settlement. A judge is going to take one look at these emails and texts and laugh us out of court. We *cannot* litigate this."

"Understood."

I created a new client folder as a second email popped up with three sample complaints attached.

I opened the first one, written on behalf of the wife of a famous athlete who was suing the publisher of her memoir for breach of contract. The second complaint was for the founder of one of the most popular social media platforms. The third was for a legendary morning-show host who was suing the TV network for ageism.

All Leo's clients.

I felt an unshakable wave of imposter syndrome.

It took all of ten minutes to read through Sterling's documents. It seemed the only undisputed fact was that the film fund had approached Sterling to make an investment in a slate of four movies with budgets of $5 million each for a total of $20 million. He'd wired the money in one lump sum. Other than that, it didn't look like he received any formal agreement papering the investment or copies of the movie budgets, and it didn't even look like he'd asked for them. It was going to be difficult to meet the minimum standard for a bona fide complaint with such sparse supporting facts.

I quickly summarized the emails and texts into a coherent memo, then began carefully reading each sample complaint and researching breach-of-contract cases with similar fact patterns. There weren't any.

I went to bed late and woke up early. I hadn't seen Charlie in almost a week. I was already used to having someone I could say anything to inside our office bubble. I texted him as I got off the subway to see if he wanted Joe's and was disappointed when he responded he was out the whole week for depositions somewhere in the Midwest. He promised to send tallies of oversized SUVs and American flags.

The meeting with Sterling was scheduled for one o'clock the next day on Greene Street in SoHo. A black car would pick me up from the office at noon.

I arrived a few minutes early and buzzed the top floor of the loft-style building. There was no concierge, but an elevator attendant appeared a few seconds later and scanned a key to the penthouse. The elevator door opened directly onto a massive loft with garage-style windows and a woman sitting behind an Apple monitor.

"Hi, I'm Samantha DeFiore from Abramson & Klein. I'm here to meet with Sterling Solomon."

"Oh, hi, Samantha. I'm Grace. Sterling is just wrapping a call, but let's head to the meeting space, and he'll be over in a few."

I settled into a camel-colored leather swivel chair and powered up my MacBook to review my notes.

Sterling was nothing like I imagined. He didn't look more than twenty-five. He was barely taller than me and wearing ultrafitted black jeans, an oversized black denim jacket, and green sneakers.

He extended a hand. "Sterling. Thanks for coming by. I know we have real work to do here, so let's dive in."

I handed Sterling a copy of the outline I prepared.

"Leo sent over the documents," I began, trying to sound confident, though I was painfully aware I was going into this meeting completely solo and transparently inexperienced. I needed to stick to the facts. If he asked about strategy, I'd have to punt to Leo.

Sterling grinned. "Leo is fucking awesome. If he was on my team when these assholes asked me to invest in their bullshit movies, I wouldn't be in this position. I guess live and learn, right?"

The logline to the story of my life, I thought, *only my lessons hadn't cost $20 million.*

"We're going to do everything we can to minimize your exposure," I assured him. "I think it would be helpful to go over a few preliminaries. Your background is in tech, right?"

An hour later, I had a pretty good idea of the picture I wanted to paint about Sterling's decision to invest $20 million in a slate of art-house movies. In his own words, Sterling was generally bored day-trading tech stocks and needed to "switch it up." His favorite pastime was going to the movies alone in the afternoon, and he was frustrated studios only seemed to be making big Marvel movies. The film fund that solicited him for money was represented by a shark of a Hollywood dealmaker who saw Sterling coming a mile away: a young tech guy with lots of cash and no experience in the movie business. Sterling thought he could be the guy to prop up smaller and more tasteful movies. There was zero transparency with respect to the financials. Unbeknownst to Sterling, the fund had already burned through an initial round of money from Dubai, then pivoted to Silicon Valley, where the wealthiest players were under thirty and eager to pay for celebrity access.

"As you know, the emails and texts aren't a lot to go on. But I looked up the box office numbers for each movie, and they were actually pretty strong. The $5 million budgets should have been recouped from the sale of the movies and the box office numbers. But given how little information they gave you, I have a hunch the budgets were actually a lot more than $5 million. And if they took your money, then turned around and inflated the budgets, you would potentially have a fraud claim. And that's a much more intimidating claim than breach of contract."

"It *was* fraud! Those assholes stole my money. They can't get away with it."

I nodded sympathetically. "Just to confirm—you never saw copies of the budgets, right?"

"Nope."

"Did you ask for them?"

"Nope." Sterling continued doodling along the margins of his notepad. "But I heard that one of the guys paid himself a million-dollar producing fee and fucked off. No one even knows where he is."

Sterling rubbed his jaw. He looked like a frustrated kid who lent another kid lunch money then found out they spent it on a new video game. Even though we were from completely different worlds, I felt how shitty the situation was. Sure, he was a trust-fund kid who burned through $20 million trying to make movies. He wasn't relatable in theory. But wasn't the point of being a lawyer to help someone who was wronged? It was clear who the bad guys were in this mess.

He nervously clicked the bottom of his pen. "Look, I'm going to level with you. My dad is going to cut off my balls if I don't get this money back. He told me not to give those guys a penny, and I didn't listen. He doesn't even know yet that the money's gone. Last I heard, they were telling me to go after the original backers in Dubai. He's gonna kill me."

I was still trying to wrap my head around $20 million.

I promised Sterling I'd have a draft of the complaint to Leo as soon as I could.

I picked up a salad on my way back to the office and started going over my notes from the meeting. Leo was right: There was no way to file a complaint for breach of contract that would pass muster. We'd been taught in the first year of law school that lawyers have an obligation to only file lawsuits where the facts meet the standard of pleading; otherwise, you get sanctioned, maybe even disbarred. Unless we uncovered some more helpful facts, we weren't getting close.

I wished Charlie was back so I could complain about the cards being stacked against me on my first assignment for Leo Hirschman. No one could draft a compelling complaint for this client, let alone someone with zero experience.

I lost track of time as I plodded through page after page of sentences that I knew would be ripped apart by the other side's lawyers. The office felt cold and empty.

"How is it one a.m.?" I muttered. But I was wired. The city was sleepier than I was.

My office line rang, jolting me back to reality.

"Knew I'd find you there," Charlie said. I smiled and wondered how he knew that I needed a friendly voice.

"You're manifesting my reality when you call me this late."

"I don't know what that means."

"It means the universe knows you're going to call, and it makes sure I'm sitting here waiting for the phone to ring."

Charlie clicked his tongue. "I don't think you need me to manifest your workaholic lifestyle. Pretty sure you do that all on your own. Anyway, I'd bet a lot of money that whatever's keeping you at the office this late is better than what I've been doing all day."

"How many pickup trucks did you see today?"

"Let me just paint the whole picture. I landed in some bumfuck town, then drove three hours to some even more Podunk town, where I spent the day in a *warehouse* trying to find FOIA documents in a filing cabinet that was built when Teddy Roosevelt was president. Then I carried *one* box back to my car and drove thirty minutes to make copies. You can guess what happened next. Meanwhile, you're going to barbecues in Malibu. I'd ask, 'Where did I go wrong?' but I don't think I can handle the answer right now."

I smiled at the image of Charlie stuck somewhere in Middle America. "What's FOY-UH?"

"Freedom of Information Act. Someone mentioned it once during orientation—it's like the best and worst tool to request government docs. Tax filings and all that stuff. They literally respond with everything under the sun, and you have to wade through the mountains of paper they generously send to find the one thing you actually need."

"Sounds like an environmental crisis."

"No shit."

"Well, thanks for the pick-me-up. I know you don't believe me, but I needed it."

"Figured you missed me."

I nodded silently. "You'd think I'd love having this view to myself, but the truth is, it's starting to feel a little creepy. Especially late at night."

Charlie groaned. "Fuck, how is it only Wednesday? My flight back isn't till tomorrow night. We're due for a proper catch-up. I want to hear all about LA and this new case and whatever new yoga class you found."

I hung up and stared at my screen, imagining Charlie in a Midwestern warehouse wading through bureaucratic sludge. *FOIA*. The acronym felt burned on my brain.

I needed a break from the complaint, so I opened my research document and read through the notes I'd taken on the four movies Sterling invested in. Curious, I typed "Tokyo Summer movie" into Google and clicked the "News" tab. A few reviews popped up at the top of the page. One headline caught my eye: "New Indie Production Shoots NYC's Chinatown to Pass for Tokyo." I read the first line of the article: "While New York State may be more tax-credit friendly than Japan, the producers are being crucified for assuming Americans are that stupid . . ."

I sighed. Sterling couldn't have gotten involved with a less legitimate group.

And then it hit me.

I swiveled behind me to the bookshelf where I kept three textbooks and all the books on entertainment law I had bought before law school. I grabbed *The Biz* by Schuyler Moore and scanned the table of contents for the tax-credits chapter. It was only a couple of pages long but enough of a refresher to know what I needed to find out.

I grabbed my phone and excitedly texted Charlie. You're a freaking genius.

Chapter Seventeen

Our first meeting with the prosecutors on Andie's case was the following Monday. I was more anxious than she was. Most of the arguments Eddie was planning to make were based on documents that only *I* had reviewed and research *I* had done. I didn't want to let either of them down.

I woke up early and ran to the store to get water bottles and granola bars—the "secret weapon" advice given to me by the senior associate who mentored me when I was a summer associate: Be the first-year who always has snacks handy. Something about it felt sexist, but I did it anyway before hailing a cab downtown to meet Eddie and Andie, who were coming separately.

Twenty minutes later, I got out at 1 Saint Andrews Plaza. The building was surprisingly nondescript, considering it was headquarters to prosecution of the country's most high-profile cases. I followed Eddie and Andie as we placed our bags on scanners and walked through metal detectors. A security officer led us to an interrogation-style conference room with bright fluorescent lights.

The all-male team of prosecutors assigned to Andie's case reminded me of what Eddie promised Andie in our first meeting: My presence would ensure there would always be another woman in the room.

"Fellas," Eddie acknowledged coolly.

Andie looked calm and collected. I could learn a thing or two.

I pulled out a folder with Eddie's talking points so I could follow along. He barely looked at them. He knew exactly what he wanted to say and didn't miss a beat. It was like watching a movie. Twenty minutes later, he finally took a breath.

"Look, guys. We're about a month into this now, and that's a month more than anyone should spend in defense of a baseless indictment. There isn't a shred of evidence that would support the felony you're accusing her of. We all know what this job is about, and it's going after the bad guys, not a woman who, at worst, showed some bad judgment by dabbling in an elite poker game. This is a fool's errand."

The prosecutors stayed expressionless throughout Eddie's impassioned monologue.

"Thanks, Eddie. That's helpful. We do have a few questions for Andie, but why don't we all take five first."

They gave us the room, and Eddie handed me back the talking points.

"These were great, thanks." I wanted to jump for joy like a little kid. Instead, I finally let myself breathe out fully.

"I brought some water and granola bars, if either of you needs anything."

Andie nodded. "Water would be great. I feel like it was *me* talking for the last half an hour."

I grabbed a bottle and handed one to her.

"Eddie, thank you. That was gr—" I heard the deafening *whoosh* before I saw it. My stomach dropped and everything around me seemed to move in slow motion. Carbonated water exploded out of the bottle, drenching her hair and face and now-see-through blouse.

She froze, a look of shock crossing her face just as the prosecutors walked back in. My heart hammered in my chest. *Did that really just happen?*

Andie dabbed her face with her palm. "Uh . . . excuse me for just a moment, I just need two minutes—can you point me to the nearest restroom?"

I jumped up, feeling my face flush with heat. "I'll go grab paper towels . . . oh my god, I can't believe this. I'm so sorry . . ."

I realized I had grabbed sparkling water instead of flat.

She laughed nervously. "Great icebreaker."

The shorter prosecutor looked at the open water bottle and smirked. "The women's bathroom is down the hall on the left."

I was dying.

I followed Andie in the direction of the restroom. When *the fuck* had Smartwater started selling carbonated water?

The bathroom door closed behind us and Andie erupted in giggles as I stood there stoically.

"Oh my god, your face is priceless. Sam. Do *not* beat yourself up over this. Someday we're going to tell this story. Only first, I really need paper towels. And maybe a hairdryer."

I was still too embarrassed to feel relieved.

"Andie. I—I don't even know what to say . . ."

"That's okay, I think Eddie has enough to say for both of us. Damn, that man can talk."

I removed the entire stack of paper towels from the dispenser. "I am . . . so sorry. This is the last thing you need right now."

She started laughing all over again. "Honestly, it might be exactly what I needed. Stop apologizing. I'm just glad my mascara's not running."

"I really wanted today to go smoothly. *Fuck*," I moaned, covering my face.

She tossed the towels and straightened her pencil skirt, then grabbed my hand. "Today is going to go however it goes. What matters is the work you put into getting Eddie ready for this meeting. Did you hear him in there?"

I smiled faintly. "He was really channeling *My Cousin Vinny*."

She swung open the door decisively. "Let's do this. I've already forgotten about you trying to drown me in seltzer."

~

I planned to go home to change before meeting Connor and Emilie for dinner at Empellón on West Fourth Street, but by five o'clock, I was more than ready for the biggest margarita they had. I texted to say they could find me at the bar.

They got there half an hour later, dragging me to a corner table where Connor immediately announced he'd rented us a house upstate for the weekend.

"I'm sorry, why would you think I could just pick up and go away for the weekend?" I asked, taking the last sip of the Don Julio margarita I'd ordered while I was waiting.

"Sam. Come *on*. It's barely forty-eight hours. We're picking up the car in Midtown on Friday. You can jump in the back seat with your laptop and work the whole way. The house is fully stocked. The views are stunning. And we'll have you back by Sunday night."

I looked at Emilie, who just shrugged. "I know, neither of us does nature well. But he promised to never bring up again how we forgot his birthday."

"Your birthday was a *week* before the bar—which you weren't even taking," I objected. For Connor, law school had always been just another thing to add to his résumé.

He grinned. "You are so right, Sam. Anyway, Emilie is in. Gillian is in. And—"

"Wait, the girl from yoga?" I gave Emilie a *did you know that was still a thing?* look.

"The *woman* from yoga," he corrected me. "We also do SoulCycle now. But you should both know before this weekend that Gillian from yoga and SoulCycle is now my girlfriend," Connor said proudly.

"As in, you're not sleeping with anyone else?" I said doubtfully.

He looked crestfallen. "Do you both have such low opinions of me?"

Emilie coughed. "Lower, probably."

"Ladies, please come to the Catskills. Observe me over the course of a weekend. I've changed."

I shook my head as Connor held up his hand. "Observe me over a *short* weekend. Em, tell her you're in so she'll go."

Emilie gave a resigned nod. "I have so much work that at this point, I'm just hoping self-sabotage will save me."

I knew what she meant. "Ugh. Fine. But only if there's Wi-Fi at the house, and you don't force me to play a single board game."

Connor smiled triumphantly. "Drinking games only."

Chapter Eighteen

On Friday morning, we received another set of emails from Andie, so I posted up in the back seat of the giant black Suburban Connor had rented from the Hertz on Forty-Eighth Street and powered up my hotspot so I could review them on the drive upstate.

We'd barely hit the George Washington Bridge when I got to an email that I realized was directly supportive of one of our thinner defense arguments.

"Holy shit," I muttered, immediately forwarding it to Eddie with a declarative "We need to talk to this Emerson person. He's in LA."

Eddie responded two minutes later that he was still in Los Angeles and I should plan to fly out Monday.

"*Fuck*," I groaned loudly.

Connor was driving as if we weren't in the middle of Friday rush hour in New York City.

Gillian turned around. "If you want to sit up front, I'll switch with you," she offered sweetly.

I winced. "No. I need to fly back to LA on Monday. But there's no way I'll be able to get home in time to pack and make the flight. Which means Monday is going to be the longest day ever."

"Sorry, Sam, but all I'm hearing is that you have to go back to being a lawyer on Monday, just in LA, instead of New York. Why is this a Friday afternoon problem?" Connor asked as he swerved, cutting off at least the fourth car since we'd left.

"The point is I need to prep *before* Monday, and I have to go into the office to do it. Sometimes your insensitivity to the demands of my job is really fucking annoying," I whined. I emailed Patricia to please book a late flight on Monday. I'd leave from the office.

Three hours later, we pulled up to a rustic, two-story wood cabin Connor landed in a last-minute Airbnb deal. I silently wished I was there for the cozy fireplace and view of the snowy Catskills. Instead, I dropped my bag next to the stairs and settled into the oversized couch to work on another interview outline.

I didn't move until Emilie came over a few hours later with a glass of red wine.

"Dinner's ready, no thanks to you," she said.

"Shit, I'm sorry. I'll make breakfast tomorrow," I promised as I closed my laptop and took a long sip.

I stopped in the half bath off the living room to freshen up before heading to the dining room. The table was set with champagne flutes, wine glasses, and a massive pine-cone centerpiece.

"Wow. Nice table, guys, but are we inviting the neighbors?" I asked, counting six place settings.

I heard a loud *pop* and turned to see Connor holding a magnum of Moët just as everyone shouted "*Surprise!*"

My brain couldn't catch up. I looked around and saw Caroline standing next to Emilie, and I saw a third person behind a giant balloon that said "**THIRTY?!!**"

"Happy thirtieth, Sam. You don't look a day over twenty-one." Charlie handed me the balloon as Emilie put a champagne glass in my other hand.

"Wait, what? Is this actually happening?"

No one had ever thrown me a surprise party, let alone a surprise weekend. I couldn't stop laughing as Connor raised his glass.

"We knew you'd never agree to a birthday weekend, so we found the only people you'd actually *want* to celebrate with. So I guess in the end, this is more of a toast to everyone who made the cut. To us, guys."

I went around the room clinking glasses.

"You're all excellent liars," I said.

I couldn't believe Charlie was there. "Weren't you still in Texas yesterday?"

Charlie raised his glass. "When there's a will, there's a way. Emilie emailed me a few weeks ago, and I knew I couldn't miss it. You keep me sane and caffeinated, and there's no one else I'd want to celebrate surrounded by strangers and snowdrifts."

I was so happy to see him. In a short amount of time, he had become a dependable part of day-to-day life. He knew that I kept face wipes in my drawer, and I knew he stashed nicotine mints in his. We were eyewitnesses to the insanity of life as a first-year associate.

After rib eyes and mashed potatoes, we each carried a bottle of wine to the living room to play Cards Against Humanity. I'd never seen Emilie laugh so hard. Even though Caroline and Charlie were new to the group, it felt like we'd all been friends for decades. I felt happy, almost blissful. I'd never celebrated a birthday surrounded by a group of my closest friends.

By midnight, everyone had either lost or decided to call it except me and Charlie. Caroline, the most responsible of the crew, was the first to head to bed. Emilie followed suit, and soon no one could ignore Gillian's exaggerated yawns, especially Connor.

"Finish it out?" Charlie asked as he refilled his wine glass.

"The game or the bottle?" I asked.

"There has to be a winner," Charlie said competitively. "Officemate playoffs."

"Okay, fine. If you think I'm heading into this decade a loser, you don't really know me."

I watched as Charlie shuffled the cards. He looked like he hadn't shaved in a week, and I realized he probably hadn't been back to his apartment in that long.

"Thanks for being here," I said sincerely.

He kept shuffling. “Of course. It’s been weird living our separate lives recently. I have no idea what you’ve been up to. Good thing we have the whole weekend to catch up.”

I nodded and took another sip of wine, thinking about how I’d drunkenly ended up in bed with my ex-husband. A wave of embarrassment flushed through me. I was there with every one of my closest friends, but I hadn’t told any of them.

“Yeah . . . it’s been weird. I actually saw Ben a few weeks ago.”

He looked at me sideways. “Ben, Ben? I thought he still lived in DC?”

“He was in the city.”

“Wow. How was it?”

I took a deep breath. Maybe telling someone would defuse the emotional bomb that kept going off in my head. “It could have been fine, but I fucked it up. We went to dinner and got super drunk.” I tried reading his reaction, but his face was entirely neutral, as if I was telling him about a memo I’d written. “And we slept together.”

He went from poker face to startled and I immediately wished I could backtrack.

“Believe me, I regret everything about it. It wasn’t the right move at all. I know that.”

Something about Charlie’s face told me he wasn’t going to try to make me feel better about it.

I took another sip to stall. “Sorry, let’s change the subject . . . I feel like a schmuck for having done it, and I don’t need anyone else to tell me that.”

Charlie stared at the cards. “Your move, counselor.”

I refilled my wine glass and checked if he needed a top off.

“Do you still have feelings for him?” he asked.

“Despite the very bad choice I made to sleep with him, no.”

“Have you dated anyone since you guys got divorced?”

“Not seriously.”

“Casually?”

I smiled ruefully. "I have no clue what I'd do on an actual date. I was either dating Ben or married to him for most of my twenties. When we got divorced, the only way I could bring myself to interact with men nonplatonically was by drinking. A lot."

I hoped Charlie could read between the lines that it had just felt too strange, or too vulnerable, to be intimate with someone after I had been someone's wife.

"So what you're saying is, you've only gone on drunk dates?"

I felt my face flush. "I wouldn't even call most of them dates. Just hooking up with guys I kind of knew from school and felt comfortable with."

I paused. "I actually haven't had sober sex since I was married to Ben."

Charlie looked stunned again, then quickly recovered. "Well DeFiore, I'd offer to help you out with that tonight, but . . ." He nodded toward the collection of empty wine bottles on the table.

"That's generous," I said lightly, feeling my face get warm.

"Your move again." Charlie rubbed his jaw. "I'm sure he still thinks about you in that way. Ben, I mean. You're the one that got away. Not a lot of beautiful and funny girls out there, in my experience."

I blushed again and mumbled, "Oh."

He looked embarrassed. "Should we call it? I'm feeling a rough morning if we keep this up. Gotta be ready for ice-skating tomorrow," he said.

I groaned. "Ice-skating hungover isn't how I want to spend my surprise thirtieth birthday, so I accept your resignation. Besides, I could fall asleep sitting up right now. I hope they figured out the heat upstairs, because it's freezing down here."

I went to stand up and gravity pulled me back down.

"We should let this last log burn out before we call it a night. Safety first." He sat back against the couch.

I wasn't ready to try standing up again, so I nodded and wrapped my arms around myself.

"I might just fall asleep right here." I yawned and rested my head on the back of the couch. He passed me a blanket.

"Happy birthday, Sam."

~

I woke up on the couch, tucked in a warm blanket with a pillow under my head. There was a glass of water and two Advils on the coffee table. I smelled coffee and bacon coming from the kitchen and tried to put my finger on what I was feeling. I remembered telling Charlie about Ben. The memory of his reaction was fuzzy, but I felt a warm, unjudged feeling. There was something else I couldn't put my finger on. Something I'd felt right before Charlie went to bed.

"Rise and shine, birthday girl."

Emilie appeared from the kitchen with a mug in one hand and the paper in the other. "Brought you the morning paper. That's what people do in the Catskills," she said proudly.

I squeezed one eye shut. "That doesn't make any sense to me, but I drank my weight in red wine last night, so . . ." I said, grabbing the coffee.

Emilie plopped down next to me. "Yeah—the housemates are on the verge of rioting because we gave you the master bedroom, and you slept on the couch."

"Believe me, that wasn't my plan. Charlie and I stayed up way too late trying to finish the game, and I don't even remember falling asleep."

"Was it fun?" she asked.

I nodded. "I need this coffee, though." I sighed loudly. "Are we really going ice-skating? Is that like reading the paper here?"

"Connor isn't letting anyone go back to the city without trying it."

I finished the coffee, then sprinted upstairs to shower before breakfast. I wondered if Charlie felt uncomfortable about how much I'd shared. The end of the night was spotty. I remembered it feeling cathartic the night I first told him about Ben, after the gala, when he asked me pointedly about having been married. But sharing that I'd recently slept with my ex-husband—who I had no plans to reconcile with—felt like TMI.

I was about to turn on the hairdryer when I heard a light knock on the door. Charlie was there bright-eyed and showered, holding out the folded blanket and pillow.

"Figured I'd return this before the natives notice you didn't sleep in the only room with a king-size bed," he said.

I felt my face turn shades of crimson at the memory of Charlie tucking me in. "Emilie already found me. But thanks. Think I'll lay low on the wine tonight."

Charlie grinned. "See ya downstairs."

After breakfast we bundled up and piled into the Suburban.

I hadn't ice-skated since I was a kid. Every time I fell, I laughed so hard I could barely get up. Either Caroline (who grew up ice-skating) or Charlie (who grew up playing ice hockey) pulled me up before gracefully gliding past me. After thirty minutes, I decided to let them have the ice and went to join Emilie and Connor in the café.

"Caroline and Charlie would dominate Olympic couples skating, huh?" Connor announced as I sat down with a hot chocolate.

Emilie grabbed a sip of my hot chocolate. "Oh, that's good. We really curated an idyllic winter weekend up here."

"*I* curated," Connor said indignantly.

I nodded. "Yes, great surprise, both of you. Crazy you kept it under wraps so well. I always thought I'd be impossible to surprise."

"You're full of surprises. I'm just glad we were able to fool the master," Connor said as he scrolled distractedly through Reddit.

"How am I full of surprises?" I asked.

"Well for one, you're a divorcée."

"That's not a surprise anymore. And can I please start my thirties with a clean slate?"

"*Maybe* you should start with a romp to clean the palate? 'What happens in upstate New York . . .'" he said, nodding in Charlie's direction.

I looked at Emilie, who quickly came to my defense.

"She's got a bit much on her plate, mate. I don't think she needs to jump into another relationship."

I wrinkled my nose. "And not everything revolves around finding a partner."

"Well, looks to me like Charlie's lookin' for love," Connor sang. "Caroline's been laughing her arse off out there all morning."

I shrugged. "Why are you so obsessed with everyone else's love life anyway? Focus on your own."

"I just think everyone could benefit from my expertise. But I actually don't think Charlie and Caroline need any help at all."

I felt a twinge thinking how easy it would be for Charlie and Caroline to have a tidy weekend hookup. The idea of something so casual as a "romp" was anathema to the path I was on. Every day I wondered if I'd ever feel like a normal thirtysomething and not someone who already had a failed marriage. I didn't know if I'd ever learn to trust myself again.

Chapter Nineteen

Early Monday I headed to the office with my suitcase in tow, feeling surprisingly energized from the weekend away.

"So, what's a Virginia girl's take on the Catskills?" Charlie asked as I rolled my suitcase under the desk.

"I mean, you can't get to Manhattan in under two hours from the Blue Ridge Mountains, so I guess I'm a Catskills girl now," I said, powering up my laptop and logging into the review database.

"Did you feel properly celebrated?"

I nodded. "I still can't believe you made it all the way there from Missouri or Texas or wherever you were on Thursday. I felt *very* special."

He grinned. "And now we're back here. Like it never happened."

I scrolled through my calendar. "I have to leave here at three for JFK. Let me make sure Patricia booked a car," I said distractedly.

He headed out for coffee with his firm mentor, and I spent the morning organizing documents and drafting questions for Emerson. By 3:15 p.m., I was in a car to the airport.

Early the next morning, I woke up in Los Angeles jet-lagged and booked a last-minute boxing class next to the hotel. I went back to my room to shower, threw on a navy skirt suit with a cream-colored blouse, and took an Uber to meet Eddie and Andie for a preinterview lunch.

Eddie got right down to business. "After we finish these interviews and Sam updates the timeline, I'd like to talk about whether it makes sense for you to consider pleading guilty. There are over two dozen people in the indictment, and the longer it takes you to plead compared to the others, the less favorably the court looks on your decision to accept responsibility. A sixth defendant pleaded out yesterday. I still don't think the government has anywhere close to enough evidence to convict you if you were to go to trial, but it's always a gamble."

Andie shook her head. "I'm the *only* woman involved in this. I know I made bad choices, but I never meant to break the law—isn't that worth fighting them on?"

Eddie folded his arms. "The straightforward answer is no. I've seen thousands of these mass indictments. I wholeheartedly believe there's an exception that takes you outside of 1955, but judges are always more lenient when someone pleads guilty early on."

"Should we wait for the Second Circuit's ruling on whether poker is a game of skill?" I asked.

"When is the court hearing arguments?" he asked.

"Next week. I'm scheduled to go and watch."

He nodded. "Let's see how long it takes for the decision to come down. But if it's delayed, or they reverse the lower court's decision, I don't think you should keep waiting to plead. I've been in this situation many times, and my gut is telling me you need to be able to move on with your life, not tie yourself up in court for years for an outcome that's far from certain."

She paused, and I could tell she was nervous. "I want to be able to move on too. I guess that's as good a time as any to run something by you guys."

She reached into her bag and put a folded letter on the table. "I got this from a publisher last week. They're offering me a book deal."

Eddie looked more concerned than usual. "Andie—"

"Wait. Before you say anything, I just need you to know I'm not actually interested in writing a book. But I am so outrageously broke right now, and they're offering a *huge* advance. I've had offers before, but everyone wanted names, and I won't do that. This one is interested in my side of the story. Please . . . I need your blessing, but I need to find a way to do this."

Eddie unfolded the letter and read it silently. I gave Andie a sympathetic smile.

He looked at Andie with a serious expression. "You cannot bullshit me on this, Andie. I need to know right now: Have you started writing this book? I have to know if there's a manuscript out there. I've said it before, but I'll say it again: I cannot do my job if you withhold things from me."

Andie shook her head. "I spent a few hours outlining some chapters, just to see if this was even something I could do. But I meant what I said. *I don't want to write a book.* I just don't see how I say no to this. It feels like my only chance for a fresh start."

Eddie folded his napkin. "If you write this, we're going to have to disclose it to the prosecutors. I get that you need money. But if it fucks up your case, the money is moot."

He looked at his watch. "I need time to think it through. I have to get on a call, but I'm asking you to hold off for now. Here's my credit card. You two can finish up here. Sam, I'll see you upstairs for the three o'clock."

Andie dropped her head into her hands. "I didn't think he was going to react that way. I guess I just don't understand how this could hurt my case."

"I think he's worried that if you write something that contradicts what we've said to the government, they'll either bring new charges or use it as a reason to reassess a more lenient sentence."

She shook her head. "I need an income. I'm just planning to tell the truth. I've *been* telling the truth."

"I'll try my best to make sure he gets back to you quickly," I promised. I signed the check and hugged her goodbye.

~

I skimmed emails on my phone as I waited for the elevator up to the office. Leo had seen my name on the firm's visitor list. Did I want to discuss Sterling's case over drinks?

I was still trying to detox from the Catskills. It was becoming impossible to remember a time when drinking wasn't part of my life, even though it hadn't always been that way.

I was twenty-six the first time I got drunk. It was Thanksgiving break of my first year of law school. My brother Artie was in town for Thanksgiving, and he wanted to go out Wednesday night. Ben and I drove to the bar because neither of us planned to drink a lot. Some of Artie's DC friends showed up, and I felt my first real taste of social anxiety. I'd never self-medicated with alcohol until that night. Someone bought a round of vodka sodas. After the first drink, the vodka stopped tasting like medicine and the conversations felt lighter and almost fun. I shed my suburban housewife hang-ups. I felt like a typical twentysomething, not someone who had gotten married younger than everyone else.

By my second year of law school, I realized that my marriage was a ticking time bomb. Each time I thought about being honest with Ben about my unhappiness, I drank. I had never been a wine o'clock person, but I'd pour a glass while I was cooking dinner, then another one during dinner. Maybe one more while I did laundry or finished reading for class. I became a pro at functional drinking. I went from being someone who drank iced tea with dinner to a full-on wino. Ben joked that we needed a wine-club membership. I thought I just needed to figure out my life. Only when I finally leveled with Ben and we separated, alcohol became useful for an entirely new set of problems.

I was never single in my twenties. When I interacted with men after I separated from Ben, I didn't even know how to flirt. Drinking helped me relax. If I went to a networking event, drinking made me feel like less of an imposter in this electric new world I wanted desperately to fit into. It was the simplest way to numb my discomfort. And unlike most of my peers, I hadn't destroyed my liver in college, so my body tolerated it like someone a decade younger.

Starting adulthood as a housewife turned New York lawyer ratcheted up my social insecurity just as my drinking became seemingly orthodox. There seemed to be an acceptable reason to drink every night of the week. It was almost like being hazed: How many hours can you bill while firing on all cylinders socially and professionally? Lines were blurred between associates who were routinely out until 2 a.m. or later, only to find themselves in a meeting at 10 a.m., ties straight, heels on, discussing litigation strategy. A Tuesday night of networking with drinks followed by a dinner with more drinking. Career suicide to miss the firm's 7 a.m. "team-building" SoulCycle the next morning.

Even as life normalized social drinking, I knew there were pitfalls. The spectrum of what was acceptable, even encouraged, felt endlessly vast. Drink functionally, but don't be *The Girl on the Train* drunk.

Despite desperately needing a liver cleanse, I immediately said yes to drinks that night with Leo. We met at six o'clock. Cocktails turned into appetizers and appetizers turned into dinner with a bottle of wine. We talked about our shared impression of Sterling as sympathetic despite being privileged and Leo's failure to convince him that the best course would be settling out of court.

"My wife tells me I need to take something to trial one of these days. She's a jury consultant, so she lives for the courtroom. She's amazing at what she does. But believe it or not, I get shy in court. I'm just not a litigator at heart, and I don't want to cede the spotlight to the Perry Masons of the world, like Eddie. So I'm wired to settle."

I imagined Leo's wife as an Amal Clooney type: flawless, ambitious, effortlessly handling it all. I wondered what it would be like to be half of a power couple.

"We have twin boys, Aldous and Kingsley. A&K. An homage to the firm that's given them a comfortable life."

My EQ antenna sensed that someone like Leo didn't always get the chance to share things about his personal life. Something about how easily he was opening up made me feel self-conscious in a way I tried masking by asking more questions.

"Do you think they'll grow up and become lawyers?" I asked.

"I wouldn't rule it out. Jessica was a lawyer before she started jury consulting. But yeah, I'm afraid it's in their blood."

"Is it difficult having two at once?" It felt like a good balance of personal but also something I was genuinely curious about. One sounded impossible enough.

"Unbelievably. They terrify me. They're five and already lecturing me about pronouns. The other day, they found out their preschool teacher is having a baby. When I asked if she was having a boy or girl, Aldous said, 'They have to be born before they can decide, Dad.'"

I laughed. "That's amazing."

"We can't keep up. We both have careers we love. Neither of us thinks we'd be good parents without fulfilling careers." He paused. "But honestly, both of us trying to balance demanding careers with parenthood could all blow up in our face."

I admired how seamlessly he melded personal and professional success. "It sounds like you're being thoughtful about it all, which is the most anyone can do."

He nodded. "What about you? Do you want kids?"

There were at least a dozen more pressing questions I needed to answer for myself before I could even think about kids. "That's hard to answer. I've never been sure. But, if I imagine myself sitting here in twenty years, telling you that I never had one, I feel this sadness that I can't explain. Which makes me second-guess *not* having kids. Does that make sense?"

I blushed at the honesty of my answer.

Leo took a sip of wine. "I was never sure I wanted kids before Jess got pregnant."

He looked at me sideways. "What about the boyfriend you mentioned the other week? The one you left behind. Did he want kids?"

I shifted uncomfortably, taken aback that he remembered. "We were married. He's my ex-husband."

He raised one eyebrow. "Jesus. You *are* interesting. I'm not allowed to ask how old you are, but just know I'm wondering."

I usually hated feeling like divorce made me interesting, but something about the way Leo said it made me feel wiser and more mature.

Besides Charlie, I hadn't talked to anyone in my "new" life about Ben and was still trying on ways that made me feel like I was in control of the narrative.

"I was very young," I said slowly. "And he was a great guy. But we didn't grow in the same direction." I cleared my throat. "You know, things I should've thought about before walking down the aisle at twenty-two."

He looked surprised, and I suddenly felt self-conscious. Had I overshared? Was I putting myself at risk of being taken less seriously? I couldn't imagine someone like him relating to the choices I'd made. There probably weren't any other thirty-year-old divorcées in his orbit.

Leo studied me carefully without saying anything. He picked up his wine glass and set it back down without taking a sip.

"It's crazy to admit, but I almost got married in my early twenties too. I was even engaged. No one told me 'all the things' either, but I don't think it would have mattered. Maybe we would have eventually evolved in different directions, but I never got the chance to find out."

"Did she call it off?" I asked.

"She was killed in a car accident the summer after we graduated from college. Two months before our wedding."

I felt the wine slow my ability to react. It was a devastating thing to share. It almost felt too personal to know.

"Oh my gosh . . . Leo. I'm so sorry. I don't know what to say. I shouldn't have been so flippant about marriage," I said lamely. The look on Ben's face when I left for LA flashed in my mind.

He shook his head. "Don't be sorry. It was a long time ago. Life goes on, and mine has been good. It took me a long time to find someone who measured up to Anna. But the fact that I had very few personal distractions allowed me to focus on my career, and now I'm forty-four, and my parents are finally happy I didn't go into politics," he said with an ironic smile.

I was having trouble finding words that didn't sound like I was trying to be overly sincere.

"I guess what I'm saying is that it worked out. I didn't have another relationship until I met Jess in my mid-thirties. I learned quickly that this job takes everything we have to give. I'm sure leaving was a difficult decision, but I promise you, it's easier being on your own. You're building something. It takes intense focus to do it right."

He smiled. "And, selfishly, I'm glad you made the decision that you did. The firm is lucky to have you." He looked at his watch. "Jessica's been tied up with a monthlong trial in Santa Barbara. I should get home before she goes to bed."

"I should get some sleep too. It's about one a.m. for me right now," I said.

"Burning it at both ends is a good thing. Just keep doing what you're doing."

I felt validated. I loved Connor and Caroline, but neither of them seemed to understand that now wasn't the time to figure out my personal life.

Ten minutes later, I rolled down the window of my Uber to take in the warm California air as my phone pinged with a text from Leo.

> Thanks for a fun night. Client gallery opening tomorrow night on Melrose—if you're still in town, join me?

I responded I'd love to join.

Chapter Twenty

Eddie and I sat in silence on opposite ends of a conference room as I typed up notes and he answered emails. I wondered if he'd gotten back to Andie yet about the book. His phone buzzed, and he sent it to voicemail.

"Samantha, there's only one way Andie can write a book and not compromise herself, and that's if we stay involved in the process. I don't mean that we should write it *for* her, but she would need to show us drafts as she's writing so we can determine if the material will be problematic."

He tapped his fingers on the table as he thought about what he wanted to do. "You've read all the documents and emails firsthand, so you know the facts we're presenting to the government even better than I do. If there's anything that contradicts the information we've disclosed to the government, we have an obligation to let them know."

"Do you want me to review the material as she writes it?"

He nodded. "It's the only way this can work. The issue is you won't be able to bill your time doing it, and there's no way this won't become a time suck. If you want to take it on, I can ask the firm to let you bill half the time on a pro bono basis, but even if they say yes, it's a lot of pressure for you."

I tried to mentally calculate how it would work. Even if the firm wouldn't let me bill any of the time, I knew I couldn't say no.

"I'd be happy to do it. I can have her send me chapters as she writes them, then flag any possible issues for you to look over. Would that work?"

"I think so. Let's see if Andie's okay with it. But I don't think she'll take no for an answer, and this is the only option I can think of to make sure everything is aboveboard. Let's try her now."

I dialed her on speaker. Eddie made sure she knew he still thought it was a bad idea, but he understood that she needed to get back on her feet, and if she was willing to do it our way, she could take the book deal.

Andie squealed with excitement. "Guys, a thousand times, yes. This sounds way better. Sam, you can tell me when I sound vapid, and I'll rework it so the book appeals more to the 'intellectual' crowd."

Eddie chuckled humorlessly. "Okay, we're in agreement. But Andie? You have to promise us that the manuscript you deliver to the publisher will be the version we've vetted. Not a word different. I get that you're going to want to editorialize, but if taking creative liberties poses problems for your case, there's no point to any of this."

Andie promised not a single word would go unvetted and that everything she sent to the publisher would be blessed by us.

Eddie rushed off to another meeting across town. The gallery opening was in three hours, and I hadn't packed anything other than suits and athleisure. I packed up my laptop and walked to Nordstrom across the street. I found a simple black tea-length dress with pale-pink pumps, then zipped back to the hotel and spent an hour updating Andie's case timeline before I took the elevator to meet Leo downstairs.

He arrived in a black car at 6:15 p.m. sharp in a navy suit and gray wool tie. I waited nervously as he got out and walked around to open the door for me.

This is just a work event, I told myself, feeling the butterflies in my stomach dictating otherwise. I needed to keep reminding myself that he was just as much my boss as Eddie.

The opening was a who's who of LA's high-end art scene, but I quickly realized Leo was the one person they all wanted to talk to. Everyone knew his clients from *Variety* or the *LA Times*. I felt like an invisible voyeur as I sipped champagne and moved from one group to the next.

"LA's art doppelgängers try to measure up, but Manhattan culturati are just inherently superior," a woman wearing a fitted leather jumpsuit quipped as she flashed Leo a smile. I took another sip and thought, *I'll never wear lipstick that well in my life.*

"Alexandra, Samantha's a rising star from our firm's New York office, so I'm sure she'd agree with you." He winked at me.

Alexandra skimmed me up and down as she lightly shook half of my hand. "Well, Samantha, you're not in terrible company if you're already working with Leo Hirschman," she said approvingly. "Where do you live in New York?"

"In the West Village," I answered, feeling a small sense of pride. It didn't matter that my apartment was a shoebox with a bum stove. It was the West Village.

Leo seemed to have the inside scoop on every deal happening in Hollywood. He handed me another glass of champagne as we listened to a group of studio executives venting about the viability of the theatrical business.

"What about the studio that shall not be named? Is there any chance they rebound from last weekend's $250 million flop?" one of them asked.

Leo scoffed. "It would have been cheaper to put all the film reels into Bob's Aston Martin and push it off a cliff than to release that movie on twenty-five hundred screens."

Everyone laughed as I caught the eye of the woman from earlier watching me closely. Something about the way she was looking at me made my face burn.

Suddenly, everything about the gallery opening—dressing up, Leo picking me up in a car, introducing me to everyone—seemed obvious. I looked like the girl on his arm. It felt like the contours of our working relationship had bent when we'd veered into personal territory the night before.

"I should get back to the hotel," I whispered. I needed to regain ground.

"Is everything all right?" he asked, looking concerned.

I nodded. "I just have an early meeting tomorrow. And I think the late nights at the office might be catching up to me. But this was really fun. Thank you for inviting me. I can find my way back to the hotel," I said, wishing for a more graceful exit.

I suddenly felt his hand on my lower back.

"Traveling between coasts is exhausting. I'll wait outside with you until your car comes."

I ordered an Uber, grateful that the car was only a minute away. I thanked him again for inviting me. He leaned in to hug me, and I felt him kiss my cheek.

"Good night," I said quickly, hurrying into the Uber before my face caught fire. I could still feel the heat from his hand on my back.

I rolled down the window, my heart pounding anxiously.

There was no way he didn't assume I had a crush on him. Every woman in that room seemed to know.

The inevitability of this all ending badly weighed heavily as I slid the hotel key into the door and kicked off my heels. I grabbed an Evian from the minifridge and sank onto the foot of the bed, staring at myself in the mirror opposite me. I wanted to jump out of my skin.

I jumped as my phone buzzed with a text.

Figured you'd appreciate this.

A picture of an empty Grand Central Station followed. It was after midnight in New York. The idea of Charlie burning the midnight oil in New York made me feel homesick.

I tapped the image with a heart emoji.

Back tomorrow. Hope you didn't give my desk away.

~

I landed in New York late the next afternoon. My apartment was a disaster, so I invited Caroline over to drink wine while I got my life together. It took one glass for me to confess my crush.

"I've never met anyone like him," I said as we sat on the floor, a bottle of sauvignon blanc in between us. "He's a *partner*. And he's married. It's impossible."

"When was the last time you had a crush on someone?"

I aimed the wine cork at the wastebasket and missed. "Probably the bartender poet from Vin Rouge."

"I think it makes sense. You're just not a typical thirtysomething. You were a housewife while the rest of us messed around in our twenties. So realistically, you may not be into guys your own age, because they're all immature assholes."

"So that explains why I'm attracted to Leo?"

"I don't know anything about Leo beyond what you've just told me, but my guess is that you're into him because he's mature and impressive. And he has life experience. That's attractive."

I sighed. "He lives in this world full of brilliant and successful people, but he made me feel like I was the interesting one. It was intoxicating. Especially when part of me still feels like the housewife making turkey sandwiches for Ben to take to work," I said pathetically.

Caroline made a face. "Okay, you're the only one to blame for doing that. That's not a married person thing, that's a *you* thing. Do me a favor and never make anyone's lunch ever again."

"I can't stop thinking about him," I said, instinctually unlocking my phone to check my emails.

"But you're not actually considering it, are you?"

"What do you mean?"

"Crossing a line with a married partner. It's a little counterproductive to the cause, don't you think?"

"What 'cause'?"

She gave me a hard look. "Do I really have to spell it out? You're a first-year associate who wants a future there. I'm sure it's obvious how much you want to work with him. Crossing a line is only going to end up making *you* look bad. No one ever called a man a home-wrecker."

The word landed like a brick.

Caroline reached for the bag of pretzels on the counter.

"All I'm saying is it's a waste of all the progress we've made in the last few years. You're accepting the attention of a powerful man, and somehow your brain isn't sending you predatory signals."

I ironed the crease in my jeans with my hand. "That's a lot to unpack. What if *I'm* attracted to *him*? You're basically saying that I de facto lose all agency—and he's automatically a predator—just because we work together."

"I just think you're not thinking this through. It's the quickest way to lose the confidence of all the other people in power. Especially women. I've seen it happen before. Even being seen as *encouraging* a flirtation with a married partner is the fastest way to make enemies."

"It just felt . . . nice. We both shared personal things. It was weirdly comfortable talking about my past with him."

"In my experience, this kind of thing never ends well. If I were you, I'd keep things on a professional level. And don't drink too much around him. That's where lines always get crossed."

I put my face in my hands. "That's another thing. I've never drunk so much in my life. I'm starting to worry about long-term health effects. I read an article on the number of drinks per week that qualifies as alcoholism, and I think I'm there," I said despairingly.

Caroline shook her head. "I've been in finance since I was twenty-one. It's the same kind of drinking culture as lawyers, plus recreational drugs. I never understood the appeal, but I've seen the best and worst of it for over a decade, and the key is learning to be fun and social without blacking out."

"Not helpful health advice. You're basically just telling me to get better at being an alcoholic."

She looked at her watch and finished her wine. "I should go. I have a 5:30 spin class."

"Roll those spin class dice."

She blew me a kiss. "Think about what I said. You're better than that."

~

I woke up the next morning to Andie's first three chapters. Her voice on the page was crisp, clear, and funny. Even though I already knew her story backward and forward, I quickly became absorbed in the material and barely noticed the time.

Charlie texted as I was waiting for the subway.

> You going to show up today? I might give your chair away and then you'll have to stand at your non-standing desk.

I typed a one-handed response.

> On my way in. Don't touch my chair.

He responded with a picture of my desk chair with a massive box on top of it. I couldn't remember ordering anything.

Special delivery from . . . New York Dept of Taxation and Finance?

I dropped my phone on the platform as my brain put it together. It had to be documents from the FOIA request. Was it possible my idea to help Sterling was actually going to work?

Oh shit! Guard that for me. There in twenty.

Chapter Twenty-One

"So what you're saying is, I'm the reason you're making partner. In fifteen years," Charlie said triumphantly as he chewed the rim of his glasses.

"If I pull this off, yes."

"Well DeFiore, I'm humbled that my daily slog was the source of your creative genius."

I proudly held up the piece of paper I'd found after three hours of digging, my fingers covered in ink. "The smoking gun."

Charlie clapped. "This job keeps getting sexier."

I stared in disbelief at the yellow notepad covered in my left-handed scribble. "This piece of paper just gave me what I needed to do *this* math equation."

Charlie peered over the desk divider. "The work of a mad genius."

I sank into my chair. "I killed thousands of brain cells trying to figure out the movie budgets without having to file a complaint. And each brain cell was worth it."

"So you figured it out?"

"Lawyer 101. You can't subpoena information or documents without filing a lawsuit. But we can't file a lawsuit, because his case sucks. And the only way to scare them into settling is to prove we *know* the movie budgets were more than $5 million, because that's the max he agreed to for each movie."

"I see."

"Enter Exhibit A. The New York State tax filing that the producers filed, claiming a thirty percent tax refund on the total budget of the film. And see this number here?"

He squinted. "Too small."

"*$3.6 million.* That's the refund they requested in the tax filing." I held up the notepad. "And this is the sixth-grade math that tells me $3.6 million is thirty percent of *$12 million.* That's sixty percent of his total investment in just one movie. Which was not the deal."

He stood up. "Boom!"

"I would have never gotten the idea for the FOIA request if you hadn't called me the other night to complain."

"Glad my misery could be helpful."

My cell phone vibrated somewhere under a stack of papers.

"Hey, Em," I picked up, trying not to lose my train of thought.

"Hey. Can you meet me for lunch? Please say yes."

I cradled the phone with my shoulder. "Is everything okay? You never leave the office to eat lunch," I said suspiciously.

"No. I'm just . . . I don't know. I'm freaking out a little. I know we haven't really talked much lately, but work's been such a nightmare. I actually think I want to quit," she said, her voice sounding small and strained.

I leaned back in my chair and stared down Park Avenue, wishing I hadn't picked up the phone. I'd experienced a few of Emilie's panic attacks in law school, and they were usually short-lived.

"I can't really leave right now. I have two feet of documents to get through. What happened?"

"There's a Sweetgreen three blocks from your office."

"You're not really thinking about quitting, are you?" I said distractedly, organizing documents to send to the copy center to be scanned. "Does your dad know?"

I'd only met Emilie's dad once, but I knew he was usually the source of her anxiety. He would be apoplectic if she quit her job after just a few months.

Emilie breathed heavily into the phone. "There's just constantly another emergency coming down the pipe. I can't deal with the nonstop panic. I've been having the 'Sunday scaries,' or whatever it's called, ever since I started. I thought about going back on my anxiety meds, but they make me feel foggy, and I can't write when I take them. This morning, I freaked out and told the partner I needed a mental-health holiday. And I've only been there a month. I know they're going to sack me if I don't buck up."

"Is that a thing? A mental-health holiday?"

"Probably not. But if I don't figure it out, I'll snap. I feel like I have the makeup of a tiny little bird, and the wind might just blow me out to sea if I'm not careful."

"Remember that time you freaked out right before our Torts final? You took one Ativan and were fine. Try taking, like, half."

She was quiet, and I stared impatiently at the stack of documents I still had to get through.

"I know you, and I *know* you're killing it. Even if you don't *feel* like it. Just take some deep breaths and maybe a walk around the block."

"I wanted my friend to meet me for a salad," she snipped.

"I know. I'm just in the middle of something timely. Can we talk more this weekend?"

"My dad will kill me if I quit," she said, her voice quiet again.

"So don't tell him anything yet. Just do what you have to do to get through it."

I looked down at my phone to remind myself what day it was. "Hey. Let's go out tomorrow night. Caroline booked a table for eight people at this restaurant on Bond Street, and she only has five others confirmed so far. Let's take the last two spots. Her friends are always a good time."

Emilie scoffed. "Meaning she just makes a big reservation and assumes people don't have plans?"

"People like us?"

"Ha. Okay, fine. I can't remember the last time I had Saturday night plans."

~

Charlie and I worked in comfortable silence the rest of the afternoon. I started drafting a proposed settlement memo for Leo, explaining how we could use the FOIA evidence to allege fraud, the only claim that might intimidate the other side into settling.

At seven o'clock, I slid my laptop and charger into my Longchamp. Charlie was playing poker on his phone with Bob Dylan blasting from his earbuds.

"Is this what you do all day when I'm not here? Send me desperate text messages and play poker?"

Charlie smirked. "Work is weirdly slow today. Want to grab sushi?"

We hadn't spent time together outside of the office since my birthday weekend. I was worried things would change after my big confession about what had happened with Ben. I didn't want him to see me differently.

"I could. But can we go somewhere besides Hatsuhana? I don't want to run into anyone from the office. I'll feel like I should be working late."

Charlie raised his eyebrows up and down. "You do know it's Friday, right? But challenge accepted. I know the perfect place. We can go out the sketchy Lexington side to this basement sushi bar on Forty-Third Street."

"Sounds appealing," I said.

"You'll love it. Dollar sake bombs. No way any partners know about it."

Charlie was right—there was no way anyone from the firm knew about this sushi bar. It was two flights below street level with zero atmosphere. We settled into a corner table and ordered Sapporos and sake.

Charlie clinked his bottle against mine. "Okay, spill. What's happening on Andie's case? How'd it go in LA?"

I told him about editing Andie's chapters. "I get to log pro bono hours for half of the time, which is cool. And I mean, how crazy is it to get to see a book get written from the beginning?"

Charlie poured soy sauce for each of us. "I swear you have some kind of 'it girl' halo around you. But like a nerdy one, just for lawyers. How many first-year associates can say they ghostwrote a client's memoir?"

"I'm ghost *editing*. Very different."

"Call it whatever you want, but it's fucking awesome. And what about working with the LA partner? Did you blow him away yet with the FOIA stuff?"

I shook my head. "I'm kind of hoping I'll see him in the next few weeks so I can pitch it in person. I want the full dramatic effect."

"Channel the halo." He grinned. "Do anything fun in LA?"

I told him about dinner with Leo and the gallery opening. "I'm not exaggerating. Every person in that room was hanging on every word he said. To be fair, he's unbelievably charming. He's not even forty-five and one of the most successful lawyers in the country."

"'Unbelievably charming'?"

I blushed for being overly effusive. I was supposed to be talking myself out of this crush.

"Sorry, I spent the last week drafting that complaint and got way too comfortable with hyperbole."

"Watch that, DeFiore."

"What about you? How's your week been?"

"I won't even pretend to compete with you. While you were sipping champagne, I second-chaired a deposition somewhere in Delaware. What else . . . I got super high a couple nights ago with some of my law school buddies and almost adopted a cat. I guess the highlight was I went on a forty-eight-hour date. Pretty surreal," he said, looking both pleased and exhausted by the idea of a date lasting that long.

"Awesome, tell me more about the deposition."

"We weren't even close to the one Delaware town you've heard of. I had to rent a car at the train station and drive another hour."

"Yikes. And the date?"

He took a long sip of his beer. "She works with a friend from college. It was a blind date that started Monday night and ended yesterday. We haven't talked since then, and I can't decide if that's normal or a sign that the connection maxed out at two days."

He looked honestly unsure, and I laughed without meaning to.

"Sorry, but it can't be *that* hard. If you liked her enough to spend forty-eight hours with her, then text her. If you didn't like her, maybe also send her a text that says you were only in it for the story."

"I know what my communication options are. I'm just not sure which of the two I'm feeling," he said, feigning offense at my advice.

I threw my hands in the air. "Trust me, I'm not trying to be preachy. I have *nothing* to preach to you."

I briefly considered the idea of Charlie liking someone enough to spend two nights with them. I suddenly wanted to know everything about her. Did he have a "type"?

Charlie motioned to the waiter for another Sapporo. "What about you? Ever think about 'gettin' back out there'?"

I must have given him a look, and he immediately looked embarrassed. "Sorry. Was that a weird question?"

"Siri, what's a synonym for 'weird'?"

He splashed my soy sauce with a chopstick. "Don't be a word snob."

I leaned back and sighed. "I can't even think about dating. Besides, there should really be a dating grace period after losing your humanity to the bar exam. At least a year."

"Fair. And truthfully, it might be why my dating life has sucked so much."

"I don't know if you can put that on the bar exam."

"Another fair point. Goddammit."

"I mean, can you imagine that conversation on a first date? In New York? It'd be different if I stayed in DC or some other city where people also got married when they were barely old enough to buy beer."

Charlie's eyes widened. "Fuck, that's true. There should be a regional dating app for twentysomething divorced people. Probably wouldn't get much traction in a place like New York, though."

"Does anyone ever put 'divorced' in their Bumble profile?"

He looked like he was really thinking about it.

"I was just joking. But I bet you'd swipe left."

"I don't know. I never thought about it."

I paused. "Honestly, I never saw myself as a selfish person until I left Ben. But things got to a point where I needed to be selfish to go after what I wanted. It scared me a little bit. In five years, I wanted something completely different than I thought. The person I was when I left was completely different than the person that married him. Like, unrecognizably different."

"Because you grew up. Like most people do in their twenties."

"Right. But I was supposed to be growing *with* someone."

"Siri, what's another word for 'supposed.'"

I rolled my eyes. "You know what I mean."

He looked frustrated, like he was trying to put words to something he could only feel.

"I just think you're not actually that different from anyone else, Sam. I mean that in a good way. We all become ourselves in different ways. You happened to get married in the middle of it. None of us are the same as we were five, ten years ago. When I was in college, I thought I wanted to manage a Boston sports team. Now I'm a schmucky Big Law associate wishing I *hadn't* grown past that dream, because it would probably be a lot more fun than what I'm doing now. But you know what I'm saying? Realizing your ambition couldn't thrive in your marriage doesn't make you selfish."

He looked so earnest, like someone who could stumble into a forty-eight-hour date because life just happens to them.

I wondered what it would be like to date someone for a month, or six months, or years. Or spend forty-eight hours together and never see them again. Either way, it was enviable how normal all the options were for someone like Charlie. He could learn about himself through natural channels of experience. I felt like that ship had sailed.

"I can't get past the idea that becoming myself meant hurting someone else."

"And maybe one day you'll find yourself on the other end of that. You don't know."

"Maybe. I guess I'd deserve that." I took the last sip of Sapporo. "Caroline thinks I won't be interested in someone my own age because they don't have as much life experience as me or whatever," I said, flailing to regain sure footing.

"Is she defining divorce as 'life experience'?"

"Okay, lawyer, I don't know how she's defining it. But it's true. I can't really go about dating like everyone else does. Including you."

Charlie looked wounded at being grouped with all the others. "But who will you date then? Will you just be single until you meet someone with the same 'life experience'? No offense, but that doesn't sound like the right strategy."

I bristled. "It's not a 'strategy.' I'm just thinking out loud. Because *you* asked."

He looked contrite. "You're right. I'm sorry."

I poked a spicy tuna roll. "I don't want to get sidetracked by dating someone who wants more from me than I can give right now. I just need to keep my eye on the prize. And not fall for unavailable older men, like Leo."

Charlie looked confused. "You're into that partner?"

I immediately regretted the tipsy slip. "He *is* 'unbelievably charming,' remember?" I said, trying to laugh it off.

"That's a little cliché, don't you think?"

I shot him a look. "At this point in my life, I could be a little more cliché."

"Not one of your better ideas. But you don't need me to tell you that."

"*Obviously* it's a terrible idea. I work for him. It's a terrible, cliché idea."

"Not just because you work for him. Isn't he married?"

I felt my eyes narrow. "Maybe he's not even happily married. I'm not necessarily saying he's *unhappy*, but marriage shouldn't be a death sentence."

He rubbed his jaw, looking frustrated again. "I never said it should be."

"I just think no one should be stuck in something that isn't making them happy. Which is basically what you just said a few minutes ago."

I was projecting so hard we could both taste it.

"Look, I have no idea how we got here. I'm just saying that being divorced doesn't give you the right to become an asshole who can't see right from wrong. Like getting involved with a married guy."

"Right from wrong? I didn't realize I was back in Sunday school."

I was quickly unraveling and indignant at the thought of Charlie lecturing me. I made a show of digging into my bag to find my wallet.

"It's late. I have to get home and go over notes for a nine a.m. call with Eddie," I said coldly.

"Tomorrow's Saturday."

"Work doesn't stop on the weekends for some of us."

Charlie crossed his arms. "Look, you're doing what you always wanted. Working for people like Eddie and Leo. Just don't fuck it up by becoming some young associate who falls for a partner. You're better than that."

I pushed my chair out a little too aggressively, and my bag dropped heavily onto the floor. "I have to go," I said. I could tell I was on the verge of tears.

"I'll get this. Good luck with the call tomorrow."

~

I walked all the way back to the West Village, alternating between feeling angry and anxious. I was embarrassed for being so reactive. Was he right? Was I jaded—or worse, morally bankrupt—because of my past?

It was almost 11 p.m. by the time I turned right on Perry Street. As I crossed West Fourth, I saw the shape of someone sitting on the step of my building. I gripped my keys as Charlie stood up.

"I didn't want to leave things like that."

I put my keys away. "I shouldn't have gotten so defensive."

"Yeah, but I overstepped. Your personal life is none of my business. I guess when you confided in me about Ben, something got crossed in my brain. I don't know. Maybe I thought you wanted my opinion on everything else. But I really didn't mean to come off self-righteously," Charlie said, looking earnest again, and ten years younger than he was.

I sat down heavily. "I've felt so out of control since I slept with Ben. Now I'm just casually throwing around that I have a crush on a married partner. I don't even know who I am anymore. Maybe I don't have a moral compass."

Charlie squeezed my shoulder. "You're just figuring it all out, and anyone in your shoes would be doing the exact same thing. Everyone gets a pass for growing pains when we go from adolescence to adulthood, but no one ever talks about what happens after we're technically adults. But we're still growing. And we're going to keep making mistakes."

"Hollywood should really make more 'coming-of-adulthood' stories."

"They do. It's called every Duplass brothers movie."

I laughed. "This night really turned dramatic. You're on my steps at midnight. We should both get some sleep."

He stood up quickly. "Let's just pretend tonight never happened, okay? Except the part where I finally got you to my secret sushi spot. We have to go back and cleanse that place. Or maybe never leave the office. We seem to be good there."

I smiled. "Deal."

We shook hands, and I watched him disappear toward the subway that would take him back to Brooklyn.

Chapter Twenty-Two

By the time the sky brightened, I felt more mentally drained than sleep deprived. I worried our symbiotic officemate bubble had been punctured, and I was the only one to blame. He had been so thoughtful, almost in a vulnerable way. What had acting so defensively gotten me?

I grabbed my phone and booked a last-minute spin class. I needed to get out of my head. I neatly folded a work-appropriate outfit into my gym bag and walked east toward SoHo. The city was beautifully still, and I made a mental note to try getting up earlier.

The MetLife Building was completely empty at 8:30 a.m. on a Saturday. I wished it was Monday, and Charlie would be in the office. I wondered if by Monday morning, we'd brush it off like nothing happened.

My cell phone rang extra loudly as I walked down the empty hall toward my office. No one called this early, unless it was Charlie trolling me at 2 a.m.

"Morning, Andie," I chirped.

"Hey, editor. I'm in town. Can you meet for lunch at the Four Seasons?"

I cradled the phone under my chin and dropped my gym bag next to my desk. "Today? I think I can do lunch—is it just us or is Eddie coming too?"

"Just you. I didn't tell him I was coming to the city."

I had no idea why Andie was in town, but I sensed it had to do with the book. Her publisher was in New York and pressing her to get down five thousand words a week. The problem was no one knew how the story was going to end.

I worked quietly for a couple of hours. Charlie hadn't texted, and I couldn't decide if that was normal or not. Maybe he was annoyed after the intensity of last night.

The Four Seasons was twelve blocks up Park Avenue. I arrived at the hotel's main restaurant at 12:30 p.m. sharp.

"Reservation for two, under Reese," I said as I scanned the restaurant for Andie.

"Reservation for three," the hostess responded with a succinct "come along" wave.

Andie jumped up when she saw me. "*Love* your jacket," she said, giving me a warm hug.

"Thank you! Did you end up inviting Eddie?"

Andie waved to someone behind me as I turned around to a man who was not Eddie being led to the table by the same hostess.

Andie reached out to shake his hand. "George, it's such a pleasure to meet you in person."

She turned to me with a proud smile. "I want to introduce you to my defense attorney, Samantha DeFiore. Sam, this is George Brenner."

I knew immediately who he was, but I had no idea why he was there, or why *I* was there. I extended my hand and tried to look like this lunch meeting was the most normal part of my day.

"George Brenner, it's so nice to meet you," I said, hoping everyone called him by his full name.

We sat down as I looked at Andie quizzically, hoping she would explain why we were meeting one of the most famous writers of my generation for lunch at the Four Seasons.

"Sam, I'm sure you're familiar with George's work," Andie said, giving my forearm a tight squeeze.

George Brenner was Hollywood and Broadway royalty. Even his older TV shows still streamed. He had multiple Emmys and at least one Oscar and was probably nominated for more Golden Globes and Tonys than most other screenwriters or playwrights. Now in his fifties, he seemed more relevant and prolific than ever.

"Yes, of course. Most of my law school classmates became a lawyer because of you," I said. It was true. One of his longest-running TV shows had tapped into the most idealistic version of what it meant to be a lawyer, turning him into a perennial law school icon.

"That's very kind of you. My family is filled with lawyers. I was the only one who went another way."

Andie ordered a bottle of Pellegrino for the table. "George, are you based here now? Or Los Angeles?"

He nodded. "I have a house in Los Angeles but spend half my time here."

"Samantha is becoming something of a bicoastal figure herself," she said proudly.

"As you should. It's the only way to work in the business and stay sane," he said.

I nodded along, but I had absolutely no idea why he was there, or why I was there.

Andie looked like she could read my mind. "I didn't have a chance to update Sam yet—do you want to go first, or should I?"

He took a piece of bread from the bowl at the center of the round table and started buttering it. Everything felt so maddeningly casual.

"Sure. I'll start. First, I just have to say that it's an absolute pleasure to meet you, Samantha. It sounds like you and Eddie Kaufman are two of the best things to ever happen to Andie. I know you're both working tirelessly toward the best possible outcome."

"Eddie is the best there is. She chose well," I said with as much poise as I could muster.

He nodded thoughtfully. "A few days ago, I got a phone call from my old college buddy, who heads up one of the more successful publishing houses. He said he had an early manuscript he thought I'd find fascinating."

George Brenner took a sip of Pellegrino. "I read what was on the page in one sitting. Obviously, we won't know how the story ends until the case is resolved. But I called my agent and said I'd found my next project. Between the story itself and Andie as a protagonist, the screenplay basically writes itself. I already have half of it mapped out in my head."

My head was spinning. "Oh, wow. That's incredible news. The book isn't even published yet—Andie, you should try to negotiate a higher advance," I said, only half joking.

"I'm thinking about it," she said lightly.

He looked pleased. "Andie has agreed to work with me on fleshing out the story and characters. I'd like to tell the story through the lens of the legal proceedings. Which is why I asked Andie if the three of us could meet."

I glanced at Andie. I had no idea what he was about to say, but it felt like I was floating out of my body, watching the scene unfold like in one of his movies.

"I have a self-defeating obsession with writing about things I know nothing about. But I've gotten pretty good at finding the best people to help me overcome whatever the subject-matter handicap is, and that's where you come in—because to be able to write the story I really want to tell, I need to know everything about the law Andie is accused of breaking and all the inside baseball of a federal indictment."

He finished the last bite of bread. "I'll get directly to the point. I'd like you to work for me as a story consultant, meaning I would pay you hourly to answer all my questions. With Andie's permission, of course."

The words hung in the air as the waiter returned to take our order. Andie ordered the Nicoise, and George ordered the burger with fries. I'd been too distracted to look at the menu but figured every hotel had some version of a Cobb salad.

"This is a once-in-a-lifetime opportunity, for both of us," she said to me.

The rest of lunch was a blur. He excused himself immediately after picking up the check, and I promised to figure out a way to work with him that wouldn't get me fired from my day job by violating attorney-client privilege and confidentiality. Even if Andie gave her blessing, like the book itself, this felt like another gray area that was likely to spook Eddie. Not to mention I was already spending a lot of time on nonlegal work by editing the book. I worried whether even asking the question would make me look less serious about the work I was actually there to do.

Andie walked me back to the office to debrief.

"You know this means my book has a shot at selling more than one copy," she said as we walked south down Park Avenue. "George doesn't make bad movies."

"This is unreal."

She smiled proudly. "I said I'd help you meet the right people in Hollywood."

I shook my head. "This transcends Hollywood. He's a creative genius. No one even comes close."

"The publisher is really delivering, huh?"

"Seriously. *College buddies*?"

"What are you going to tell Eddie?" she asked.

"I have to figure out a way to convince him to be okay with it so I can get the firm's blessing. I'm more worried about that."

"Do you want me to send an email saying *I* want you to do it? Doesn't the firm have to do what the client wants?"

I could easily see the firm telling me it was either my job or Hollywood, but not both.

~

When I got back to my desk, Patricia had emailed a large PDF file of documents to review for the Film at Lincoln Center pro bono matter. This one's picking up next week, the email said. I hadn't even thought about Lincoln Center in weeks.

I tried my best to focus while mentally plotting the best way to talk to Eddie about George Brenner's offer. I wanted him to take me seriously as a lawyer and not come off as flighty or distracted by the shiny things that somehow kept coming my way. It seemed like no matter what, I wasn't going to be able to balance everything.

At 4:30 p.m., I gave up trying to focus and texted Emilie that I'd be at her apartment by seven for a predinner cocktail.

I went home, showered without washing my hair, then put on black jeans, a white top, and a cropped black blazer.

I could hear hip hop blasting from her apartment before the elevator even opened. I held up a bottle of sparkling rosé. "It's French," I announced.

"Oh god. *No*, thank you," she said, handing me a martini. "It's dry. It's clean. It's what grown-ups drink."

She cracked the window to smoke a cigarette. I realized I hadn't checked in since her panicked call the day before.

"Has work let up at all?" I asked lightly.

"I didn't quit," she non-answered. "Moving on." She exhaled the cigarette inside the apartment.

"Between your parents' wallpaper and that cigarette, I'm finally living out my dream of being a New Yorker in the eighties."

She coughed. "Seriously, *what* is this obsession with New York in the eighties? You've mentioned that more times than I can remember." She exhaled thick smoke. "I never cared enough to ask why."

I shrugged. "Some weird combination of Nora Ephron's movies and Jill Clayburgh in *An Unmarried Woman*. Although I think that was technically the late seventies."

"I'll never understand American cinema. It's too on the nose. No wonder you got married so young." She put out her cigarette against the brick under the windowsill. "You do realize New York was crime-ridden in the eighties," she continued.

"Okay, okay. Let's shake off the week, shall we?" I held up the martini glass and took a sip. It tasted like gasoline. I looked longingly at the thirty-dollar rosé it had taken ten minutes to choose.

At 8:30 p.m., Emilie slipped her doorman a twenty, and he hailed a cab to take us to the restaurant on Bond Street.

We were the last ones to sit down. Caroline handed our jackets to a waiter as she launched into short but thoughtful introductions that somehow put everyone at ease.

By the time we got to the part where we all pretended to be too full for dessert, it was like we were eight former sorority sisters who still made time for monthly dinners.

One of the girls, Margaret, had just gone through a breakup after a five-year relationship with her college boyfriend. They'd been broken up for three months, and she wasn't shy about how much she still missed him. He'd been the one to end it. She was taking her therapist's advice to "just get back out there," but dating was, so far, an underwhelming venture. Each guy was more superficial than the last. All they wanted to talk about was their stock portfolio, how many people were in their Hamptons share house, or the podcast they were making with their friends. She worked at a nonprofit for underprivileged Asian American youth and lived in Park Slope.

Maybe it was the Brooklyn address or the wine, but before I knew it, I was announcing in an exaggeratedly self-aggrandizing voice, "I know someone *great*!"

Encouraged by the hopeful expression on every face at the table, I committed the cardinal matchmaking sin of failing to undersell and overdeliver.

"Seriously, he's perfect. I promise he doesn't even know what the Nasdaq is—but like, in a good way—and I'm pretty sure he's never even been to a group fitness class. Not to say he isn't fit, just naturally tall and lean. Hates the Hamptons. Total diamond in the rough," I heard myself say in a voice that didn't even sound like mine.

I offered to see if he'd be interested in a setup. She nodded enthusiastically as Caroline euphorically clasped her hands as if to say she'd really nailed this group.

The restaurant split the bill eight ways, making it a unicorn New York establishment. I opened the bill holder, and my eyes landed on a handwritten note scribbled at the bottom of my receipt. The waiter's name was Alex, and he wanted my number.

I blushed as I tried to covertly show Emilie the note, but the girl seated on the other side of me saw it first.

"I *knew* he was into you!" she whispered. "He was reading the specials *to you*."

Margaret looked delighted. "This is *exactly* how you should lose your Manhattan dating virginity. Blind dates are terrible."

I reached uncomfortably for my credit card. "This would be a blind date," I corrected her.

"Not really. We just spent three hours with him. He's *so* cute."

"And funny!" Caroline added.

I could tell it would be new friend suicide *not* to leave my number.

As soon as we left the restaurant, I got a text from a 646 number asking if I'd be up for a drink sometime.

I stared at the text for a few seconds, wondering if I'd ever be that person again—someone who got excited about someone cute asking for my number. I put my phone away without responding. I'd been in New York less than three months, and life already felt like drinking from a fire hose.

We tagged along with the group to a nearby speakeasy for another drink. Emilie excused herself while I ordered a round of cocktails. I checked my emails absentmindedly as the bartender made the drinks, then looked over and saw Emilie coming from the direction of the door.

"Were you smoking again? You said you were going to the bathroom," I said as I handed her a martini, my voice sharper than I intended.

She looked guilty. "If I say yes, will you leave it alone?"

"I don't know. Two cigarettes in one night makes you a smoker."

She sighed and dropped her head dangerously close to the glass. "I wasn't smoking. I was on the phone."

"Ah. Why did you say you were going to the bathroom?"

"I haven't been completely honest with you," she said, her British accent more pronounced the slower she spoke.

"I don't know what that means. You didn't need to go to the bathroom?"

She lifted her head and blew a strand of hair out of her eyes. "I mean when I called you. When you refused to step out and meet me for lunch."

"Meaning, you don't actually hate your job?"

She nudged me down to an emptier part of the bar.

"There's a man at my firm. A much . . . older man."

"And?" My mind flashed to Leo. Was Emilie living my fantasy?

She swirled the cocktail without taking a sip.

"We've been seeing each other for a while now. It started last summer."

"When we were studying for the bar?" No one could pull that off, not even Emilie.

"No, the summer before that."

"When you were a summer associate?"

She nodded. "And all through last year. He'd come down to DC, or I'd take the train up here for a weekend. Sometimes we'd meet at the halfway point, at a bed-and-breakfast on Baltimore Harbor."

"So he's a partner?"

"Yes."

"A married partner?"

"No. He's never been married."

"How old is he?"

"Fifty."

I couldn't believe I had been clueless for well over a year. Then again, I hadn't exactly been forthcoming with her about sleeping with Ben or my feelings for Leo.

She said they both decided to keep the relationship a secret once she got to the firm, but then they started working together eighty hours a week on a complicated appeal, and it was Emilie who realized she couldn't handle it.

"Every time I try to talk about *us*, he uses work as a weapon. He says, 'When am I supposed to think about the future? When I'm home at two a.m. after editing your work?' That's always his excuse. And he always says 'the' future. Not *our* future."

She looked distraught. I couldn't believe she'd been able to keep all of this under wraps. It was so layered. I felt sad that she hadn't trusted me enough to bring me into the fold.

"What are you going to do?"

Her eyes were wet. I wished I'd made time to meet her for lunch.

"I don't know, but I'm just so miserable. I haven't known what to do since the first time we met that summer. Sam, you know me. I'm not someone who falls for a guy and loses my head. He's a career bachelor whose world revolves around work. And yet somehow, my feelings only get stronger, and . . ." Her voice sounded strained. "It's started to feel like the opposite for him. He doesn't even look at me the same way anymore. It's like I'm a . . . distraction. It's so incredibly painful. Sometimes I lie awake at night and feel like I can't breathe. If he ends things, I can't stay there. It would be hell."

I shook my head. "Man, we're really a pair. I'm divorced, and you're trying to lock down a forever bachelor." I briefly considered telling her about sleeping with Ben. I wondered if it would make her feel better to know we all had secrets. But I wasn't sure making this about me was the right move.

She made a face. "I don't even think people can have a successful career and a happy relationship. Look at my parents. If my mum had wanted to work, my dad would've been fucking miserable."

I thought back to what Leo said about focusing on work. If it was ever possible to have both, it certainly wasn't going to happen before my career had really even started.

I stared at the bartender's toolbox of green olives, cocktail onions, and cherries and almost wanted to tell her about my feelings for Leo. But after what had happened with Charlie, I was reticent to give anyone else reason to paint me as morally adrift. Even if it might level the playing field a bit and help her feel less alone.

I also knew I didn't have any good advice. All I could do was listen.

"Even if I'm coming into this story at the end of the book, tell me everything. How it started, all of it."

Chapter Twenty-Three

I arrived Monday morning to an empty office. I still hadn't heard from Charlie.

I drank three cups of coffee before heading to the forty-ninth floor for a required continuing legal education seminar for junior associates.

I spotted him come in ten minutes late and sit in the back row. I waited until the lunch break, then filed into the buffet line behind him.

"Good weekend?" I asked casually.

He smiled. "Nothing too crazy. I didn't have to work, which was awesome. I finally got through that Yeats book I've been trying to finish for three months. Saturday night, I went out with Annabelle."

"Is that the forty-eight-hour-date girl?"

He laughed. "I think we can call her by her name now that I've been on two separate dates with her."

"Look at you. Two dates!"

"How was yours?"

I told him about going out with the girls on Saturday night.

"I actually met someone I thought you'd like. One of Caroline's friends. But now that you're properly dating Annabelle, I'll try to think of another lucky guy to set her up with."

"Two dates doesn't mean we're dating. It means I decided to see her a second time."

"So does that mean you'd be up for meeting Caroline's friend?"

"Depends. What kind of music does she listen to?"

"We didn't get that far. All I know is where she works and that she lives in Brooklyn."

"Are you borough-typing me?"

"One hundred percent. If the subways and bridges shut down, and your significant other lives in Manhattan, that could be the end of a relationship."

We sat down as he cracked open a can of Mountain Dew and smeared the contents of a mustard packet on a catered club sandwich.

"Dating in New York is bleak enough without outer-borough discrimination, you know."

"Where does Annabelle live?" I asked.

"Brooklyn."

"There you go."

"Is it just me, or do catered lunches have a certain satisfying quality?" he asked.

"I'm not there yet. So, can I introduce you to Margaret? Or do you want to see where things go with Annabelle first?"

"Sure. I have two tickets to this concert in Fort Greene a week from Thursday, if she wants to go."

"Cool! I'll text her."

"It's nice to know you think enough of me to set me up with someone in my borough."

I tossed a purple grape onto his plate. "She seems great. And she's apparently been going on dates with a lot of jerks. Maybe you can show her there are still good guys out there."

"But only in Brooklyn."

"Right." I missed the easy banter. I wanted to get back to easy.

"Not totally off-topic, but I was also asked out on a date."

He raised both eyebrows. "Not off-topic, but pretty big news. Who's the lucky guy? Or girl," he said quickly.

I laughed. "He works at the restaurant I went to on Saturday."

Charlie clapped. "I'm proud of you, Sam. All the angst, and then you just made it happen."

"I didn't make anything happen. He asked for my number, and I wrote it down."

He balled up the sandwich paper and shot it in the trash can across from us.

"Buckets." He looked at his watch. "I have a call in ten minutes. You heading back to our office?"

It was our office again.

"So when's the big date?" he asked as he held the elevator door for me to step in.

"There's no date. He asked if I wanted to grab a drink sometime, but I haven't responded."

Charlie looked at me sideways.

I laughed. "What?"

"So you gave him your number, but you're just gonna ghost?"

"I don't know. He seemed nice. All the girls thought he was 'super cute.' I don't know . . . I guess he read the specials eloquently enough?"

"Ouch."

I shrugged. "I'll text back today."

We sat in our office working with earbuds on the rest of the day. It was pouring rain, and the clouds were so low you couldn't see out the window.

"Looks like we both have dates Thursday," I announced a few hours later.

"What's that?" he asked, taking out an earbud.

"The waiter. He asked if I was free next Thursday, and I said yes."

"Ah. Nice!" he said as he put the earbud back in.

I sat there and stared at my phone. I couldn't tell if Charlie was on a deadline or just over talking about dates. I texted Caroline, who I could count on being more excited than I was that the date was actually happening.

She called my cell less than a minute after.

"*Babe!* This is huge. Do you want me to come over and help you pick out an outfit? Maybe help you do your eyes a little bit more than you usually do?"

I glanced over at Charlie and wondered if I should step out, but his headphones were still on, and he didn't seem to notice I was on the phone.

"I only have mascara and concealer. I won't respect myself if I buy more makeup for one date."

She sighed. "Fine, your outfit can do all the talking. I'll bring a few options."

I hung up and started packing up my laptop to take the subway downtown to listen to oral arguments in the Texas Hold'em case.

"I'm the last guy to tell a woman what to do, but most guys don't like a lot of makeup. Just do what you normally do," he said as I threw a khaki trench over my suit.

I pretended to be distracted by my phone. "Good to know, thanks."

~

On Wednesday morning, Leo's name appeared on the New York office visitor list.

I hadn't heard from him since I'd hurriedly left the gallery opening. The fact that he hadn't reached out to let me know he was coming to the city somehow made me feel exposed. I wondered if he sensed my attraction and was keeping his distance.

I still had to plug the last few holes in the settlement strategy before I could present it to Leo. I'd backed into the budgets for two of the movies, but I couldn't find where the other two were shot or if tax credits even were involved. I searched IMDb and scrolled through the cast and crew, looking for inspiration to hit. I noticed the name Max Carlton listed as the "line producer" on both films and quickly typed an email to the firm's dedicated "librarian"—a master researcher with a reputation of being able to dig up more dirt than a private investigator—to see if he could locate an email address or phone number.

Within minutes, the librarian responded with a Pennsylvania cell phone number.

Max Carlton picked up on the second ring. I introduced myself as an attorney from New York with a few questions about two films he'd recently line-produced.

"There's a pretty tight confidentiality provision in my contract," he said. "Don't get me wrong though—if I wasn't afraid of getting sued, I'd be happy to help you nail whoever it is you're after. Those were two of the worst productions I've worked on in thirty years."

"Worst how? If you don't mind me asking," I said, trying *not* to sound like a lawyer.

"Bad people. Cutting corners, safety hazards everywhere, antiunion shit. I won't work for people like that anymore. Falls in the 'life's-too-short' bucket."

I explained I was trying to figure out if the budget of each movie was over $5 million.

He laughed in a way that told me he'd smoked every day of those thirty years.

"Let me just say this: You don't pay an actor $3 million on a $5 million movie and have anything to show for it. As for the other one, we shot it in NOLA. You can look up Louisiana tax-credit filings online."

"Thank you so much," I said. I was already googling the Louisiana tax-credit portal.

It was almost too easy.

There was no way the budget for the NOLA film was less than $8 million, making the total for just three of the four movies *$26 million*. I wondered who else's money they stole. That was someone else's problem.

I sent Leo an email letting him know I had a possible settlement strategy to run by him, omitting that I knew he was working from New York.

He responded a few minutes later, saying he was in the city for the week and free to meet the next morning. His email was polite and professional. Maybe my sudden exit from the gallery opening *had* been a red flag, and he was dialing it back down. Or maybe I'd just imagined all of it.

Chapter Twenty-Four

In brief, despite extensive expert testimony and compelling evidence to uphold the defendant's acquittal, the appeals court reversed the district court's ruling that Texas Hold'em poker is a game of skill, not chance, and was therefore appropriately considered to be an illegal gambling business under Section 1955, I concluded the email to Eddie after the Second Circuit announced its decision in the Texas Hold'em case the following morning.

The "game of skill, not chance" argument was officially a dead end.

My calendar flashed a fifteen-minute heads-up for the settlement meeting with Leo. I pulled out a flattened granola bar from the bottom of my tote bag, then gathered my laptop and notes and tried giving myself a mental pep talk.

Half an hour later, I put down the marker, looking back and forth between the conference room's oversized whiteboard and Leo's face. I felt out of breath. He hadn't said anything the entire time.

"Who represents the film fund again?" he finally asked.

"Damian Entwhistle."

He smiled. "Let's bring that fucker in for a meeting. I want to watch you tell him exactly why it's in his client's best interest to settle."

"Really? Does that mean you think it could work?"

"It's brilliant. This is your time to shine, baby."

My palms felt sweaty.

"I'll be there if you need me, but this is some *badass* lawyering. You took the things you knew and found a way to figure out what you didn't. Whether these guys are still too pigheaded to settle, who knows—but even if they don't, Sterling actually has a solid claim now."

I pressed my palms against my cheeks. The conference room felt too small for both of us. "Okay. Wow. So I'll draft the fraud claims into the complaint for you to look over?"

"Sam, excellent work. Bravo."

His phone dinged. "Shit, I need to dial into a call."

I gathered my things and headed toward the door.

"I have an eight p.m. reservation at Campagnola tonight on the Upper East Side. Join me?"

Between the flattery and the dinner invite, I realized how much I wanted to be back in his good graces. "Sure, that would be great," I quickly responded.

He winked. "See you tonight, then."

Charlie was blasting Bob Dylan when I got back.

"How'd it go?" he asked, turning down the volume.

"We're scheduling a settlement meeting," I said, trying to play it cool.

"So was he blown away by your math abilities?"

"He was very complimentary. *Appropriately* complimentary," I quickly added. I didn't mention dinner. "Can I be honest? I never thought I was great at thinking outside the box. I always felt smart in a bookish way. But I feel like I'm actually learning to be strategic."

"You're a real superstar, office buddy. Pretty soon these clients will be rolling in. Next stop, Hollywood."

That reminded me.

"I actually need advice. Big time."

He started laughing the second he picked up on where the story was going.

"No fucking way. You're consulting for *George Brenner*?"

"If I can get Eddie and the firm to say yes. That's where I need advice."

"Unbelievable. I'm serious, Sam. You're kind of unstoppable."

"This was all Andie. I never could've seen this coming when she made a book deal. Not in a million years."

"It's great PR for the firm."

"Maybe that's what I'll tell them." I needed to print copies of the talking points for the meeting later that afternoon with the US Attorney's Office. "If you were me, would you email Eddie about it? Or ask him in person?"

"When are you supposed to see him?"

"At four p.m. We're meeting the prosecutors. I'm supposed to share a car with him downtown."

"Do it then. Captive audience."

I wasn't supposed to meet Eddie for three more hours. I couldn't focus. Charlie threatened to throw every one of my pens into the industrial shredder if I didn't stop nervously clicking.

"I just have to be okay with the fact that he might tell me to fuck off," I said abruptly an hour later as Charlie came back with an eighteen-foot Italian sub in one hand and two bags of chips in the other.

"Have you billed any time today?"

"Like, an eighth of an hour."

"So, no."

"I'm mentally preparing myself to pass on the chance of a lifetime. He might tell me to pound sand."

"You can't do that and be a functional Big Law associate at the same time?"

"Could you?"

"Hell, no."

My phone rang and I nearly jumped out of my skin.

"Hey, Andie," I said, trying to sound composed.

"Did you talk to Eddie yet?"

I wondered if he had already updated her on the Texas Hold'em ruling.

"I'm going to do it from the car."

"Are you nervous?"

I chuckled. "Um, yeah. I have no idea what he's going to say."

"Don't forget to tell him how much I want you to do this." She paused. "And look, no matter how the meeting goes, I've been thinking about it a lot, and I think I want to plead guilty. Like—sooner, rather than later. I have to start planning out the rest of my life. Will you float the pleading thing by Eddie, make sure he still thinks it's a good idea?"

In a perfect world, I wanted to be able to go to bat for Andie. But there were actually reasons for her to settle—time, money, unpredictability. Her case wasn't a slam dunk, even if we didn't think a jury would find her guilty. I also understood wanting to move on with her life. No matter what she decided, there was no pretending that the case hadn't changed her life forever, in both good ways and bad. It had already changed mine.

An hour later, Eddie was waiting in the car when I got in.

"I hope you weren't waiting long," I said as I rushed into the back seat.

He smiled without looking up from his phone. "My twelve o'clock finished early, and I took the chance to catch up on things. I could sit here for another hour doing this." It looked like he was editing a legal brief from his iPhone. "Bummer about the Texas Hold'em case, huh?"

I was physically incapable of holding it in. "George Brenner wants to adapt Andie's life into a movie."

He looked up. "*The* George Brenner?"

I nodded.

"How did that happen?"

I took a deep breath. "Someone at the publisher—his old college friend, actually—sent him the manuscript, and he sparked to the story."

He shook his head. "This has been a fun one, huh?"

I laughed nervously. "There's more. He asked me to consult for him on the script. To answer questions about the indictment and negotiating with the prosecutors, things like that."

He shot me the same incredulous look as when I said George Brenner wanted to write Andie's movie.

"That's not something most lawyers get asked to do," he said in an indecipherable tone as he looked back at his phone.

I held my breath and wondered if the conversation, along with my once-in-a-lifetime opportunity, was over.

"What did you say?" he asked as he scrolled through his contact list.

"That I needed to ask you first. Of course," I said quickly.

"Would he want you to start right away?"

I told him we hadn't gotten that far.

He paused and lightly chewed the tip of his pen.

"You don't say no to that. That's a door-opener."

I nodded hopefully. "I really want to do it, but not if it means putting the firm in a bad spot."

"Yeah. Well, this would be a much easier sell if she pleaded guilty and we weren't actively representing her anymore."

I told him about Andie wanting to plead.

He nodded. "Well then, that's great news all around. I've been hoping she'd come around. There's no way we're ever going to get these prosecutors to drop the charges. She just has to take her lumps and get on with it."

"Does that mean I can tell George Brenner yes? Once she pleads guilty, I mean?"

"Make sure he knows it's ultimately the firm's decision. But if she pleads, I don't have an issue with it." He put his readers back on and looked at me seriously. "But Samantha, whether it's time spent editing the book or consulting for George Brenner, your work for the firm can't suffer. Otherwise, I won't continue to be supportive."

I took a deep breath and nodded. "Understood. I can manage."

I silently hoped George Brenner could wait.

Chapter Twenty-Five

That evening, I took the subway up to Seventy-Second Street and walked over to Campagnola, a timeless Italian eatery on First Avenue. I handed the maître d' my coat as he showed me to Leo's table. I wondered if the dinner would be business as usual. Only our past dinners had always veered away from talking business.

"You made it," he said enthusiastically, greeting me with a friendly hug. He pulled out my chair and motioned for me to sit down.

"Come up with any more brilliant ideas since this morning?"

"Let's see if it gets us anywhere," I said modestly. "Like you said, they might call our bluff."

He leaned in. "I'm going to give you some advice that it took me way too long to practice. You've got to celebrate every small win along the way. If you wait until the outcome you're hoping for, you lose sight of all the tiny moments that got you there."

He poured a glass of red wine from a carafe. "Don't get me wrong. I'm not saying take your eye off the prize. But what you did is worth a pat on the back, regardless of whether they settle."

He raised his glass. "To all the small moments."

I toasted back, feeling self-conscious as I wondered if he'd gotten better looking since the last time I'd seen him.

"How are Aldous and Kingsley?"

He grimaced. "Slowly killing me. They have more energy in an hour than I have in a month. We just hired a second nanny to tag-team, because the one we had threatened to quit."

"No kidding."

"They're not easy. Or cheap." He took a sip of wine. "I asked Jessica if we could leave them with her parents for Thanksgiving and go to Anguilla, just the two of us. She looked at me like I had two heads."

"Could you take them with you?"

"I wouldn't take them anywhere without both nannies."

"Oh boy."

"You live alone, right?"

I nodded.

"God, do I envy you. I miss the days when I was just responsible for myself." He looked down at the menu. "Can I be honest?"

I braced myself. "Of course." I wished I had left the office early and stopped for a drink to take the edge off. I felt like he was glasses ahead of me.

"I came out here this week to get away. I needed space to think."

I shifted uncomfortably in my chair. "I'm sure taking space helps to be a better partner and parent. It's a lot. You have to take time for yourself," I said encouragingly.

"It's an expensive mental-health vacation. I'm at the St. Regis. On the firm, but still."

He paused as the waiter came to ask for our order.

"They're famous for veal piccata," he said.

"I'll have a Caesar salad and the veal piccata, please," I said.

"I'll do the same."

The waiter collected the menus. I started to tell Leo that I had outlined Sterling's fraud complaint but immediately sensed he didn't want to have a working dinner.

He took a deep breath and looked at me squarely. "I'm leaving Jessica."

The words hung heavily in the air as I tried to think of something that didn't sound immature. I didn't know why, but something about Leo making such a personal confession made me feel self-conscious.

"Oh, wow. I'm really sorry to hear that," I said awkwardly, knowing nothing would have come out right.

"So many of my friends are unhappily married, but they're sticking it out. It feels like you're the only person I can really talk to about what I'm going through," he said, his voice thick with emotion. "How did you know it was time to end things?"

I fumbled for the right words. The idea that my experience could be helpful felt superficially parallel. "That was different," I said carefully. "We didn't have kids."

"Right. Of course." He took a deep breath. "It's painful saying this out loud, but I'm going to offer her full custody, and just ask for visitation rights. Weekends, here and there."

I tried to affect a neutral expression, but I felt shocked thinking he wouldn't want to share custody. I wondered how long he'd been thinking about this. Was I a catalyst? I felt embarrassed thinking it, even if I'd wondered before now if the attraction was mutual.

"Is that really what you want?"

He sighed, looking distraught but determined. "I haven't felt like myself for a while. I need to figure things out."

I didn't know Leo's wife or much about their marriage other than they were both committed to their careers. But it struck me that no matter what, his choice to leave would have a disproportionate impact on her life. In many ways, the life I was chasing would have been impossible if Ben and I had had a child.

He looked like he could read my thoughts. "Please keep this between us. Most lawyers at the firm know Jessica, and I'd hate for her to hear it from someone else. I'm planning to talk to her when I get back this weekend."

"Of course. You don't have to worry," I assured him. "I'm sorry you're going through this," I said honestly.

He took a slow sip of wine. "It's going to be a rough couple of months, but hopefully it'll be better on the other side."

I suddenly wanted to tell him how much I knew about wanting to get to the other side. I thought if I could just get through the bar, get to New York, start my new life, be my own person, I'd have it all figured out. So far, most of what had been waiting on the other side were lessons on how there really is no such thing as getting to the "other side."

"That's the thing about getting to the other side," I said cautiously. "If you're not facing things on this side, they tend to follow you."

It made more sense in my head. But I was living it.

Maybe it was Caroline's voice in my head or my own internal voice. Somehow, having dinner with Leo felt less innocent.

He smiled sadly. "I admire you a lot, Sam. It takes strength to leave someone."

I hesitated. "I don't think *strength* is the right word. I made a hard choice, and it bought me a second chance to do it right. But second chances don't always look like you thought they would. It's never a clean break."

He raised his glass for the second time. "To second chances, then."

I was grateful when he switched the conversation back to work. "What's happening with Andie Reese? Has Eddie convinced the prosecutors to drop the case yet?"

"I think she's going to plead guilty. She wants to move on."

I debated telling him about George Brenner but decided not to. It was too close to Leo's world. He probably knew George personally. "She's writing a memoir."

"Have you read it?"

I told him about the editing process Eddie came up with.

"Is there anything you can't do? Star associate, ghost editor . . . looks to me like this new life fits you like a glove."

"I don't know about all that, but thank you," I said.

"You know, it's been a long time since I met anyone like you."

Something about the way he was looking at me made me feel vulnerable and flattered at the same time. And far out of my league.

"It's been a pleasure learning from you," I said, instinctively wrapping my blazer tighter.

He chuckled and held my gaze. "What do you say to one more drink? There's a great little bar a few doors down."

I looked down at my watch. "I'd like that . . . but I really need to finish the memo from today's meeting with the prosecutors." I instantly felt guilty for lying. But despite all the mental space he'd taken up over the last month, it felt like something had shifted. His attention felt invasive. For the first time, I felt like wine was heightening my inhibitions instead of lowering them.

"Fair enough," he said cheerfully. "I'll pop in for a solo martini and make it an early night."

I thanked Leo for dinner and promised again that his secret was safe with me.

I walked across to the 6 train, stopping to look down Park Avenue at the MetLife Building thirty blocks below. I knew Charlie had a hearing in the morning and would still be working. I took a picture of the building and texted it to him.

Waving from 72nd Street (good luck tomorrow).

~

Sterling was adamant that if we were going to file a lawsuit, we needed to file it before Thanksgiving so he could let his dad know he was putting his money where his mouth was.

Leo's assistant scheduled the settlement meeting for Friday afternoon. I woke up at 5 a.m. to practice delivering my arguments. As much as I appreciated Leo's hands-off approach, the idea of making an aggressive ultimatum to another lawyer while Leo watched was a nail-biting proposition *without* the added complication of being in emotional limbo.

Charlie had a dentist appointment, which meant there was no one to absorb my nervous energy. I paced our office until it was almost time for the meeting. I found a sleeve of stale saltines in my desk and ate half before going down to set up the conference room a few minutes early.

Leo was already there, answering emails. "All the visitor offices were booked today, so I've actually been posting up here since this morning."

He winked. "I'm feeling great energy in this room."

He didn't seem at all rebuffed by my ending the night after dinner.

The visitor desk downstairs called to let us know that Damian Entwhistle and his associate were on their way up. I tried taking a deep, cleansing breath and reminded myself that I knew these arguments backward and forward.

Damian was shorter than me, with a young Joe Pesci vibe. He had a thriving law practice in Jackson Heights defending clients whose business practices often got them in trouble.

"Great view from up here. I think we can see Philadelphia," he joked in a heavy Queens accent.

We shook hands, and I took my seat next to Leo. I handed them each a set of exhibits I'd printed, marked *Privileged & Confidential/ Attorney Work Product* at the top.

"As you know, our client is intent on filing a lawsuit against your clients for breach of contract and fraud."

Damian chuckled. "We've seen the same emails and texts as you. There's no way there's a colorable fraud claim here. But please, continue."

"I assume you're referring to the emails our client relied on when deciding to invest his money, representing that his investment would be allocated across four movies, with budgets of no more than $5 million each?"

"Sure. Those emails."

"We now know your clients inflated the budgets of at least three of the four movies."

I held up the first handout.

"This is Exhibit A, with a breakdown of what we understand the final budget to have been for *Tokyo Summer*, in addition to a copy of the tax-credit filing with New York state."

Damian's associate, a petite brunette in a pale-pink pantsuit, leaned in and whispered something to Damian.

"Do you need the room?" I asked.

He shook his head. "You can continue."

"You'll see at the bottom of the chart is the budget number for *Tokyo Summer*, which we uncovered by working backward once we obtained the tax-credit filing from the state."

"Reminder that a court is unlikely to be sympathetic with a fact that you 'backed into.'"

"I'll let you read through Exhibit B and C."

Leo gave me a stealth thumbs-up as they skimmed the next few pages.

Damian looked unimpressed. "Continue."

"Respectfully, we know your clients doubled the budgets. If forced to file a lawsuit, we're going to subpoena all of their records, and the line-item budgets will be the first things we demand to see. And we're certain the documents will confirm that your clients bloated the budgets with fees for themselves, overpaid actors, used budgeted funds for frivolous Cannes parties. Then we'll subpoena each movie's financial statements, and we'll know exactly how Sterling's money evaporated into thin air."

He appeared unmoved. "So file a lawsuit, and see what you find," he said flatly.

"As I said earlier, we'll be alleging fraud, along with embezzlement, negligent misrepresentation, breach of fiduciary duty, and unfair business practices. We'll be seeking compensatory damages of at least $20 million, and another $20 million in punitive damages for fraudulently inducing our client to invest millions and knowingly devaluing our client's investment, foreclosing any possibility of recouping even a fraction of the millions he invested."

Damian smiled politely and stood up, signaling the meeting was over. "I hope you've got the complaint ready to go."

I went in for a firm handshake. "We plan to file at five o'clock a week from today, unless we hear from you otherwise."

Chapter Twenty-Six

The following Tuesday, I was drowning in documents for the Lincoln Center matter when I got an email from Damian Entwhistle's secretary saying he wanted to schedule a call.

"Holy shit. What if it worked?" I asked, my voice too loud for our small office.

"What if what worked?" Charlie asked.

"The film fund's lawyer wants to set a call."

"Rock and roll," he said, reaching over the desk to give me a high five.

I forwarded the email to Leo. He responded within minutes that he was slammed with a deal closing but to take the call and report back.

Damian's office sent a dial-in for 6 p.m. I went back to tagging documents.

At 5:45, Charlie started blasting "The Final Countdown" by Europe.

"You're such a nerd," I laughed.

"Are you gearing up for victory?"

"I'm debating if I want to take this call with you in the room."

"I'll put my headphones on. I won't make a peep."

I went over my talking points from last week's meeting, then dialed in promptly at six o'clock.

"Leo is tied up, but I'll fill him in after," I said as everyone announced themselves.

Damian postured for the next ten minutes, aggressively pointing out all the weaknesses in our claims and calling Sterling an unsympathetic plaintiff.

"Despite all of that, I'm authorized to make the following offer of settlement. Mila will follow up with the full written proposal."

The fund was offering $10 million cash and an assignment of future revenue from the four films until Sterling received the other $10 million. According to Damian, the fund planned to file for bankruptcy once it repaid the first $10 million.

It was a real, tangible offer. And the fact that it came in so fast meant the fraud argument had teeth.

"Thanks, Damian. We will discuss and come back to you. Of course, I must reserve rights on behalf of Leo and our client."

Charlie threw a paper clip over as I drafted an email to Leo summarizing the settlement offer.

"So?" he asked.

"They made an offer. I need to see what Leo says. It's half of what we were asking for, but it's not small potatoes. We really want him to settle."

Five minutes later, Leo's assistant's number came up on my phone. "I have Leo for you."

She patched him through.

"Hey, rockstar. Did you just settle your first case?"

I laughed nervously. "I mean—we knew asking for the full $20 million up front was a long shot, right? But depending on how those films are released, he could maybe recover more than the initial $10 million."

"*Yes.* That's an excellent point, actually. We need approval over distribution of the films. They need to actually try to monetize them."

I wrote down *DISTRIBUTION APPROVAL* in big letters.

"Should we call Sterling? Let's close this up, baby!"

I gave Charlie a thumbs-up.

~

The next day, I dove into the back seat of a black SUV, escaping a mob of paparazzi waiting outside of the federal courthouse.

"How do people *do* that?" I gasped, fully out of breath.

Andie was laughing hysterically. "It's official. We're buying matching outfits for the sentencing hearing and crossing every finger this happens again. I really hope those pictures end up online."

Eddie had channeled his past life as a high-profile prosecutor and curated a plan for Andie to evade the inevitable media circus waiting outside after the plea hearing. We were both petite brunettes in black pantsuits and oversized sunglasses. I'd leave the courthouse through the front as a decoy while a car waited for Eddie and Andie at the back entrance.

The plan worked perfectly. As I walked casually down the front steps of the federal courthouse toward the black SUV, I was blinded by flashing lights and requests to make a statement. I went from defense attorney to indicted celebrity. It was one of those out-of-body experiences that felt worlds away from my past life. I had never felt more part of a team. We'd really been in the trenches together.

I texted Charlie from the car, half jokingly asking him to keep refreshing the internet for my picture. It was nearly five o'clock by the time the driver dropped us in front of the MetLife Building. Andie walked toward her hotel, and Eddie and I rode the elevator up to the fiftieth floor.

"I can't believe it's almost Thanksgiving," I mused, wondering what it was about elevators that deadened my ability to make small talk.

"It's unfortunate that her sentencing will be right before the holidays, but if we do our job right, she can at least celebrate dodging prison," he said humorlessly.

Worst-case scenario, Andie was facing up to five years. Best case, she'd get one year of probation. She was choosing to plead guilty and accept responsibility for her actions, something some judges took into account when weighing a harsher or more lenient sentence.

Charlie texted to say he had to leave unexpectedly and asked if I could log onto his laptop and reset his password when I got back. The firm made us do it manually from the office once a month for security reasons, and if you missed the deadline, you were locked out until IT came to physically unlock it.

I opened the laptop, typed his current password, "Brady_12," and was suddenly staring at a blown-up screenshot of my face in sunglasses, looking down demurely toward the ground, with the giant headline:

> POKER PRINCESS FOLDS, PLEADS GUILTY IN MANHATTAN FEDERAL COURT.

The door swung open, and Charlie walked in with a bottle of prosecco and two Solo cups.

"I got a Google Alert that you finally pleaded guilty today."

I grinned. "Hilarious."

"How does it feel?" he asked as he poured prosecco into both cups.

"That literally just happened thirty minutes ago," I said, pointing to the screenshot of my indicted alter ego.

"An attractive woman walking proudly out of court after pleading guilty for running poker games? With those sunglasses? On your behalf, I'm offended it took them half an hour."

"Eddie planned that to a T. I didn't think it would work until I almost couldn't see from all the flashes."

"Celebratory basement sushi?"

"Can I ask all the dumb questions I want to about my date tomorrow?"

"What date?"

I shot him a look. "With the waiter?"

"That's tomorrow? I thought it already happened."

I put my hands on my hips. "And you never thought to ask how it went?"

He laughed. "Sorry. Now I remember."

"And you're taking Margaret to the concert in Brooklyn tomorrow. *I* remembered."

"Uh-huh. I'm going to need a few sips of Sapporo before I can answer your date questions, though."

"Deal."

~

Charlie's number-one piece of dating advice was *don't overthink it.*

On Thursday, determined to project a casual attitude, I went straight from the office to the Union Square wine bar where Alex had suggested we meet. He'd arrived early and already selected our first wine-tasting flight, which included a Pinotage from South Africa, a Shiraz from New Zealand, and a Tuscan Chianti.

"The sommelier here is off his rocker. He puts together these tastings that make absolutely no sense, but somehow you learn the craziest things, and by the end of the flight, it starts to come together."

I looked down skeptically at the pairing sheet. "Sounds like that's the wine doing its job, but I'll take your word for it. Which one do I start with?"

Alex knew a lot more about wine than me. He was a career waiter who had worked at some of Manhattan's finest restaurants. He'd trained at Le Bernardin, spent four years at Gramercy Tavern, and then did a brief stint at Momofuku. He was an effortless conversationalist who did most of the talking, but not in a way that I found displeasing. His day-to-day was filled with high-end foodies, angry chefs, and constant drama. As soon as he finished a story, I hoped he would start another.

"You should pitch a TV show about the gritty world of New York fine dining," I said, making a note that I liked the last wine best.

"If it sells, can you be my entertainment lawyer?"

"Good question. Do I get a credit on the show for convincing you to pitch the idea?"

He laughed good-naturedly.

We each ordered a glass of Primitivo from the flight and agreed to share a few appetizers. I was starving and feeling the wine.

Even though he knew nothing about working in a law firm, he seemed fascinated by my job. He wished restaurant gigs were a little more stable. He wanted to know what drew me to entertainment law. I told him about my love for independent film. *Memento* was his favorite movie.

At a certain point midway through a story about a Michelin-starred French restaurant on the Upper East Side, I realized it didn't even feel like we were on a date. It felt easy. He asked good questions and had good stories. I found myself wondering if Charlie would think he was pretentious about food and wine.

He excused himself to use the restroom, and I reached instinctively for my phone to skim emails. The top one was from Charlie, sent ten minutes earlier, forwarding me an invite to a Fordham Law recruiting event next week.

> Hoping you can get on board with recruiting some of the more hardworking / less snobby kids.

I hit reply. Sure. But why are you emailing me right now?? Enjoy the concert!!

When Alex got back to the table, he accepted my offer to split the bill, and we walked out onto Broadway.

"I had a lot of fun," he said kindly. I suddenly felt shy and had the urge to just shake his hand and jump in a cab. I was grateful that he wasn't leaning in or standing too close. I figured I'd know when I wanted to be kissed on a first date.

I had no idea if I'd see him again but was relieved that the whole thing had been totally pleasant and even enjoyable. And I could tell Connor and Caroline that I actually went on a proper date.

A minute after I got in the cab, my phone lit up with a text from Charlie.

So?

I smiled at the screen.

Nice guy! Knows lots about wine.

Ouch.

What??

Do you tell people I'm a nice guy?

All the time, why?

Exactly.

So? Your turn . . .

Nice girl.

Chapter Twenty-Seven

The next day, I was scheduled to prep Eddie for a meeting with the New York Film Festival board members.

A few hours before, Patricia called to say Eddie wanted to see me in his office. I wondered if Leo had told him about the settlement.

I walked the internal staircase up to the fiftieth floor. Eddie motioned for me to sit down and close the door.

"The lawyer for the city just called. The permit applications we sent over for the film festival were dated incorrectly, and now we're right up against the deadline. We're helping the festival negotiate with the city on a pro bono basis, but we need to be just as buttoned-up as we are for paying clients. If the city uses this as an excuse not to permit the festival, we're fucked."

I felt lightheaded as my mind was racing.

I looked at the stack of documents he had printed.

It was a blatant fuckup—the kind that made me physically nauseous. After all this, I couldn't be the reason the New York Film Festival wasn't happening.

"Please double-check your work. We could lose all credibility."

I wanted to crawl into a hole and never come out.

"I'm so sorry. I'll do everything I can to make it right."

He nodded soberly. "I know that mistakes happen, especially when technology is involved. But for lawyers, mistakes have catastrophic consequences. Our profession can be very unforgiving. One mistake could tank your career, and you might not get a second chance." He turned back to his laptop. "I guess that's the only takeaway I've got."

I walked like a zombie back to my office. Charlie was out all day for another deposition, which left me alone with the looping echo of Eddie's words. How could I have made such a careless mistake?

By the time I got home, I was running on fumes. I dropped my keys to the floor, stripped off my clothes, and turned the shower knob all the way to the left, letting the small bathroom fill with steam. I stepped into the tub, standing still with my eyes squeezed tightly shut.

Eddie was right. This was a world where no mistake was inconsequential. I felt unprepared for such a weighty reality.

I toweled off and realized I hadn't eaten anything all day. I found my phone and hit the reorder button on my Seamless app without looking at what I'd last ordered.

My eye landed on the open bottle of red across the room.

The first summer that I spent in New York away from Ben, I'd romanticized lonely Friday nights like these. Alone, no responsibility to anyone but myself. Whatever takeout I was in the mood for. All the rom-coms my heart desired. Wine on my couch.

I turned on the movie adaptation of Emily Giffin's *Something Borrowed* to drown out the quiet. Twenty minutes later, the buzzer sounded, and I felt around for my slippers.

"Come on up," I automated as I pressed the button and reached for a clean wine glass.

Minutes later, there was a light knock as the door handle jiggled.

"Just a sec . . ." I said as I peered through the peephole and saw Connor's face.

I cracked the door so he wouldn't get the full view of my depressing Friday night.

"Jesus. I thought you were the Seamless guy, but they usually don't try to open the door themselves," I said with a nervous chuckle.

"Since I'm not the Seamless guy, can I come in?"

I kicked my slippers off behind the door. "Sure."

Connor took off his shoes outside and settled onto a kitchen stool. "Seamless and wine, is it? And you didn't think to invite me? You know we're only young once."

I rolled my eyes. "What's *up*? You don't live close enough for a casual pop in."

"No Friday night plans? In the greatest city in the world?"

"It was a long day."

"They're all long, Sam. They'll be long for the rest of our lives. What won't last forever are wild Friday nights."

"Maybe we have different versions of wild."

"Anyway, Gillian's out of town, but 'the French' are in town, and I'm heading to meet them at Art Bar around the corner. And clearly saving you from a sad Friday night."

I shook my head. "I don't know 'the French' but I'm about to drink a glass of wine and go to bed."

Connor sighed. "I'm not loving this for you, Sam. You need to meet people. Interesting people. Some sophisticated Frenchies. Just come out for one drink. If you're not having a blast after an hour, you're only five minutes from home. It'd be a mistake not to even *try* having fun."

The Word of the Day hung in the air.

"Everyone makes mistakes," I said dryly.

"C'mon. I need a wingwoman. My ex is going to be there."

"Which one?"

"Get dressed, and I'll give you the skinny on the way."

"I'm not in a social mood. And I just ordered food."

He looked unconvinced. "Is Caroline at home? She can bring it in for you. There's food at Art Bar."

"She's in Iowa," I said.

"Sam. I never ask you for anything. Please."

I stared at the wine glass on the counter. I didn't know if drinking alone was going to make me feel better or worse. He didn't seem to be taking no for an answer. If it involved a subway or cab ride, there was no way. But he was basically asking me to cross the street. I could bail as soon as I dropped him off with his friends.

"Okay, fine. But just *one* drink."

He waited in the hall while I threw on black jeans and a burnt-orange sweater. I ran a brush through my hair, dabbed on concealer and light mascara, and grabbed a pair of ankle boots from the back of my closet.

"This is as good as it gets," I said, locking the door behind me.

Connor smirked. "The Divorcée takes Manhattan."

"Save that detail for yourself, please." I dug around my bag for lip gloss. "Who are these friends again? Did I ever meet them at Georgetown?"

"I went to boarding school with Stefan, who was childhood friends with George, who I'm loosely calling an ex because we dated for a summer when I was in college. Whilst working on a vineyard in Bordeaux."

"Romantic."

"The French are romantic for a summer. Then the narcissism sets in."

"So it's Stefan and George?"

"And their friend Christophe, who just moved from Paris. He's the one they're visiting."

"Would Gillian be jealous if she knew you were seeing George?"

"I wouldn't know because I didn't mention it. She's at a yoga retreat."

"Remind me not to take relationship advice from you."

We walked into Art Bar as an intimidatingly well-dressed group of guys converged on Connor.

He wrapped his arm protectively around my shoulder. "Boys, this is Samantha. An old friend from law school."

"What would you two like to drink?" one of them asked.

"Ketel and soda for me," Connor said.

"Same for me, thanks," I said.

I leaned over and whispered, "Which one is George?"

He shot me a look then whispered back, "On the right."

George struck me as the male equivalent of Gillian, only much taller.

"You have a type," I murmured as Stefan returned with our drinks.

Stefan raised a martini glass. "*Aux vieux amis et nouveaux amis.* To old and new friends." He squeezed Connor's shoulder. "Very old friends, in some cases. You look tired, man. What's this city doing to you?"

Connor pretended to be wounded. "I'll always be younger than you, lad."

Stefan chuckled. "You're working too hard."

"Not as hard as this one," Connor said, with an affectionate light pinch of my cheek.

I thanked him for the drink. "Working hard is old news in New York."

Christophe gave a small wave. "I'm the New York virgin. I just arrived last week from Paris. But I can keep the Parisian lifestyle, non?"

"As in, never working," George quipped.

"Something like that." He winked in my direction, and I noticed a small gap in his front teeth.

"What do you do?" I asked.

Christophe laughed. "That's such an American question. What do *you* do?"

I blushed. "I'm a lawyer."

"Entertainment lawyer," Connor jumped in.

Cristophe looked amused. "But what about when you're not at your job?"

It was an embarrassingly tough question. "Mental note, get a hobby," I joked.

"It's just that my experience of Americans is they are very one-dimensional," he said, his French accent making it sound even more condescending.

Connor feigned offense on my behalf. "And in my experience, that's a very French point of view."

I tried to come up with an answer that wasn't lame. "I work out, I watch movies . . . pretty standard fare," I said, feeling even more boring than when I couldn't think of anything to say.

"You go to a bar with your friends," he added. I had a feeling Christophe was having more fun than any of us.

"I was *dragged* to a bar," I corrected him.

"What would you be doing otherwise?" he probed. His eyes were intense in a way that felt like he could see underneath my clothes.

Connor jumped in. "Okay, lad, call off the interrogation."

I stood there silently as the group caught up. I eventually noticed everyone's drink was mostly empty, including mine. "I'll get the next round," I offered, looking for a chance to break away.

Christophe jumped up. "I'll help you."

Connor tapped his shoulder. "No funny business."

Christophe was a head taller than me, which proved helpful in getting the bartender's attention. He pulled out a barstool for me while we waited.

"I wasn't trying to be an asshole back there. I just feel like Americans love to hide behind their work."

"I'm not hiding behind anything. I've got my dream job," I responded defensively.

I noticed Connor across the room, waiting for me to return a thumbs-up.

"But there's more to life than work." He smiled, and I realized he had a dimple on one side. "After this drink, come to a reading with me."

I handed my card to the bartender. "Come again?"

"A poetry reading. A friend from Paris is hosting it in her apartment in the East Village."

I laughed at how European it sounded.

"Are you trying to curate a hobby for me? The one-dimensional American?"

"I just think we can spice up this night a little bit. What do you say? Have you ever heard Sappho read out loud? In French?"

I hadn't read Sappho in English. "That's the reading?"

"They're reading Anne Le Fèvre Dacier's translation. It's more beautiful in French."

I rolled my eyes. "What isn't."

"Exactly."

I glanced in Connor's direction. "This isn't really my scene. But it would be disingenuous to say a French poetry reading in the East Village is me either." I handed him two of the drinks as I juggled the others.

"But you wouldn't know, because you've never done it."

He set down the drinks and checked his watch. "I'll have you home by midnight." He extended his hand. "The French keep their word."

Chapter Twenty-Eight

I promised to text Connor if I needed to be rescued and followed Christophe out to Eighth Avenue.

Christophe touched my arm and pointed to a cab coming across Horatio Street.

"So, are you ready for some French poetry?"

I reached down and zipped my purse. "Sappho was Greek."

"Whatever you say, American girl. I think you will love it."

We got in a cab, and I watched him watch the city go by, admiring the way his mouth was consistently set in a playful smile. The novelty of escaping my comfort zone was oddly satisfying.

The weight of my mistake from earlier still loomed, but it was beginning to feel more abstract.

"I probably should have asked before, but—do you have a boyfriend?"

I looked instinctively down at my left hand. Even after a year of not wearing my wedding band, I still expected to see it.

"Why?"

"Because it might be, I don't know, weird to ask another man's *copine* to a romantic poetry reading."

"Ah. No boyfriend."

"So, how do you feel?"

"About being single?"

He laughed. "I mean, how do you feel right now? In this moment?"

"Is this like 'what do you do' except you don't actually want to know the answer?"

"It's just a question, Samantha. How do you feel?"

"It's Sam. And I feel . . . open. But I'm not sure why," I said honestly.

He laughed. "*Open* is a funny word. But I like the way it sounds."

The cab pulled up to a brownstone on East Tenth Street. We walked up to the parlor floor apartment where a woman with long black hair and a stylish black jumpsuit greeted us both with a double air-kiss.

"Amelia, this is my new friend Sam. She's an American lawyer." He winked and picked up two glasses of white wine from a waiter holding a tray of wine glasses.

"I didn't think people hired waitstaff for house parties anymore," I whispered, watching a tray of figs and blue cheese pass by.

"Like I said, we keep the Parisian lifestyle wherever we go."

Christophe was a kind and attentive date. He introduced me as his "newest New York friend" and insisted that everyone speak English.

I felt like the subject of my own social experiment. Maybe it was knowing I'd probably never see most of them again, but I wasn't overthinking.

It hit me that Alex hadn't texted since the wine bar, but I hadn't texted him either. The realization somehow made me feel worldly in a way that I liked. Whether we went on another date or never saw each other again, I was proud of myself for stacking new experiences.

Amelia shepherded everyone into the "salon." We settled onto a shag rug while we waited for the reading to start.

"So where were you before New York?" Christophe asked.

"In law school, in DC."

"Did you have a boyfriend in law school?"

After two cocktails and two glasses of wine, I didn't even flinch.

"I was in a relationship, yes."

"Tell me about him."

I looked at him curiously. "Is this how the French flirt?"

He shrugged. "I just think it's an interesting way to get to know someone."

"We were married," I said. "Does that make me less one-dimensional?"

He laughed. "See? We're getting to know each other."

"You probably haven't met many divorced women my age."

He leaned in. "I don't even know how old you are."

"I'm thirty."

"That's a great age for a woman. It's when you finally figure out what you want. *You* figured out you don't want to be married. Bravo."

"You sound like a therapist."

He gave me a knowing look. "I like the idea of being inside your head."

Amelia clinked her wine glass and thanked everyone for coming. "The wine will continue to flow, but we ask that you stay seated while someone is mid-poem," she said with a subtle French accent.

Each poem was more lyrical than the last. The whole thing was like a masterful recital.

I felt Christophe nudge me as I reached for a third glass of wine.

"It's 11:30. I promised you'd be home by midnight," he whispered.

"Let's stay."

"As you wish."

The reading finished just after midnight, and the apartment quickly emptied. We thanked Amelia for hosting, and I accepted Christophe's arm as we walked outside.

"My apartment is on Astor Place. Do you want to come home with me?" he asked with a confidence that I found undeniably attractive.

"You don't mess around."

"I've enjoyed your company tonight."

He held out his hand, and I took it.

~

I woke up and fumbled around for my phone. The light in Christophe's apartment was nonexistent. I had no idea what time it was.

My throat was so dry, I could barely swallow. I was fully clothed but had the feeling we'd made out for days. My lips were chapped. I really needed the backlight of my phone to find the bathroom. And water. And fucking Advil.

I got up cautiously, trying not to wake him. I sat up and steadied myself on the bed. I didn't have a shot in hell at making it to yoga.

I couldn't tell if we were in a basement apartment or a penthouse. There was no light from the street. He must have installed blackout shades. I didn't so much as project a shadow as I felt my way around for a wall or a doorknob.

I finally found a wall and felt my way across. I landed on a light switch and flipped it briefly on and off. Bingo.

I shut the door quietly behind me, hoping I could find the kitchen and a glass of water next. I buttoned up my jeans and felt around to wash my hands.

I turned back to the doorknob, but it didn't move. I tried turning the other way, then pulling. Nothing. I was either half asleep or still drunk, but either way, I started to panic. I took a step back. The light switch was outside the bathroom. I didn't know if it would be worse to wait out the night in the pitch-black bathroom or bang on the door and wake him. Both options felt equally humiliating.

I gripped the handle again and pulled harder, a doomed sense of claustrophobia setting in. The alcohol was fueling my anxiety. I took a deep breath and pulled with everything I had. It finally gave way with a deafening rip, the force throwing me backward, landing me sideways on my left wrist. The panic gave way to shooting pain as I sat there trying to figure out what happened. Seconds later, I heard footsteps and a concerned knock on the door.

"Samantha? Are you okay? What the hell was that?"

I felt my right hand wrapped around the cold piece of metal.

"Can you please turn on the light? And open the door?"

The light came on as I saw the doorknob was still there.

Then I realized what had happened.

He knelt down next to me. "Holy shit!"

I dropped the wall fixture I was still gripping with my right hand and cradled my wrist. "I didn't want to wake you, so I left the light off . . . and I thought the door wouldn't open. But—I must have mistaken the towel rack for the doorknob."

"Are you hurt?"

"Just my wrist. I fell back when this came out of the wall, and . . ."

We both looked at the gaping hole in the bathroom wall and then back at each other. I could see he was trying not to laugh, which made me want to laugh. Soon we were both laughing hysterically.

He put his hands on his face. "You're a tornado. Stronger than you look," he said with a huge grin.

Something about the word *tornado* made me laugh even harder.

"I'll get you some ice. Stay here."

I rested my head against the wall and tried bending my wrist. "*Fuck*," I whimpered.

I held the bag of ice against my wrist for a few minutes while we each finished a bottle of water.

"What time is it?" I whispered.

"Three a.m. That's the devil's hour in America." He smirked. "We could finally . . . you know."

I looked down at my swollen wrist. "I think the moment passed."

He smiled sympathetically. "You're a cool girl, Sam. It was fun helping you find some fun for a night."

I resisted the urge to retort.

We fell back asleep for a few hours. I woke to the smell of coffee and a fresh bag of ice next to me.

"You're sweet," I said when he asked if I took my coffee with cream or sugar.

"That's the opposite of a compliment in France."

"If you say so."

I was out of lines. I finished the coffee and freshened up in the bathroom. When I came back, he was sitting in a corner chair next to the window, reading *The New Yorker* in a bathrobe and slippers.

"I should get home," I said.

He smiled. "Thank you for a lovely evening."

I suddenly felt shy again. "Well. It was nice meeting you."

He snorted. "Oh, no. Please—don't say that."

He set down the magazine and I held up my hand. "Don't get up. You're a picture of the perfect Saturday morning right now."

"If you insist."

I bent down and gave him a kiss on the cheek.

"Thanks for helping me find some fun last night."

Chapter Twenty-Nine

I was eating a salad at my desk on Wednesday when Charlie and his suitcase rolled into the office from yet another Texas deposition.

"Did you come back just for the Fordham recruiting event?" I asked.

"You bet. You're still going, right?"

"You think I'd miss the chance to help the firm recruit the next Charlie Bronstein?"

He looked at my bandaged left wrist, which I'd self-wrapped to avoid taking time to go to the doctor. It still hurt like hell four days later.

"Shit, what happened to you?"

"I'm fine. I tripped over a pair of shoes in the middle of the night. It's just a sprain."

There was no way to explain ripping a towel holder out of a wall without sounding like a deranged drunk.

"Did you get an X-ray?"

"I'm just icing it."

He looked suspicious. "You tripped, huh?"

I nodded. "You can add 'clumsy' to the list of adjectives when you introduce me to all the awkward law students tonight. The worst part is I'm a leftie, so I can't write, and I'm typing like a five-year-old."

At six, we packed up our laptops and took a cab to Fordham's Lincoln Center campus. The security guard pointed us toward a banquet hall filled with black suits. We found our name tags and stood awkwardly off to the side.

"Drink?"

I shook my head. "I'm going to try doing this without alcohol. I want to see if I can win people over with my unaltered personality."

"Seems a little unfair to the firm. We're here to recruit the best and brightest."

"Then *you* can bait them with your personality, and I'll swoop in and talk about how magical the work is."

"Just don't forget to tell them you're consulting for a famous screenwriter. It's the only reason I invited you."

He grabbed a Heineken and surveyed the room.

"Divide and conquer?"

I wasn't so into that idea—I thought we'd at least be fielding stilted conversations together—but said sure anyway as I watched him cross the room.

Half an hour later, I was sandwiched between two international students running through a synchronized script of questions. I couldn't tell if it was my problem or theirs, but I'd never been more bored. I really wanted a drink.

I finally excused myself and escaped to the restroom. I locked myself in a corner stall and texted Charlie an SOS.

My phone buzzed with a text from Emilie.

He just broke up with me. It's over.

I texted Charlie again.

OK now I actually have to go. Friend emergency.

Still no response.

Fuck it, I muttered as I exited the restroom and picked up a prosecco from a table of prepoured glasses.

I scanned the room and spotted him in a corner talking to a blond who looked like a potential recruit.

He looked over and gave me a wave. I pointed toward the door to signal I was heading out. He held up two fingers and mouthed, "Two minutes."

I wasn't feeling patient. I drained the prosecco and unpinned my name tag. I shot an irritable look back in Charlie's direction. It looked like she was putting his number in her phone.

He strolled over and held up his empty beer bottle.

"Did you see a recycling bin anywhere?"

I laughed despite my agitation. "Over there. Did that student just give you her number?"

"She did."

"So that you guys can talk more about life at the firm, or . . .?"

"I can't tell if you're making a joke."

"I'm making a point. She's a law student who might be an intern next summer. Remember the summer bubble?"

"She's interested in real estate and asked if we could have a follow-up conversation." He shrugged. "She seems like a great candidate, and it sounds like she's considering multiple firms. She's third in her class. I can swing a phone call if it helps the cause."

I pointed to the empty bottle. "Okay Mr. EPA. Chuck it so we can go. Emilie texted an SOS, and I'm trying to track down where she is."

"Wait! Almost forgot—we have to check out the rooftop before we head down. That girl said the view is unbelievable."

I still hadn't heard from Emilie where she was, but I couldn't say no to someone who'd lived in New York for years and still got excited about a view. I could imagine a slightly younger law student being charmed by someone like Charlie. A high-powered lawyer who recycled.

The top of the Empire State Building seemed so close you could almost touch it. We stood there quietly as I texted Emilie again.

"Can I ask you a question?" he asked.

His face was backlit by the city. I tried mirroring his look, but it was unreadable.

"Yes, counselor?"

"Have you really not slept with anyone—sober—since you got divorced?"

I shot him a look. "How many beers have you had?"

"Three."

"Is that where this is coming from?"

He looked puzzled. "What do you mean?"

"I just mean your question feels like it came out of nowhere. Like a three-beers-in question."

He shrugged. "I was just thinking about it."

"Why?"

"What about the date you went on a few days ago, with the bartender guy?"

"Waiter. Are you asking if I slept with him?"

"I guess I am."

"We didn't. And no, I wasn't exaggerating about the sober sex. Or lack of it."

"Damn." He looked away. "It's just that . . . I don't know. Sober sex is so much better than drunk sex. Personally, I've had enough drunk hookups to last the rest of my life. At a certain point, it just feels like masturbating with someone else in the room."

My mind was trying to decide if I was comfortable having this conversation. "That's . . . visual."

He shook his head. "Sorry. Forget I asked. You know how nosy I get after a few beers."

I smiled sympathetically as we rode the elevator down to the lobby. "I really need to get home, but I have to find Emilie first. And then there's a screenwriter waiting for me to blow him away with my explanation of federal sentencing guidelines."

"How many times a day do you use that line?"

"I've lost track."

He grinned. "Get on the sober sex train, Sam. You won't regret it."

"Bye!" I rolled my eyes as I jumped in the next cab.

I still hadn't heard back from Emilie, so I decided to stop by her apartment to see if she was home.

"West Twelfth and Fifth, please."

I stared out the window, Charlie's question repeating in my head. It was an intimate question, but it didn't feel intrusive. The idea of him thinking about my sex life made my heart beat a little faster.

I needed a male perspective. Before I could change my mind, I dialed Connor.

Gillian answered in a whisper. "Hi Sam, it's Gillian. Connor's asleep. He pulled an all-nighter."

I heard a groggy voice ask who was calling as she passed him the phone.

"Sam? Is everything okay?"

"Looks like someone is still burning it at both ends even though you rejected lawyerhood."

"Yeah, yeah. Seriously, what's up? I don't think we've ever talked on the phone before, and if I can be completely frank, I'm much more of a texter."

"I just wanted some . . . guy advice," I said, feeling lame.

I could almost hear him sit up straighter.

"Well, Sam, I've been waiting for this moment. I'm your one honest male friend, and I've been massively underutilized."

"This is your time to shine, then," I mumbled, starting to regret the decision to call.

"I heard that you and Christophe made a night of it. Very proud of you. So are we talking about him, or that waiter Emilie said you went out with?"

I took a breath. "It's about Charlie."

"Officemate Charlie?"

I told him about the drunk confession I'd made in the Catskills and how Charlie randomly brought it up tonight, out of nowhere.

"I just wanted your thoughts on why he would still be thinking about it. The conversation happened over a month ago."

Connor didn't respond for a few seconds, and I held the screen up to see if he was still there.

"Hello?"

"I'm thinking. I guess there's a chance he's hearing you tell him that you haven't had good sex in a really long time, and now wires are getting crossed, and his brain is telling him that *he* needs to be the guy to save you from your dry spell. Totally possible."

"For the record, I said it was a sober sex dry spell."

"Are you into him?"

I scoffed. "No! He's my *officemate*."

"I thought you guys were friends."

"We are. But it's not like that."

"It isn't till it is, love."

I sighed exasperatedly. "It's *not*. And I don't think any wires got crossed. I just wanted your thoughts on why he brought it up again."

"You asked and I answered. Either he's crossed from the friend zone into the attraction zone, or he's just swooping in to save your arse from more drunk sex—either way, my point is that you should figure out how you feel about him before you ask, because it could get pretty awkward if you're not on the same page."

"The same page of what?"

"You're painfully overthinking this. I'm hanging up."

I swiped my Amex as the cab pulled up to Emilie's apartment.

"Okay. I can't say this was helpful, but I'll let you know if I figure it out."

"Just stop putting rules on everything. Charlie's a nice laddie, but all guys fantasize about their lady friends at some point. I know you girls still binge *When Harry Met Sally* like it didn't come out the year you were born."

I got out of the cab as the doorman waved me up. Charlie *was* more than an officemate. He had quickly become one of my closest friends. I knew from the basement sushi dinner gone south just how destabilizing it was to be knocked off our easy camaraderie. I couldn't imagine gambling with the idea of crossing an emotional or physical line.

The doorman waved me up to Emilie's floor. I knocked lightly on the door and waited. No answer. I dug around in my bag for a Post-it. I was mid-note when the elevator door opened and Emilie stumbled out, her left arm draped around the shoulder of a man I intuitively knew was Stephen.

"Almost there," I heard him say as I stood there uncomfortably. There was nothing good about this situation.

"Hey, Em," I said.

"Oh, fuck," she slurred, stopping short when she saw me.

I looked at Stephen. "What happened?"

He sighed heavily. "She'll be okay, but she's very intoxicated. I don't think she should be alone." He ran his hand through thick, wavy hair. "Can you stay with her tonight?"

I nodded. "Yes, of course."

He looked pained. "I just don't think I should be the one . . . given I'm the *one* . . ."

"I get it."

She stared down at the hallway carpet, swaying back and forth. I hated that he was seeing her like this.

"She told me she took a Valium, so she should fall right to sleep. I just wanted to make sure she got home safely."

"Thanks, I can take it from here."

I could tell that he was trying to make the best of a miserable situation, but I also knew how bad this was for her, on so many levels.

"The keys should be in her bag," I said.

"I've got one." He looked embarrassed. "I should leave it with you."

We helped her onto the bed. Neither of us said anything. I was struck by how normal he looked, like a younger version of Ed Harris with corporate clothes and lots of hair.

"You must be Sam."

I nodded. "And you're Stephen."

"Thanks for staying with her."

He nervously cracked the knuckle of his right index finger. "I'd appreciate your discretion on this. Our world is very small."

Emilie was passed out with her head on the pillow and her feet still on the floor.

"I'd ask the same of you, I guess. For her."

"Of course. She's a brilliant mind. It would be a shame if she left the firm."

I winced, thankful she wasn't awake to hear that.

"I should go." He held up the key. "I'll leave this next to the door."

"Thanks. I'll make sure she gets it."

I didn't even know about Stephen two weeks ago, but somehow he had a key.

I watched him leave and waited until I heard the door close behind him.

"Jesus," I muttered.

I carefully took off her boots and covered her with a blanket. I poured a glass of water and left Advil on the nightstand, then took an extra pillow and made a small makeshift bed on the floor next to her.

I went to the kitchen and opened my laptop to answer an email from George Brenner, then went back to check on Emilie. I stripped down to my bra and panties and pulled the couch throw over me. I lay there staring at the ceiling, wondering if she'd remember anything in the morning.

My phone lit the room with a text from Charlie.

Emilie OK?

I sent back a thumbs-up.

She will be. See ya in the morning.

Chapter Thirty

I woke up to the sound of Emilie throwing up in the bathroom. I folded the blanket and put the pillow back on her bed and braced myself.

Her eyes were barely open when she walked back in.

"Morning," I said cautiously.

She stopped short, holding her stomach. "Hi . . . When did you come over? And how did you get in?"

"Stephen had a key."

She looked confused. Her eye landed on my bandaged wrist.

"What's on your wrist?"

"It's a long story. But it's just a bad sprain."

"Aren't you a leftie?"

"Yeah, not ideal."

She sighed and held a pillow over her face.

"You should go see Jane," she muffled.

"Who?"

"My acupuncturist."

"I didn't know you did acupuncture."

"You didn't know about Stephen either."

"No, but I get why you didn't tell me."

"Do you?"

I still couldn't see her face.

"I mean, I think I do . . . You didn't want anyone to know. I get that."

"Connor knew."

"How come Connor and not me?"

She sighed. "Look, Sam. I love you, but you haven't really been top notch in the friend department. And like, I know that we met at a really tough time in your life. And I accepted that we were in law school, and you were getting divorced and all that . . . but I sort of hoped that would change when we got to New York."

"Are you saying I'm a bad friend?" My back hurt from sleeping on the floor all night.

"I guess it sometimes feels like we have a one-sided friendship. There have been so many times when I wanted to tell you what was going on in my life, but somehow we were always dealing with *your* crises, not mine."

"Why haven't you said anything until now?"

"Fuck, my head hurts." She propped herself up on her elbow. "As much as I think of myself as a straight shooter, it's hard to tell someone you care about that they're self-absorbed."

I flinched. "Ouch."

"See? This isn't a fun conversation. But I'm glad I'm still drunk for it."

I stared down at the bandage and pulled at a loose thread.

"How can I change if I don't know what I'm doing wrong?"

"Sam. I know you're a good person, just trying to find your way . . . but so are the rest of us. It's not like your being divorced in your twenties is worse than someone else's problems; it's just different. But sometimes it feels like you don't really get that."

I swallowed hard, processing Emilie's honesty. My face burned.

"Well, this is really embarrassing. It's not the way anyone wants to see themselves. You've gotten me through some pretty dark times. I wish you could say the same about me."

She smiled sadly. "Now's your time to shine, babe."

I went to sit next to her on the bed, wrapping my arm around her bony shoulder. "I'm here now. I've been here since last night."

She planted a kiss on my cheek. "I think a bagel would be a great place to start. And the biggest iced coffee they have."

I shot up. "On it."

I threw on my clothes from last night, then grabbed the key Stephen left by the door and ran to the corner deli on Fifth. I tucked the bag of bagels under my arm and balanced the coffee tray in my right hand, setting everything down on the floor to open Emilie's door.

She stared at my wrist. "Oh, Jesus. You really need to spill how that happened," she said dryly.

"Nope. Today's about you."

"Honestly, right now I'm just so sick of myself. I regret telling you to stop being so self-absorbed. Wait until tomorrow to fix yourself."

"I can work from here this morning. Keep you company."

"Have you been typing with one hand?"

"Yes. It sucks balls."

She grabbed her phone and texted me the contact for Jane Acupuncture Gramercy.

"See if she can fit you in today. She's an actual miracle worker. You'll feel better after one session. I go to her for everything. Like, even if I'm just super sore after Pilates."

"I always saw you more as a pill person. I figured you'd be pushing an old Vicodin stash on me."

She looked confused. "Shit—did I take a Valium last night?"

"You told Stephen you did."

"Ugh. I do not want to know."

I gave her a sympathetic pat. "This too shall pass."

She huffed. "If I'm not sacked first."

I dialed Jane Acupuncture Gramercy. Her first opening wasn't until Saturday morning.

"Bummer," Emilie said when I hung up.

"I've been living with it since early Saturday. I can hang on a few more days."

"What the *fuck* were you doing? I demand to know."

I caved and told her the whole story.

"Oh my god. Are you freakishly strong? I never would have guessed," she said between fits of laughter.

"Just a drunk idiot."

"A *brutishly* strong drunk idiot. Do you think you'll see him again?"

I shook my head. "I really don't. It was like, a time and a place. A Friday night in the city. If he called me up and wanted to do something off the wall, I might say yes. Nothing beyond that."

She looked at me quizzically. "Well, there you are. Our girl is growing up."

I felt another twinge of guilt for having let her down.

"I swear I'm going to get my shit together."

She squeezed my right hand. "I know you will. No one thinks you're intentionally a narcissist."

"Keep piling it on. It's good penance."

"Next favor."

"Anything."

"Will you come to my firm holiday party with me? I really can't bear the thought of being there dateless in front of Stephen . . . and it would be way more fun if we could sit and judge everyone."

"I wouldn't miss it. I'll be your proud plus-one."

She sniffled quietly into a tissue. "Do you think it will hurt less by then?"

"I don't know," I said honestly.

"He's such a prat."

I nodded. "For what it's worth, he made sure you got home safely and then asked me to stay with you."

She bit her lower lip. "I guess that makes him a little less bad."

"Maybe just a little bit."

Chapter Thirty-One

The acupuncturist was a block down from Gramercy Park. The doorman waved me up a small set of stairs toward a sign that said **Dr. Jane Chiang and Dr. Dennis Wu, Acupuncture & Chinese Medicine.**

I opened the door to a dimly lit waiting room with a wall fountain and a faded Van Gogh poster hanging over a dark green couch. I was ten minutes early. I sat quietly next to a side table covered in pamphlets titled *Acupuncture for Fertility* and *Using Herbs to Conceive.*

I scrolled Instagram to distract myself when a petite blond in a beige peacoat and Nike running shoes flung open the door and sat down across from me, pulsating with an energy I didn't recognize.

A minute later, a man in a black linen tunic and scrub pants appeared, smiling warmly in her direction. "Elizabeth, come on back."

She bounced out of the chair, all but knocking him sideways with an aggressive hug.

"Dr. *Wu.* Oh *my god.* Dr. Wu." She held up a picture on her phone with shaky hands. "It worked. *Two* positive tests." She looked like she was going to cry. "You got me pregnant!"

I watched the scene unfold like a Bravo reality show about conception. He reached for a box of Kleenex next to the couch. She caught my eye and gave a knowing smile before they disappeared.

I stared at the wall fountain, transfixed by the flowing water, feeling numb. Fertility wasn't something I had ever thought about in more than an abstract way. I wondered how old Elizabeth was.

Dr. Jane appeared a minute later, rescuing me from my mental spiral on whether fertility was something I'd ever need to think about, or how it was even connected to acupuncture. We spent fifteen minutes on my health history: no smoking, no drugs, social drinker, sometimes more. I gave her the PG version of how I'd sprained my wrist. She unwrapped the bandage and gingerly felt around the ligaments. She did something with an electric pen, explaining she was measuring my energy channels. Then she handed me a sheet and told me to undress.

When she came back, she deftly pricked me with needles everywhere except my wrist, dimmed the lights, put on calming music, and said she'd be back in half an hour.

My foot twitched, and I felt a sharp pain in my ankle. I willed myself to lie still.

As I closed my eyes, the conversation Ben and I had in Lake Anna came back to me. I fidgeted uncomfortably. Four years later, I was divorced and getting acupuncture for an injury that happened during a drunk hookup. Weren't things like that supposed to happen *before* marriage and conversations about children?

The feeling of having massively regressed hit me like a brick.

I don't know if it was Elizabeth's unbridled emotion or my lacking energy channels, but I lay there immobilized as tears started streaming down both sides of my face, hitting my ears, pooling onto the table. Then I was laughing but still crying. By the time Dr. Jane knocked lightly, some of the needles had fallen out.

She moved methodically around the table without making eye contact, carefully removing the rest. When she took out the last needle, she patted my forearm. "Most new patients become emotional during their first session. Finish getting dressed and we'll conclude the appointment."

I sat up weakly and blew my nose, catching my swollen reflection in a small side mirror next to a window AC unit. My stomach hurt from laughing. I flexed my wrist. It felt slightly better.

Dr. Jane came back and motioned for me to sit in the chair opposite her. She typed a few notes as I reached for another tissue. She swiveled the iPad toward me, showing a chart of my meridians.

"There's an imbalance in your liver qi. For women, it's one of the most important things to pay attention to. Responsible for the smooth flow of energy and emotions." She swiveled the iPad back toward her. "Do you often feel irritable or stressed?"

"I have a stressful job."

"Most people in New York have stressful jobs. My advice is to improve it with diet and nutrition. I'll send you home with some herbs that will help, but you should also reassess your nutrition and alcohol intake." She grabbed a folder from the shelf next to her. "Here's a handout of things to avoid."

She circled *alcohol.* "Try cutting back for a few weeks. I promise you'll see a difference."

I nodded, feeling embarrassed. "And for my wrist—how often should I come back?"

"Once a week should be fine for now. We can reevaluate in a few weeks."

I had an hour to kill before meeting Emilie and Connor on Twenty-First Street for the guided meditation Emilie wanted to try because she was trying to be "mindful" about her breakup. I felt emotionally hungover from acupuncture.

I arrived at the studio fifteen minutes early. I felt a muscular arm loop around my waist as I signed in.

"Early bird," Connor sang in my ear. I squeezed his forearm, relieved to see a familiar face.

"How's the patient?" he asked.

"Acupuncture isn't for the faint of heart."

"Dope."

"You should try it sometime. It really opens you up." I tapped my temple. "Here."

"The floodgates are already open."

I hung my coat and unzipped my hoodie.

"Do people wear workout clothes for this?" I asked.

He shrugged. "It's just a mind workout, love."

I staked out a cushion directly behind Emilie. A loud *gong* signaled the start, and the instructor's voice filled the dome-shaped room.

I tried my best to emulate cleansing breaths, but every time I closed my eyes, my mind was a turbulent montage of fragmented memories. Our favorite neighborhood restaurant in DC. Telling Ben I wanted a divorce. Moving out of our house. Leo telling me he was leaving his wife. Charlie accusing me of being morally adrift. Emilie calling our friendship one sided.

I fidgeted with a button on the cushion. My eyes kept opening no matter how tightly I shut them. Everyone looked like they'd found momentary inner peace. Even Connor was completely still.

"Wasn't that fantastic?" Emilie asked as we walked outside.

"Mind numbing, in the most zen way," Connor said.

There was only one right answer. "Great call, Em."

She smiled proudly. "So we can make this a Saturday thing?"

"Like, every Saturday?" Connor sounded panicked.

She linked her arm with mine. "How was Dr. Jane?"

"Good. I can already bend it a little more than I could this morning."

"Lovely. Shall we brunch?"

~

Brunch turned into Connor dragging us to a Murray Hill pub to watch Chelsea versus Manchester United. Emilie immediately ditched us to catch up on reality TV. Gillian arrived ten minutes later, dressed in head-to-toe Lululemon and looking just as out of place as I felt.

I was nursing a watered-down iced tea when Charlie texted a picture of his desk.

Hope you're somewhere more fun than this.

I felt an unfamiliar current at the sight of his name.

I sent a frown emoji.

Not really. Stuck at some pub that plays English soccer games.

He tapped my response with a black heart emoji.

Connor slid into the empty chair next to me. "How's Jim Halpert?"

I put my phone away. "I knew I'd regret asking for your advice."

He grinned. "Why don't you invite him to come watch?"

"Are you trying to tell me I'm no good as a third wheel?"

"Yes."

"Oh my god. *You* invited *me*. I hate soccer."

"But that was before I knew Gillian was going to meet us."

I rolled my eyes. "Well anyway, he's stuck at the office."

Connor nodded knowingly. "Definitely thinking about his next move to get you out of the office and into bed."

I could feel my face turning red. "I'm going to the bathroom. And then I'm going to finish my iced tea, like a responsible person who listens to their acupuncturist, and you lovebirds can cozy up."

It was four o'clock and somehow almost dark. I paid for the tea and hugged them goodbye.

I was on the subway platform downtown when he texted that he was done working and needed fresh air.

Quick walk in CP?

I really wanted to take a walk in Central Park with Charlie.

Without thinking about it, I crossed over to the uptown line and got off at Fifty-Ninth Street/Columbus Circle.

Ten minutes later, I exited the subway and immediately spotted him, his left shoulder weighed down by a heavy laptop bag. "Figured you might need some air, too, after that dank bar," he said.

"You're in slacks," I observed.

"Don't know if you've noticed, but there's nothing relaxed about being a lawyer. Not even on Saturdays."

"It's brighter than I thought it would be at night," I said, self-conscious of my robotic commentary. Maybe our banter only extended to the office and basement sushi bars. "I've just never walked through the park after dark," I added.

"Isn't it cool how the building lights shine through the trees? I always walked to class through the park after work. It was the best way to switch headspace."

"I always forget you went to night school. So impressive."

We stopped in front of a bench. "Ever notice that all the park benches are inscribed?" He pointed to an inscription.

I peered closer. **WE WOULD MAKE THE SAME MISTAKE ALL OVER AGAIN!—VIC & NANCY SCHILLER. STILL BEST FRIENDS.**

"What do you think the mistake was?" he asked.

"Having kids?"

He laughed. "So I take it you're on the fence." He looked at my wrist. "How's it feeling?"

I flexed it gently. "Getting better. I went to acupuncture this morning. I think it actually helped."

"I hear it's super calming."

I laughed. "That wasn't really my experience, but I wouldn't trust my review."

"Are you one of those people who thinks Eastern medicine is a hoax?"

"No. It was just . . . weird. But in a way that was totally specific to me."

He chuckled. "Can you be a little more specific for *me*?"

We sat down. I wrinkled my nose, weighing if Charlie would be empathetic to a retelling of my erratic emotional spiral, then decided to try. He was an active listener in a way that made me want to keep talking.

"Afterward I had to pull myself together and pretend to meditate in a room full of people."

"Oof. Emilie must really hate you."

"That's what I was thinking."

I shifted carefully on Vic and Nancy's bench. "I haven't thought about kids for a while. I don't know how to explain it. It just felt . . . jarring. I *was* on that path, and now I've never been further from it."

He nodded thoughtfully. "I think I want a family. My parents had their issues, but I can't remember ever seeing them fight. Not once."

"You're joking."

"Nope."

"I don't even think that's healthy! You missed out on a formative life experience."

"Dysfunction looks different on everyone."

"I don't remember a time when my parents weren't fighting," I admitted. "They were from totally different worlds. They never put in the work to understand each other."

"There's probably some healthy medium between your parents and mine."

"Probably Nancy and Vic."

It was starting to snow. I wrapped my coat tighter. "I kind of want to keep going back to acupuncture just for the emotional release. It beats being in my head all the time."

"Is that how you feel? Like you can't get out of your head?"

I nodded and dug my hands into my pockets. "I think this is why you're supposed to be middle-aged with kids when you get divorced. No time to be self-absorbed. You have to focus on not fucking up your kids."

"I don't think kids make someone less self-absorbed when they're going through something like that."

"Maybe not, but it still just feels so heavy. Physically, I'm *here*, doing all the things I dreamed about. But I don't know how to separate myself from it. It's like it stunted me."

Charlie stood up. "For what it's worth—from where I sit, you're not divorced Sam or Sam the lawyer. You're just Sam." He smiled and held out his hand to pull me up. "Today you're Sam with a sprained wrist who had a crazy meltdown at acupuncture."

I wanted so badly to just be Sam.

"Stay out of your head for a little bit. We can check out a few other benches before I send you home."

Chapter Thirty-Two

"Guess what three months of shitty real estate cases just got me," Charlie announced Monday morning as he strolled into the office, proudly waving a small envelope.

"Courtside seats to the Knicks," I guessed without looking up from the billing tracker. I had completely forgotten to track my time the day before and was now trying to reconstruct billable hours from emails.

"Think bigger, DeFiore."

He pulled out two tickets and slid them across the desk.

"Orchestra seats to *The Nutcracker*. This Saturday. And not just any *Nutcracker*—the OG Lincoln Center one."

I raised my eyebrows. "Just so I'm clear: You *are* saying that *The Nutcracker* is cooler than—"

"Yes. That's what I'm saying. I'm from Boston. We live and die for the Celtics. Larry Bird, not Patrick Ewing."

"Oh, right."

He leaned back in his chair, his hands folded behind his head.

"So . . . you free this Saturday?"

I looked down at the ticket. "Why would you waste a completely baller night on me?"

"Friends don't let friends talk about themselves that way."

"I'm serious. Annabelle's not free?"

He gave me a look. "I haven't gone out with Annabelle in almost a month. Not since the date with that girl you set me up with."

"Margaret."

"Not since the date with Margaret."

"So Annabelle's shelf life was forty-eight hours and . . . two dates?"

"Why aren't you jumping on this? Have you even seen *The Nutcracker* before?"

"What about Margaret?"

He shook his head.

I inspected the tickets. "Orchestra seats, wow. This is fancy. I heard women wear gowns."

"I'm sure we can find you something."

"Between now and Saturday? I don't know."

"Come on, Sam. I'm starting to feel like you just don't want to go."

"I'd love to go. But maybe take a beat and think if there's anyone else you'd rather go with besides your *officemate*."

"Nope. And after we're done classing it up, we can meet my sister and her friends at Scallywag's in Midtown for some Guinness and tater tots."

"Your sister's going to be in town this weekend? You don't think she'd want the ticket?"

"They're all coming down to play indoor golf at Five Iron. They do it every few months. They always end up at Scallywag's because it's close to her friend's apartment. They'll probably be blacked out by the time we meet up, but it'll still be a good time."

His persistence felt genuine. I was aware of how easy it was to spend time with Charlie. But I wasn't ready for another relationship, and he wasn't someone I could treat casually.

He tapped his fingers on the desk. "So?"

He looked *so* hopeful and earnest, I almost felt guilty.

"Okay, if you insist. And no, I've never seen it."

He looked pleased. "You'll love it. And in the interest of full disclosure, my ex is going to be at the bar. She's still in my sister's group of friends."

"Which ex?"

"Kristen, my college girlfriend. We broke up right after she started law school."

"Are you guys still in touch?"

He shook his head. "I was pretty beat up about it for a while. We actually haven't talked in years."

"How come you broke up?"

He rubbed his jaw. "She slept with a guy from her 1L section. Like, the first week of law school."

"Ugh. Not cool."

He nodded. "I think she does employment law for a local firm somewhere on Newbury Street." He paused. "Honestly, it was for the best. I couldn't see myself staying in Boston."

"Is she dating anyone now?"

"No idea. I don't ask Perry for updates."

"Perry is your sister?"

He grinned. "You'll like her. She's two years younger than me but way more mature. She got engaged last year."

I held back the unsolicited opinion that being engaged doesn't necessarily equate to maturity.

I texted Caroline asking if she knew the appropriate attire for *The Nutcracker*. She responded immediately to book an appointment with Rent the Runway on Fifteenth Street.

I stopped by on my way home later that evening, hoping they could fit me in. A tall, stylish brunette walked over with an iPad in hand. I told her I needed a last-minute dress for *The Nutcracker* and wasn't sure where to start. She disappeared and came back with four dresses. When I tried on the last dress, we both knew I'd found the one: a deep-red floor-length sleeveless dress with an open back and a high neckline. As I waited for the stylist to process the gown rental, I texted Charlie.

Crisis averted. Found a dress. I'm going to look insane at that pub.

He responded immediately.

They'll all be too drunk to notice. Actually, no. They'll be just drunk enough to think THEY'RE underdressed.

~

"All I can say is *that* is a dress," Charlie said as I climbed gingerly out of the Uber Black I'd ordered for the occasion. I hadn't been this accessorized since my wedding. The gown was slightly too long. I was wearing the tallest heels I had, my three-and-a-quarter-inch black suede pumps I'd gotten on sale at Bloomingdale's in SoHo. I had dug out a pair of vintage clip-ons I'd gotten years ago from an estate sale. I wasn't used to wearing earrings, and I'd only worn the heels once before.

"You have five minutes to show me I'm not the most overdressed person here."

"I already went inside to use the restroom. You're the least dressy in the two- to eight-year-old demographic."

"Humiliating."

I hiked the gown as we approached the steps up to the David H. Koch Theater. Charlie extended his arm.

"Do I look that unsteady?"

He shook his head. "You just look like a woman who is supposed to be escorted up these stairs. Is that sexist?"

I laughed. "Probably. But if I trip and rip this dress, I have to buy it."

"You rented it?"

"It was Caroline's idea."

He reextended his left arm. I took it lightly and pulled the dress up with my other hand.

The orchestra seats were from a real-estate partner whose wife decided she'd rather go to a fashion designer's holiday party.

"My mom took us to *The Nutcracker* at the Boston Ballet every year when we were kids," he whispered as we walked through the lobby.

"You can tell me what happens then. I don't like surprises."

"No way. The suspense is the best part."

We ordered two glasses of champagne, and I sipped it slowly as we watched New York's elite bribing dolled-up children to pose for pictures.

"I don't think I ever realized this, but *The Nutcracker* is actually not the place to be if you don't have kids," Charlie marveled as he handed a third iPhone back to a parent asking for a family photo.

I chuckled. "I still say this would be an incredible date night if you wanted to impress someone."

"So you're *not* impressed."

The bells chimed as the lights flickered.

We found our seats in the third row of the middle orchestra. There wasn't a child in sight, but we were surrounded by much older couples.

"Think you can make it to intermission?" he asked.

I noticed Charlie's eyes were glassy.

"Are you—high?"

He patted his pocket. "Edible. Want one?"

I shook my head. "I can't mix champagne and edibles."

All I'd eaten since lunch was a protein bar. The warmth of the theater was making me feel sleepy. I sighed and relaxed into the chair. A few minutes later, I looked down and felt Charlie's knee pressed against mine.

I didn't move. We were used to spending hours a day sitting a few feet apart in our office, but we'd never sat *this* close. I looked at him from the corner of my eye to see if he noticed. I wasn't sure if it would be more awkward to move away or just pretend like I wasn't paralyzed by the sensation.

The stage moved in and out of focus. I studied his left hand resting on top of his knee, suddenly feeling the urge to move my right hand closer to his.

I replayed Connor's self-satisfied words about *When Harry Met Sally*.

I was tipsy and he was high. It felt like the room was getting hotter.

My knee burned.

I sat completely still and reminded myself our friendship was more important than whatever tricks my body was playing on me. As soon as the curtain went down for intermission, I jumped up.

He stood up and shot me an amused look. "You kicking off an early standing ovation?"

I tried to think of something clever to say, but I was shaky. I really wished I had eaten something.

I turned toward the aisle before he could see how flushed my face was and excused myself to the ladies' room.

The hallway leading to the restroom was lined with mirrors. I kept checking my reflection to see if I looked as manic as I felt, but all I saw was a dolled-up version of myself in a long red dress. Had I just hallucinated that entire first act? I wondered if the last forty-five minutes had been anywhere close to the same experience for him.

I washed my hands and splashed cold water on my face. I climbed the stairs up to the lobby, almost tripping twice, wondering if I should make up an excuse to leave. If I made it through the next act, my pragmatic approach to our friendship was going to be crushed.

He was waiting by the door to our section. He handed me a granola bar. "Snagged this for you," he said with a huge grin.

I was sure I'd imagined everything.

"Shall we? The second half is the best part," he said with so much conviction, it made me laugh.

It seemed like he was intentionally angled away from me for the rest of the ballet. Even without the physical distraction, I could barely pay attention. My body was there, but my mind was a million miles away, trying to regain the pragmatism about our relationship that had been decimated by his physical proximity.

I tucked my clutch and the program under my right arm and mimicked a sincere ovation.

"Want to grab a slice of pizza before we meet up with Perry and her friends?" he whispered.

I nodded. I needed food and fresh air.

We walked a block south of Lincoln Center and hailed a cab going down Broadway. I watched him turn on his iPhone and realized he'd turned it off during the performance, rather than just switch to silent like everyone else. I had no idea why, but something about that made me smile.

Chapter Thirty-Three

We walked into Scallywag's half an hour later.

"I don't think that edible knew it was going from Lincoln Center to a pub," Charlie said as he huffed air onto his glasses to clean them.

"This dress definitely had no idea," I said, scanning for an opening at the bar. I needed a mixed drink badly.

"If I'd known that dress was a rental, I might not have suggested we end the night at a place called Scallywag's."

I laughed. "It just means I won't be dancing on the bar, which isn't a bad thing."

I pulled a miniature hand sanitizer from my clutch.

"How does that even fit in there?" he asked, holding out his hand for some.

"It fits *one* key, *one* credit card, and this hand sanitizer."

"The essentials."

I'd never felt more overdressed in my life. We walked past a line of confused stares toward the back of the bar, where Perry and her friends were spread out over three pub tables backlit by hanging TVs playing the Celtics game.

"Charlie!" a brunette shouted, waving us over. Perry was almost as tall as Charlie, with tanned skin, long brown hair, and a warm smile.

Perry hugged Charlie tightly and ruffled the back of his head. "I won't tell Mum you still haven't found a barber in New York," she teased as I noticed she had an even stronger Boston accent than Charlie.

"This is Sam. She works with me at the firm, but that's where any similarity between us ends. I drew the short end of the stick, and she's killing it."

I held out my hand as Perry leaned in. "I'm a hugger," she said cheerfully.

She stood back and looked at both of us. "I totally zoned out when you told me what you guys were doing earlier, but I've never felt more like a slouch in my life. You two clean up nicely!"

"We were at the ballet," Charlie reminded her.

"Oh boy. I keep telling you, women don't actually want you to try so hard."

I felt myself blush. I realized I had no idea what he'd told her about us.

"I guess that's why I'll be a bachelor for life," he said agreeably.

Perry waved a bartender over.

"What can I get you guys? I have a tab open."

Charlie ordered Guinness on draft, and I went with a vodka soda with extra ice.

Perry made the rounds introducing us.

"We always end up here because it's right by Jen's apartment," Perry explained.

"Do you think you guys will class up this weekend when you're in your thirties? Maybe splurge for an Airbnb?" Charlie asked.

"*No*," she moaned, looking past us. All I could see was an oversized tray of shots.

"Okay seriously, guys, who ordered these?"

She looked at us sheepishly. "Guess we're doing tequila shots."

I wanted to say I'd done enough tequila shots my last year of law school to last two lifetimes, but I also didn't want to be the girl who shows up at a dive bar in a gown and refuses to take a shot.

Charlie leaned over. "I think we should station ourselves behind this table so your dress has a chance of getting out of here alive. This crowd can get rowdy."

"*Fore!*" someone shouted as I squeezed my eyes shut and quickly chased the shot with a lime.

Charlie pushed his shot glass across the table. "Our older, wiser selves are going to look back on this and wonder why we didn't know these are disgusting."

"I don't need to wait until I'm older and wiser."

I spotted the bartender coming back with our drinks and snatched the vodka soda, taking a long sip to mask the lingering taste of tequila.

"Which one is Kristen?" I whispered.

He looked around. "The short blond. Over there in the pink polo shirt."

"Are you going to say hi?"

"If she comes to our neck of the woods."

Perry ordered a platter of tater tots.

"I guess I'll be doing a double at SoulCycle tomorrow," I lamented.

"Just take the day off. Sunday's a day of rest."

"Not after pizza, vodka, and tater tots."

He shrugged and took a sip of Guinness. "You really do look stunning in that dress."

I tried tilting my face down so he couldn't see me blush.

He laughed. "You're sort of facing the wall now."

I cringed. "I'm going to find the restroom. What are the chances it's not all the way across the bar?"

He tapped Perry's shoulder. "Do you know where the bathrooms are?"

She pointed at a sign hanging on the opposite side of the bar.

Charlie nodded defeatedly. "I'll walk you."

I wanted to walk over solo to give my face time to go back to its normal color, but he was already standing up.

Halfway across the bar, I heard Charlie mutter something under his breath and saw a blond heading toward us on her way back from the restroom.

"Was hoping you'd come say hi," she said as she went in for a hug.

He suddenly looked like a tall, awkward teenage boy, uncomfortable in his own skin.

"We've just been camped out in the corner trying not to ruin our Sunday best," he said, his voice sounding tighter than I'd heard it before.

She looked at me and held out her hand. "I'm Kristen."

I responded with a short handshake and my best attempt at a polite smile.

"Sorry—this is Samantha," he added.

I made a dramatic gesture toward the bathroom. "I think I can make it the rest of the way. I'll let you guys catch up."

I breathed a sigh of relief when I realized it was a fairly clean single bathroom. I locked the door behind me and leaned against the wall. My face was still flushed.

"Damn tequila," I muttered.

Stop overthinking things.

Fucking Connor.

I wondered if Kristen thought I was Charlie's girlfriend, then wondered if that's what he *wanted* her to think.

Did I want her to think I was his girlfriend?

I jumped at the sound of a light knock on the door.

"One minute," I squeaked.

I swung open the bathroom door to see Perry waiting.

"I think he's welded to the floor over there. He's been miserable since you went to the bathroom."

I laughed. "Why?" I asked, trying to sound breezy. I looked over to see Charlie in the same spot I left him.

"Did he tell you that's his ex?"

"Oh, yeah. I just figured I should give them a beat to catch up."

Perry shook her head emphatically. "Go save him. I'm sure he'd much rather be talking to you."

She winked and disappeared into the ladies' room.

I was a pawn in the chess game of Charlie-sees-his-ex-for-the-first-time-in-forever. But he also looked genuinely happy to see me coming back.

"Hey, you," he said with a relieved smile that reached all the way to his eyes. "Was starting to worry the dress got caught in a vent or something."

"Okay, enough dress jokes."

He pretended to inspect the front of my dress. "Phew."

Perry caught my eye as she walked back toward the group and winked again.

"So, another drink? I still taste tequila," Charlie said, making a face.

"Me too. I'll get this round," I said quickly.

"Coming with you."

"I really didn't want to interrupt your catch-up," I said to him as I handed the bartender my card.

"Actually, *she* interrupted me walking you to the bathroom," he corrected me.

I gave him a sympathetic look. "Seeing an ex for the first time is awkward for anyone."

"Maybe, but I'm having a great time standing in that corner over there, dressed like freaks."

I folded the receipt and tucked it into the clutch.

"Back we go then."

The Celtics scored in overtime, which led to another round of tequila shots.

"Next weekend's my birthday, so I convinced everyone to go karaoke-ing in Koreatown. You guys better come with us," Perry insisted as she stood in between us with one arm draped over each of our shoulders. I felt four feet tall next to her.

Charlie pointed to his right. "Koreatown is right there. Should we do a karaoke nightcap?"

I hesitated, and he put his hand on my shoulder. "Charity karaoke nightcap. It's been kind of fun watching Kristen stare at us every time she thinks I'm not looking. What do you say?"

I looked over at Kristen looking in our direction. "I guess I never say no to a nightcap. Not even the karaoke kind."

~

The karaoke bar was on the top floor of an office building with only one elevator working. Charlie and I were the last two to go up. The smell of his aftershave was making me feel lightheaded.

I looked over and caught his eye. "What a fun faux date," I said. After two cocktails and a tequila shot, I was finally out of my head and having fun. It felt like we were dressing up and role-playing.

He laughed and repeated, "Fun faux. Faux fun?"

Perry had booked a dimly lit room with a small stage and a fully stocked bar with two bartenders.

Charlie handed me a five-dollar bill. "Can you grab me a whiskey soda? I never made it to the bathroom at Scallywag's."

My eyes were having trouble adjusting to the dark. I walked cautiously to the bar and ordered a whiskey soda and a vodka soda with a splash of cranberry. I stuffed his cash in the tip jar and grabbed both drinks, then nearly collided with Kristen.

"Woops, it's so dark in here!" she said, raising her hands apologetically.

"Hey again," I said, trying to sound friendly.

"Sam, right?"

I nodded.

"So, how do you know Charlie?"

Without Charlie, I wasn't sure how much I was supposed to commit to the bit, but I wanted to follow through.

"We're officemates, actually," I mumbled.

She raised an eyebrow. "Officemates, that's cute."

"I put my song in the queue," I heard Charlie announce as he rejoined the group.

I handed him the whiskey soda. "I'm going out on a limb here, but having been hostage to your Spotify playlists for the last few months—"

"His go-to was 'Sweet Thing' by Van Morrison when we were in college," Kristen interrupted.

He shook his head and looked at me. "Nope. Sam?"

"Dylan?"

"Which one?"

"'Mr. Tambourine Man'?"

"Nailed it."

Kristen gave a superficial smile. "Lawyers don't have officemates in Boston."

"Makes it more fun," Charlie said defiantly.

I was feeling the shots and the need to kick off my heels.

"I think I'll grab a seat over there." I pointed to the leather bench against the side wall.

"I'm up next, but I'll join you after," he said.

Perry was finishing a dedicated rendition of "I'm the Only One" by Melissa Etheridge. Her voice was surprisingly good. I sank into the bench and squinted to see if Charlie and Kristen were still standing where I left them, but I only saw Kristen. I followed her eyes as she watched Charlie try holding the mic in one hand and his drink in the other.

"One sec, guys," he said into the mic, then jogged over to where I was sitting.

"Can you hold this for me?"

I caught Kristen's eye as he walked back toward the small stage. I wondered if she had wanted this to be her night to reconnect with Charlie.

"Hey! Mr. Tambourine Man, play a song for me . . ."

I felt tiny goose bumps form on my arms. Charlie could sing, too, but in a different way from Perry. It was like watching someone who'd spent years perfecting an impression of one of America's greatest folk voices. He knew every note by heart and went for each one.

When he finished, I jumped up for a standing ovation.

"That was like something straight out of *America's Got Talent*," Perry gushed.

"Jeez, Per, I always wondered if you hated me, but now I know," he said, sitting down to catch his breath.

"Kristen ordered a round of birthday cake shots. Last ones, I swear."

I knew one more shot would take me straight to blacking out in a cab.

Charlie caught the look on my face. "No more shots for us. But maybe we'll do a birthday duet just for you."

He looked at me and raised his eyebrows.

"Only if I get to choose the song!" Perry demanded.

Kristen's shots came out as Bonnie Raitt came on. We both burst out laughing. Charlie coaxed me, barefoot, onto the stage. We were at that part of the night where neither of us had enough self-awareness to wonder if we looked stupid. We took turns belting the chorus while Charlie played air guitar.

The song finished, and Charlie high-fived me. My face hurt from smiling.

Perry's last song came on, and she squealed all the way to the stage.

We both collapsed onto the bench and leaned against the wall.

"That was fun," he said between sips of water.

I nodded, feeling like my face didn't know how to do anything but smile. He looked over at me and laughed.

"I don't think I've ever seen you this smiley."

"Maybe you've just never seen me after this many drinks."

"You were pretty toasted that night in the Catskills."

"We didn't have shots."

"Think you'd beat me in Cards Against Humanity right now?"

"For sure."

I stared ahead at Perry singing "Don't Stop Me Now" by Queen.

"She's really good," I gushed.

"She thinks I have a crush on you. She texted me this a few minutes ago."

He took his phone out of his pocket and handed it to me.

Sam is awesome. I can feel ST a mile away 😉

I turned my head to the side. "I'm scared to ask," I said, handing him the phone back.

"Sexual tension."

"Is there?" I asked, feeling like the room was spinning but in a pleasant way.

"Is there what?"

I nodded toward his phone.

He chuckled. "I can only speak for myself here."

"And?"

"Sure."

"Just tonight?"

"I think you can answer that one."

It was difficult to process so many thoughts at once. It was as if by playing the role of his date, my brain had forgotten the danger of crossing a line with Charlie.

"Probably," I said quietly.

Neither of us said anything. I could feel heat coming from my bare shoulder next to his.

"I'm really glad you came with me tonight," he finally said.

I took a deep breath. "So what now?"

"Another duet?"

"Don't tempt me. That was just a warm-up."

"It was nice seeing you, Char," I heard Kristen say as she waved and walked toward the door.

"You too," Charlie said halfheartedly after her.

It was obvious that in Kristen's world, I was going home with Charlie. I felt a faint sense of pride thinking that was what Charlie wanted her to think.

I turned to face him directly. "What happens Monday morning?"

He studied my face and pushed a strand of hair behind my ear. The familiarity of it made me shiver, and I could tell he noticed.

"I guess I'll treat you to Joe's. It's probably my turn."

I never imagined Charlie being close enough to feel his breath on my face. I didn't want to move away.

"But don't you think . . ."

I didn't know how to finish the sentence.

"Want to get some fresh air? I keep thinking someone's going to put on NSYNC or some other garbage song that's going to turn you into a pumpkin."

Charlie signaled to Perry that we were leaving. She came over and hugged me tightly.

"I hope we see much more of you," she said affectionately.

I fiddled with the buttons on my coat as we waited for the elevator to reach the twelfth floor.

For what felt like the tenth time that night, I was acutely aware of my body. My heart was racing. I could hear both of us breathing. I felt shy and confident and hot and cold.

The doors opened, and we moved wordlessly into the elevator, each of us standing with our back pressed against the wall behind us. I was afraid of what would happen if any inch of me shifted forward. I could feel him looking at me as the elevator started to descend.

"Sam . . ."

Whatever anchor was holding me dissolved, and I suddenly felt his hands on my face, my hair, my shoulders. I bit my lip and searched his eyes for a signal. I felt his hands move to my lower back and press me against him. His mouth grazed mine, and I pulled him toward me, feeling the weight of his body against me. I closed my eyes and let myself kiss him, softly at first and then with an intensity I didn't recognize.

The elevator opened. Neither of us moved.

"You're shaking," he whispered.

"I don't want to stop kissing you."

"Then don't."

He hit a random floor and cupped my face in his hands as he kissed me even more deeply than the first time. I could feel my heart pounding against his chest as the doors closed and he pressed me gently against the elevator wall.

"I want you," he whispered, taking his lips off mine and brushing them softly against my neck.

My whole body was on fire.

He hit the stop button and stood back to look at me.

"I want you too," I said huskily, not recognizing the sound of my voice.

He bent down and kissed me again gently, then hungrily as his hands firmly traced my shoulders, my arms, my back, my hips. I watched him kneel down, his hands running over the sides of my legs down to my ankles, gently taking the hem of my dress and slowly pushing it up past my knees. He kissed the outside of each knee, and I shivered.

He looked up at me as he carefully pushed the dress farther up toward my thighs, then my hips. I met his gaze as he deftly held the dress up over my thighs with one hand and moved my thong to the side with the other. I opened my legs slightly and watched him softly taste me. I gasped as I closed my eyes and tilted my head back against the wall. All thoughts stopped, and my body took over. I came so intensely I almost couldn't hold myself up.

"Take me home," I whispered.

He took me in his arms and held me against him.

"I really, really want to."

He stood back and looked at me. His eyes were bright. I resisted the urge to melt back into him.

"I want to take you home," he echoed, taking a deep breath. "But not like this. I want it to be different with me."

I nodded wordlessly, feeling a swell of affection as I realized what he meant.

He reset the elevator button.

"Can I come over tomorrow?"

"Yes."

He put his arms around my waist and pulled me to him. I was struck by how strong his arms were. I reached up to kiss him one more time and told myself we'd figure the rest out later.

Chapter Thirty-Four

I woke up the next morning with my pillowcase soaked in sweat and the dress crumpled next to my bed.

My hair hurt.

The image of Charlie pulling up my dress flashed in my mind. I buried my face in the wet pillow.

My phone buzzed somewhere under the covers.

You OK this morning?

I scrolled up to read the last few texts we'd sent at 3 a.m.

Counting the minutes until tomorrow (today?), I'd texted from the cab.

You have no idea. Text me tomorrow when you want me to come over and I'll be there.

Night ❤.

My face was on fire rereading our texts in the cold light of Sunday morning.

I bit my lip and tried to compose a response neutral enough to see where Charlie's head was.

I'd finally stopped thinking and let my instincts and desires take over. I had wanted Charlie. I knew it didn't make sense. But I wanted to feel all of it again. Starting with the weight of his knee against mine.

I laid in bed and tried to process the fear and uncertainty and desire.

The intercom buzzed, and I jumped.

"One second," I called out to no one, grabbing my robe from the bathroom and groaning at the smudged mascara looking back at me in the mirror.

I pressed the call button. "Yes?"

"Delivery from Ralph's for Ms. Samantha," a familiar accent from the corner deli downstairs floated back to me. Had I placed an order in my sleep? I grabbed a few dollars from my wallet while I waited for him to come up.

I set the bag on the counter and pulled out a bacon, egg, and cheese on a roll, along with greasy, oval-shaped hash browns, a large black coffee, and a note scribbled on the deli's order pad: *called in from Charlie B. for Samantha D.*

I breathed a sigh of relief that it wasn't Charlie showing up unannounced, even if so much of me wanted to see him again.

I took a picture of the food and texted it to him.

Much better now, thanks for asking.

I could see him typing immediately.

Good. Hope you're not too tired today.

I ate two bites of the sandwich and went back to bed.

I woke up an hour later to my phone ringing.

"How was it?" Caroline's voice asked against the sound of New York traffic.

"I'm basically still asleep. Can I call you later?"

"Are you hungover? What'd you guys do after?"

I paused, and she jumped back in. "I'm just at the farmers market picking up a few things. I'll drop this stuff back at my place and come by in fifteen or so. Want to hear all about it."

She hung up before I could say I wasn't ready to see someone who'd already been to the farmers market. I stared at the phone as my fingers went back to Charlie's texts. I shivered rereading them a second time.

I knew Caroline would show up even earlier than she thought, so I made the bed and zombie walked my way to the bathroom cabinet. I reached for the Listerine and makeup remover. I didn't have time to shower, so I threw on yoga pants and a sweatshirt and stuffed my hair under a baseball cap. I poured the coffee into a mug and reheated it in the microwave.

Caroline tapped on the door before she opened it, holding out a small bunch of wildflowers. "Fresh from some farm in New Jersey," she said brightly.

"Thanks," I said, racking my brain to remember if I owned a vase. I didn't.

"Mason jar?" she suggested, reading my mind.

The voice in my head said, *I bet she owns more than one vase.*

I pulled out one of my dad's old tomato-sauce jars from the back of a cabinet and filled it with water.

"Scissors? You should trim them first," she instructed.

I pulled the coffee mug from the microwave. "I'd offer you some, but I'm out of coffee," I said apologetically.

"I'm caffeinated," she chirped.

I sat heavily on the floor.

"Sorry. Standing is more than I can handle right now."

She plopped down, stretching her long legs in front of her. Even for a Sunday morning, Caroline was put together in a rose-pink cashmere sweater, light-wash jeans, and crisp white VEJA slip-on sneakers with no-show socks.

She looked at me humorously. "Are you going to tell me about last night? Or just stare at my outfit?"

"It's a great outfit."

"I do casual well."

I sighed. "I don't do anything well. Except for my career. That's mostly going well."

"So, it wasn't a good night?"

"No, it was an amazing night. It's just not a good morning."

It was true. If I could compartmentalize, the night itself had been perfect.

I told her everything, realizing how good it felt to relive it. I didn't leave out a single detail.

She clicked her tongue. "I *knew* there was something there. Even before I met him. Remember that brunch at Buvette?"

"I had no idea until yesterday."

"That can't be true."

"Maybe I subconsciously started to notice. But we really upped the ante. It was like zero to sixty, and now I don't know how to go back to anything in between."

"Why do you have to? Charlie's fantastic."

"Because he's not the guy to casually hook up with. I'm not ready for a Charlie in my life right now. I didn't blow up my marriage and move to New York just to settle down again."

"Sam, you guys *made out.* With a little extra. Who's talking about settling down?"

I wrung my hands. "I crossed a line."

"Do you know how many people hook up when they're drunk?"

"Yeah, I do. But not with friends that they respect. Charlie means a lot to me, and I'm just carelessly gambling with our friendship."

"Did he say that?"

"No. He's waiting for a text to say come over and make love to me sober. Maybe."

"Then he's complicit in any gambling that's happening here. You have to talk to him."

"I need a bottle of Advil." I rubbed my temples. "What do I do now?"

"Talk to him."

I shook my head impatiently. "We can't possibly start seeing each other. We share an office. That's HR's worst nightmare. And beyond that, I can't just float from one relationship to the next. Not until I know who I am in this version of my life."

"What would Charlie say?"

"I have no idea."

"So be a grown-up and start a conversation. I bet he's having the same freak-out as you are right now."

"He ordered me breakfast. Seems like he's doing fine."

"He also went down on you in an elevator. Everything I'm hearing tells me this guy is a unicorn. You should really think about what you want, because from what I can tell, he's every woman's dream."

I hugged my knees to my chest. "Last night I wanted to be with him. Like, as more than a friend."

"So text him that."

"It's eleven a.m. on a Sunday. The sun is shining. The alcohol is leaving my body. I can't text him that."

Caroline looked at me sympathetically. "You can't keep using alcohol as a crutch. You know how you feel. Maybe last night wouldn't have happened without a few drinks, but it's the morning after. And you still think you want him. Just sit with that."

I tried to imagine having a heart-to-heart with myself.

"Sometimes I feel like I've been on emotional autopilot for so long, I can't even access my own emotions, no matter how hard I try. Alcohol opens me up. I know that's not a healthy thing to admit."

"It's totally healthy to admit. Less healthy not to do anything about it."

She looked at her watch.

"Maybe we should roll the yoga dice before you guys talk. We can still make the 12:45 vinyasa."

~

Three hours later, I got out of the shower to a text from Charlie asking if I wanted to have dinner and talk.

I wrapped my hair in a towel and took a bottle of Pellegrino from the fridge.

The answer to both was yes.

I carried my laptop and phone to my bed and typed a response to Charlie.

We made plans to meet for dinner at Sushi West on Hudson Street, one of the only casual sushi spots in the West Village. I tried distracting myself by tidying up the apartment. The minutes were crawling, and I couldn't stop pacing. I threw on my coat and walked down to Bleecker Street.

The West Village was lit up with wreaths and white lights. I walked toward Pasticceria Rocco, an Italian bakery known for cannolis and sfogliatelle. I stepped in and ordered two of each, watching the teenager behind the counter place them in a white pastry box tied with red string.

I handed him a twenty-dollar bill and carried the pastries back out to Bleecker Street. I turned right to head toward Sushi West, stopping at the corner to check my phone.

"Thought that was you."

I turned around to see Charlie. My stomach did a flip seeing his face for the first time since earlier that morning.

He nodded behind him. "I just got off at West Fourth." He held out a CVS bag. "Your favorite."

I pulled out strawberry Twizzlers. I laughed, realizing we'd both done the same thing to break the ice. I handed him the box.

"For you."

We walked side by side toward Hudson Street. Charlie stopped at the next block and looked at me.

"How are you?"

I wanted to tell him that I'd spent the whole day convincing myself we'd made a mistake, but seeing him and hearing his voice was undoing all of it.

"I'm confused," I admitted.

"Me too," he said quickly.

He looked around. "Man, this is really the place to be this time of year. Should we just keep walking? Are you super hungry?"

I shook my head. "Nope. Walking sounds nice."

We turned right on West Tenth Street. "This is the dream." He marveled at the elegant brownstones with Christmas trees in the windows.

"I really think these three blocks—mine, West Tenth, and Charles Street—are the reason people move here."

"And to find fame and fortune."

He sat down on a brownstone step and motioned for me to join him.

"Think about all the people who spent their lives here," he said.

"Who do you think lived in that one?" I pointed to a brownstone across the street. Perfectly frozen in time.

"Someone who really knew how to play the piano. And in their spare time, wrote great novels and all the sheet music that still gets played. And maybe even a poem or two."

"Man or woman?"

"Both. The most prolifically artistic couple Manhattan ever saw."

I smiled. "The toast of all the dinner parties."

He looked at me seriously. "I don't want to lose our friendship, Sam."

I felt relieved thinking we were on the same page. But I also didn't know if I could keep fighting the idea of Charlie.

I felt my breath catch in my throat. "I keep wishing we'd met after I figured out how to be happy."

"No one really knows what's going to make us happy. We're just making it up as we go and drifting in the direction of people who make us feel good."

I wished my conscious mind could drift in Charlie's direction without overthinking all the reasons why I shouldn't.

"Last night made me happy," I said honestly.

"You've made me happy every day since I met you."

I swallowed hard.

"I don't want to ruin that," I said.

"I don't think you could."

"But the possibility really scares me."

He reached down for my hand.

"Let's keep walking."

We walked back to Bleecker and turned right, passing Magnolia Bakery and continuing toward the small park in Abingdon Square. He motioned to a bench faintly lit by a lamppost a few feet away.

"But we both feel something, right?" he asked.

"Yes."

"But something's holding you back."

"There's nothing holding you back?" I asked.

"Besides the fact that you mean a lot to me, and if this implodes, we still have to sit next to each other every day?"

"Exactly."

"Can I be totally honest?" he asked.

I nodded.

"I'm willing to risk it."

I could hear him breathing quickly.

"And yes, I know all the ways it's a bad idea. What if one of us gets hurt, what if you move to LA and become a big-time Hollywood lawyer and end up dating Chris Pine? What if George Brenner sweeps you off your feet? What if we end up hating each other? I've thought about all of it."

"What about the fact that I'm divorced?"

"What does that have to do with us?"

"I'm not ready for you," I said softly. "I don't trust myself. I don't know how to be the person I want to be when I'm in a relationship. Not yet."

"You don't have to know. We'll figure it out together."

He moved his knee closer to mine. "Maybe I'm being naive, but I can't remember ever feeling this way about anyone. Not even when I was infatuated with Kristen in college. Something about you is different. I love that I can make you laugh. I love how you go after everything you want. I love how self-deprecating you are, even when you're the most impressive girl at the firm."

He paused, considering his words carefully.

"Kissing you for the first time was unreal. I'd be lying if I said I haven't been thinking about it since you drove off in that cab. And not just the way it felt to kiss you. I—I can't get the sound of you out of my head. I keep replaying it over and over."

My heart was racing again. His honesty was intoxicating. Even though I was dead sober, I knew exactly what I wanted in that moment.

"Come home with me."

Chapter Thirty-Five

Charlie took my hand and led us out of the park. He pulled me gently against the window of a closed shop on Bleecker.

He leaned down and kissed my forehead, then my right cheek, then the tip of my nose.

"You're beautiful. I want to tell you that every day."

I closed my eyes and breathed in his natural scent, tilting my head to meet his mouth. It felt like the first kiss all over again. His body overtook mine as he wrapped his arms around me, and I arched my back to press myself to him. I felt him harden against me, and I opened my eyes, overwhelmed and excited all at once.

"Let's go," I whispered, shivering more from adrenaline than the cold.

We walked the block back to my apartment without saying anything. I unlocked the building door with shaky hands.

"I love getting into elevators with you," he said with a wink.

"You can't press the stop button here, or we'll strand the neighbors."

A few moments later, we were standing in the doorway of my studio.

"I'll give you the tour," I said lamely, waving a hand in each direction.

He took off his shoes and put them by the door.

I resisted the urge to pour a glass of wine to take off the edge.

"Can I get you anything?"

"Maybe just a glass of water."

I poured water for both of us. We stood there quietly for a few seconds, then I motioned toward the bed.

"We can sit down over there," I suggested.

He raised an eyebrow, and my face flushed.

"It's just—I don't have a couch," I pointed out helplessly.

"The bed looks big enough for two people."

I set the water on the nightstand and sat at the foot of the bed. Charlie sat next to the pillows and ran his hand over the duvet cover. "Your apartment smells like you," he said softly.

I took a deep breath and covered my face with my hands. "I'm so nervous. I haven't done this in such a long time."

Before I could look up, I felt his arm pulling me close.

"Look at me."

I uncovered my face and gave him a side-glance.

He chuckled. "Goddammit. You're like this cute, small creature that I just want to cuddle, and then there's the other part of you that drives me crazy. I don't know how I didn't let myself come home with you last night."

"Because then we wouldn't have this moment," I said seriously.

"I just don't want you to regret any of this."

"Let's worry about that later," I said, only half jokingly.

He pulled me onto his lap in one strong swoop. I wrapped my arms around his neck and leaned in to kiss him. After a few minutes, he picked me up and placed me on the middle of the bed, putting a pillow beneath my head before he turned to find the switch for the lamp. He turned it off and took off his glasses.

I sat up and pulled his face back toward mine. He kissed me hard, then leaned back slightly to take off his shirt first, then mine. He reached down and kissed the space between my breasts, inhaling deeply as his hands pressed against the small of my back. He gently laid me back toward the pillows and sat back and looked at me. I could only see half of his face in the moonlight.

He reached down and unbuttoned the top of my jeans.

"Is this okay?"

I nodded, watching as he carefully slid my jeans down to my ankles. I kicked them off and reached for the waistband of his jeans, but he placed my hand over my head, then moved my other hand to meet it.

He kissed my collarbone as he unhooked my bra with one hand. I lay still as he slowly covered every inch of me with his mouth, moving my thong aside as he worked his way back up toward me. I closed my eyes in anticipation. I didn't want it to end. I cried out in pleasure and tried to catch my breath.

"I want to feel you inside of me," I whispered. My whole body was on fire.

It was all Charlie needed to fully undress. He crawled toward me and placed his hand under my head. He kissed me and entered me as I came a second time, feeling the waves of my orgasm against him. He moved slowly in and out of me. I closed my eyes again and allowed myself to be swept up in the rhythm of our bodies moving together.

He grabbed my hips firmly and pulled me on top of him in one perfectly choreographed move. I ran my hands along his arms, then reached for the top of the headboard to steady myself as he let me take control. I came again. I leaned down and buried my face in his neck as he pressed me to him and thrust deeper inside me.

"Sam . . ." he whispered softly.

He moved on top of me again, and his breath quickened.

We collapsed and lay there listening to each other breathe, our limbs tangled, our bodies exhausted.

~

I woke up sweating. Maybe a studio was too small for two bodies. I wanted badly to open the window but didn't want to wake him.

I listened to the cadence of his breath, lying there enveloped in the heat of *us*.

I breathed in as deeply and quietly as I could, folding my hands on top of my bare stomach. A shiver ran through me at the memory of his lips and his tongue. I felt a swell of desire for him all over again as my mind replayed images of us together. My mouth felt dry, and I reached for the glass of water on the nightstand. I sipped it slowly, my heart racing and my body pulsing.

I turned on my side, facing away from him. I needed clarity of thought. Every time I closed my eyes, I felt him. My skin tingled.

Charlie stirred behind me. I felt his arm reach over and his hand press against my stomach, pulling me back against him. His hand moved to my breasts, and I could feel him want me again. I pressed myself closer to him and allowed my body to curve into his. Without saying anything, he entered me slowly from behind, his hand running along my thigh, my hip, my waist, then my breasts as he thrust into me over and over, hungrily kissing the back of my neck and my shoulders.

We moved together, his arm wrapped tightly around me and his other hand firmly on my right hip, his breath quickening as we came together.

Charlie fell asleep again as he held me. With every kiss, every touch, every orgasm—I was being pulled in deeper and deeper.

It wasn't just the sex. It was the cocktail of Charlie that was making me spiral.

I lay awake until the sun came up, thinking about everything that had happened. I turned to look at him, resisting the urge to run my fingers along the contour of his face.

I wished I could jump out of my skin and be someone else. Someone who could fall headfirst into this vortex.

He'd been unapologetically honest about his feelings for me. He understood my drive, admired it, didn't want to redirect it. He didn't want me to be someone I wasn't.

"Are you freaking out?"

I jumped. "Morning," I said sheepishly, pulling the sheets tighter.

He moved back toward the window to give me space. "I know every expression you make. I can see your mind working."

"It's almost Christmas," I said pathetically.

"Are you freaking out about Christmas?"

I smiled and shook my head.

"Are you going back to Virginia for the holidays?" he asked.

"We always do the Feast of the Seven Fishes on Christmas Eve with my dad's family in Jersey."

"I've always wondered about those. Sometimes I feel cheated that we were raised Jewish and not Catholic."

Were we still Charlie and Sam?

"Will you go home for Hanukkah?" I asked instead.

"My grandma will kill me if I'm not there to light the candles with her at least once."

I smiled at the image of Charlie lighting the menorah for his grandma.

He turned to grab his phone from the windowsill. "I should probably head home to shower and get dressed."

"What time is it?"

"Almost six."

I groaned. "I really hope I'm wrong, but I have a feeling that this morning is the preview session for the all-attorney retreat next month."

He clicked his tongue as he pulled up the calendar on his phone. "Yup. Ten a.m."

I realized I wasn't even wearing underwear and pulled the covers tighter.

"Did you ever go to a retreat as a paralegal?"

"No, paralegals have their own shindig. Just not in glampy corporate retreat spots like the lawyers. I've been hearing about this ranch in Montana for years."

"Something about one thousand lawyers converging on a ranch in the middle of January seems like a recipe for disaster."

"Lena told me the alcohol budget for the firm-wide retreat tops a million."

"Meaning every lawyer consumes a thousand dollars' worth of alcohol over three days?"

"I don't know how else you survive being stuck in the middle of nowhere with every lawyer at the firm."

He sat up, looked around for his shirt, and spotted it on the floor next to the bed.

I looked away. "I'd get it, but I have on less than you do . . ."

"I'm okay with you seeing me in my boxers," he said, looking amused.

Was *I* okay seeing him in his boxers? On a *Monday*?

I pretended to check emails on my phone as he got dressed. The getting dressed part felt oddly intimate.

He came over and sat next to me on the edge of the bed. I propped myself up on the pillow and tucked the duvet under my arms.

He tousled my hair. "You okay?"

I nodded. "See you at the retreat preview?"

He grinned. "Or in our office first."

He bent down and kissed my left cheekbone. He lingered for an extra second. I touched my hand to his beard.

"I'm okay," I answered.

I watched him put his keys and phone into his jean pockets, then layer on his jacket and scarf.

A few seconds after he left, I sat up and looked at the crumpled sheets next to me.

Charlie's side of the bed.

The bed looked different than it had yesterday.

"Hold the elevator!"

I could hear the elevator doors heave back open.

"I thought that might be you," Caroline's cheerful voice chirped as the elevator closed again.

I covered my face with a pillow and waited for the texts I knew were coming.

I looked out the window just as Charlie crossed Perry Street in yesterday's clothes. The morning light looked different. I felt like another person. Grown up and reckless at the same time.

So????? Caroline texted.

I smiled. Sober sex. What a mind fuck.

Chapter Thirty-Six

"The firm will arrange flights and ground transportation to and from Bozeman. If you have schedule conflicts, please email them to Lawyers Travel by the end of this week. The accommodations and retreat space are all on the same premises. Your room number will be provided when you check in. You'll have the afternoon to acquaint yourself with the grounds, and the retreat will formally kick off with a cocktail hour at six o'clock, followed by a welcome dinner."

I craned my neck to see if Charlie was there yet.

Regret prickled as I shifted in my seat. Why had I chosen the front row?

I scrolled through my emails and opened a message from Andie with the subject line Book Launch.

The book was going to be released in the spring, but the publisher was planning an official prelaunch party for the first week of January. She'd asked the publicist to set aside two tickets for me.

Charlie texted as I was mid book-launch email.

Your hair looks great today.

I stared at my grown-up version of a folded note.

The next text was from Caroline. You owe me every possible detail lady!! p.s. he looked damn cute coming out of your apartment all disheveled 😏

I squirmed again in my seat.

Can you do dinner tonight? I responded to Caroline.

We made plans to meet at Palma, an Italian restaurant on Cornelia Street.

The retreat session wrapped with a promotional video of the ranch just outside of Bozeman, Montana. It looked like a place where trouble found you.

I got up and tried casually walking toward the door while I looked around for Charlie. I didn't see him until I got back to our office, packing a stack of manila folders into his shoulder bag.

"Hi," I said softly, closing the door that we usually left open.

He looked up and smiled. "Hey."

I motioned to the bag brimming with files. "Heading out?"

He nodded. "Last-minute hearing on the REIT injunction I've been working on. Almost missed the big payoff."

"Don't miss the fireworks."

"Never. And I know we were both wondering what the first day was going to be like back in the office, but . . . I'm probably not going to be back for the rest of the day, so . . ." He flashed a guilty smile. "Ran into Caroline in the elevator this morning."

I nodded. "I heard her bombastically yelling for you to hold the doors. Right as she passed *my* door."

"Eh, I probably would've done the same in her shoes."

"We're having dinner tonight, so she'll get all the gossip."

Charlie looked down at his laptop.

"Shit, I gotta go." He grabbed his bag as I stepped away from the door.

He paused, looking at me squarely. He reached down for my hand and squeezed it.

"I'll miss seeing you today."

I stared just a little too long at his hand squeezing mine, then squeezed his back.

"Good luck with the hearing."

~

Caroline was seated at a small table by the window when I arrived, with a bottle of champagne chilling in an ice bucket.

"What's the occasion?" I asked, taking a full minute to unbundle my Canada Goose coat, wool scarf, hat, and mittens.

"You've been deflowered. By someone adorable, no less. And it's basically like I was there for the morning after. Cheers, babe!"

I sat down as she handed me a gold-rimmed flute.

"I'm the furthest thing from being deflowered. I was *married*," I contested, appreciating the warmth of the fire across the room.

Caroline waved her hand. "Didn't you once tell me that you found sex boring?"

"I have, on occasion, found it boring." I took a sip of champagne. "It was *not* last night."

She clinked my glass again. "You better tell me everything."

I didn't spare a detail. It was like a tell-all confession.

"Sam. *This. Is. Huge.* No matter where this is going. You felt a feeling, you acted on it, and you're still intact. *And* you slept with him sober."

"Three times."

"Incredible."

She filled my glass to the top.

"I'm so proud of you."

"I'm terrified."

"Of what?"

"Caroline. Come on. How can this possibly end well?"

She grabbed the menu and gave a dismissive wave. "It's either going to work or it's not."

"Sounds apropos of absolutely everything in my life."

We ordered rigatoni alla vodka, balsamic brussels sprouts, and two glasses of Sangiovese.

"Do you think you guys will spend New Year's together?"

I shrugged. "It's my first New Year's Eve in the city. He's been here for a few years, so he probably doesn't want to be *in* the city for New Year's."

"Ah, yes. The right to have disdain for Manhattan on New Year's Eve must be earned."

"What about you? Are you going back to Iowa?"

She nodded morosely. "Sadly, yes. But not because I want to. I have to be there to console my sister."

"What happened?"

"She's still depressed about losing the city council election last month."

"Oh, I'm so sorry to hear that. Was it close?"

"It was, until someone hacked her emails and found out she donated to Planned Parenthood."

"That was the nail in the coffin?"

"She was running as a Republican."

"Ah."

Caroline chuckled. "The ironic thing is that she didn't actually donate to Planned Parenthood. She signed up for this app that challenges you to competitions with yourself—work out five days a week, drink less than three nights a week, whatever—and for every goal you miss, it donates to a cause you hate."

"Your sister hates Planned Parenthood?"

"I come from a very different world than the one we're living in."

"Clearly. So her emails got hacked, and she lost the election because she didn't make all her workouts?"

"Basically. Her whole voting base turned on her."

"Wow. I hate to sound insensitive, but . . . karma?"

"Something like that."

Chapter Thirty-Seven

I woke up at 3 a.m. from a dream where I relived the entire night with Ben at Union Square Cafe and the morning after, only it was Charlie, not Ben.

I didn't need a Freudian scholar to psychoanalyze what it meant.

I was so unsettled I couldn't fall back asleep. We were never going to go back to the version of Sam and Charlie from last week. Everything had changed, and there was only one possible outcome. *It was either going to work or it wasn't.*

The next morning, Charlie texted he wasn't feeling well and felt it was safer to work from Brooklyn (don't worry, NOT contagious). After the dream and now Charlie's absence, I was starting to spiral.

The second day Charlie stayed home, I got a call from the firm's managing partner, Andre Adepo, telling me I was one of two first-year associates chosen to work on a high-profile matter involving a conservative senator with very public aspirations for a presidential run. Overnight, the scandal was on every news outlet, regardless of political affiliation, and it was throwing the Republican Party into turmoil.

Andre and the senator had gone to Harvard together. Now, decades later, the firm was hired to conduct an internal investigation to prove the story didn't have legs. We would have one month to interview everyone on the senator's staff, then turn around a comprehensive report that would be picked apart by every newspaper and cable news channel in America—and likely determine the fate of his political career.

It took one day to realize I was heading into every first-year associate's nightmare. In the typical hierarchy of most Big Law cases, junior associates report to senior associates, who report directly to partners. There was a glaring hole in my law firm experience, and it was about to be filled by Elinor Baker.

"Stock up on your supplements, ladies, because *this* conference room is home now." She made an exaggerated circling gesture around the conference table. "I know you're barely lawyers, but I assume you're aware of the highly confidential nature of this investigation. Everything stays inside this room, and that includes each one of you unless you're sleeping. You are not to speak to anyone about the work we're doing. Journalists will be camping outside the building. Do not utter a word to them. IT is bringing in screen protectors. Do not ever open your laptop outside this room without one."

Elinor's jet-black hair was pulled into the tightest bun I'd ever seen. Her makeup was flawless in a way that made me think of the permanent eyeliner I'd read about on *The Cut*. She was minimally accessorized with pearl studs, a pearl necklace, and a massive emerald-cut diamond on her left hand. She smelled like Chanel N° 5 and parsley from the green smoothie she drank every morning.

"This may sound unusual, but I can't ever be in a position where I need something from you and find out you've signed off for the evening. So even after you're dismissed from the conference room, I will expect you to let me know before you go to bed."

She sipped the smoothie and glanced at her phone.

"You'll be expected here at eight a.m. sharp every day, and I doubt any of us will be out of here before two a.m., probably later. That includes Saturdays and Sundays."

The other first-year selected to work on the investigation was a kind and introverted associate named Angela. The firm was in the final stages of clearing conflicts, and Elinor expected we would be cleared to formally start the following Monday. "So get in your doctor appointments, waxes, last spin class, *whatever*, over the next few days. Otherwise, your lives are on hold for at least the next month."

It was like stepping into a bad *Ally McBeal* episode.

The only generous thing she said was a begrudging acknowledgment that it was the holiday season, and she'd preapprove one night off ("different nights for everyone, obviously") for each of us to "shop for presents, see your family, whatever." I emailed Elinor to request blocking off the night of Emilie's holiday party and held my breath until she approved it.

Charlie was finally back in the office on Thursday. Since Monday, our texts had mostly consisted of face mask emojis and Seamless tirades, or me paraphrasing the crazy shit Elinor said and explaining how women can be sexist toward each other.

"How in the world did you end up defending that guy? Isn't he notoriously pro-life?" Charlie asked as I tried getting through an inbox full of emails from Elinor.

We were back in our office like nothing ever happened.

"Um, because the top partner in the firm personally *called* me and said he'd heard good things from Eddie and Leo and assumed I was free for a nine a.m. meeting."

Charlie shook his head. "That senator is an embarrassment."

"He's a politician. They're all bad."

"And now, you're like, his defense counsel."

"One of . . . five."

"That's a pretty elite number."

I sighed. "Anyway, you haven't even given me a chance to ask how you're feeling. You disappeared for two days."

"Better. Didn't realize I'd come back to you switching political parties on me though."

I rolled my eyes. "We *work* for this firm. Which means we work for the clients of this firm. What was I supposed to do? Would you have taken the liberal high ground in my shoes?"

"I like to think so."

"Then I guess we're different people." I smirked. "But don't forget, you're working for the same firm as me. Not exactly stumping for Bernie right now."

His face softened. "I missed this."

"Missed what?"

"You. The banter."

"To be fair, you've been MIA since Monday."

"I know. Maybe I was just worried things would change."

I nervously clicked the closest pen within reach. "Things have kind of already changed, don't you think?"

"I know. I'm not *worried*, worried. I'm just . . . aware."

"Okay."

He came around and sat down on the edge of my desk.

"Want to grab a bite with me tonight?"

I nodded, eager to recalibrate. "Let's go to our sushi spot."

~

I woke up to the alarm I'd set for 7 a.m.

I hit the snooze button on my phone, then glanced over at Charlie.

"Ugh, my train," he groaned.

"It's this afternoon," I reminded him.

He had a three o'clock Acela to Boston. Perry was picking him up, and they were meeting his parents for lobster rolls.

These were the kinds of details I knew because I was his friend, his officemate, and now his lover.

He rolled over to face me. "Well, in that case . . ."

We made love for the fourth time since we'd left the sushi bar, making out in the cab all the way back to my apartment.

I made coffee and checked emails while he showered. I had forty-two new emails since 10 p.m., all from Elinor.

"You've got to be kidding me," I muttered as I reached into the fridge for half and half.

"You say something?" Charlie appeared in the bathroom doorway, brushing his teeth with a towel around his waist. I felt myself blush. It was all just so *intimate*.

"They're calling us into the office over the weekend," I groaned.

He grinned. "What's it like to be needed twenty-four seven?"

"We weren't even supposed to clear conflicts until next week. Now we're *interviewing* his chief of staff on Monday morning. Which means I need to read a few *thousand* emails this weekend to be ready in time."

"Christmas is canceled."

I wondered what Christmas in the city would look like if Charlie and I had nowhere to be. Wish fulfillment had worked almost *too* well. I was living every associate's high-profile client dream, and all I wanted was to spend the weekend with Charlie.

"What are your plans for New Year's Eve?" he asked. I felt like he was reading my mind.

"No plans," I admitted. "I'll probably be at the office. Elinor didn't mention anything about having New Year's Eve off."

"Well. *If* you can escape, and I won't hold you to anything—would you want to go to this horrible house party in Brooklyn with me?"

I laughed. "Who says no to that?"

"It'd be a lot more fun if you were there. We could make fun of all the vegan snacks and mocktails."

"Your friends are sober?"

"It's trendy. Just think about it," he said as he disappeared into the bathroom.

All I could really think about was how quickly I could get to the office.

He reappeared behind me and wrapped his arms around my waist. "Go get 'em," he whispered.

He put on his glasses, grabbed his backpack, and tilted my chin up. He grazed my lips before leaning in for a slow kiss. I wished neither of us had anywhere to be.

"Hope we get to do New Year's together," he whispered.

~

An hour and a half later, I was the last person to walk into the conference room. On my way in, Elinor had sent an eight-hundred-page PDF that needed to be reviewed and summarized by the end of the day.

I spent the day tagging emails that were relevant to the senator's chief of staff. At 9 p.m., Charlie sent a picture of the bar from *Good Will Hunting*, with a beer emoji and the caption Perry's local watering hole.

I was unexpectedly relieved that Charlie was out of town. It was easier to commit to the pace of work with Charlie in Boston.

By the end of the weekend, I knew everyone in the senator's inner circle so well I could have written a political soap opera.

The investigation was already a top news story. Andre was booked on five different news shows starting the day after Christmas.

We were going at superhuman speed. Each day, hundreds of new documents and emails came in and needed to be reviewed within twenty-four hours. Anything pertinent needed to be added to the "Fact Chron," a timeline of relevant facts that already topped two hundred pages. If I wasn't taking notes in a witness interview, I was in the conference room, distilling Elinor's notes into a cohesive memo, adding information to the Fact Chron, and surviving on saltines, ginger ale, and black coffee. My stomach was in a perpetual knot.

The firm retreat was scheduled for January 4. I couldn't imagine how any of us could spare the time, but Elinor had said attendance was mandatory, and it was "up to us" to make it work. I daydreamed about sneaking into Charlie's room late at night. In my daydream, the room was more rustic cabin and less corporate hotel in the middle of Montana. Charlie was supposed to be back from Boston on the 30th.

At the rate we were going, it felt like the retreat might be the only way we would be able to spend time together.

It was finally the night of Emilie's holiday party at Rockefeller Center. Only instead of being excited about getting to leave early, I was exhausted by the idea of socializing with strangers. I wished I could just go to bed early.

At three o'clock, I asked Elinor's permission to run downstairs for an espresso. I needed a gallon of caffeine to stay awake and help distract Emilie from Stephen.

"Sam is making an espresso run," Elinor announced two seconds later. "Put in your orders now. I'm feeling a late night, people."

Everyone put in an order.

"You can handle it, right? We can't really afford to send two people downstairs at once," she said dryly.

I spotted a piece of parsley wedged in her front lateral and smiled. "No problem."

I raced down to Joe's.

"Five espressos, and can you please make one a double?"

Charlie and I always joked about keeping a flask of sambuca in a desk drawer for late-afternoon espressos. As I waited for the coffees, I imagined us holed up in our office, watching the holiday lights up Park Avenue in the dark. I missed being next to him.

The barista didn't have tray holders small enough for espresso cups, so I balanced two to a cup holder. I knew I wouldn't get to sleep until well after midnight unless Emilie decided to leave the party early. It felt like everyone had a say in what time I got to go to bed.

My phone buzzed as I stepped onto the escalator. I juggled the espresso tray in one arm and pulled my phone out of my blazer. As I saw Elinor's name, I felt my left leg being pulled behind me and automatically jerked to free myself. I heard a loud ripping sound as the hot espresso splashed across my light blue shirt.

"*Goddammit*," I muttered, wiping my hands on my black pants. I stepped to the side as I got off the escalator and pulled out my phone to call Elinor back.

Elinor picked up on the first ring. "Where are you?"

Her voice was eerily flat.

"I'm on my way upstairs. Is everything okay?"

I heard her take a deep breath. I'd already seen her explode twice that day on some poor soul on the other end of the phone.

"Forget the coffee. Just get back up here. *Now*."

My hands were shaking. I wanted to find the nearest bathroom and try to salvage my shirt, because God only knew the next time I'd make it to the dry cleaner. Instead, I chucked the coffee tray into the nearest bin and sprinted to the elevator.

"Shit," I mumbled as I inspected the three-inch tear up the side of my $400 Theory pants. I caught a glance of myself in the elevator mirror and burst into tears.

"You do not have time for this," I scolded myself out loud, wishing the elevator would break down so I could cry for another twenty minutes. My phone buzzed again. There was no way I could answer until I'd pulled it together.

I got off the elevator and ducked into the restroom to inspect my mascara. My shirt was soaked. I took a deep breath and screened Elinor's third call.

I charged into the conference room looking nothing like I did when I left.

She glanced at my shirt then pointed to her monitor. "Do you know what this is?"

She had highlighted row 2,110 of the Fact Chron. It was an email from the senator's chief of staff to the senator himself, recapping a phone call with a major Republican donor, venting that the local city council members weren't "toeing the line."

"I went through your outline from the chief of staff's interview, and not only *wasn't* this document pulled—it appears the outline didn't even include a question about it."

I blinked hard and looked again at the Fact Chron. *How could I have missed that document?*

"I—"

"I have no idea how far back this puts us, Samantha, but this is an unacceptable lapse. Your entire *job* here is to be a master of these documents. If we publish a report that has holes in it, we're fucked. If someone leaks this email to the press, and our report omits any mention of it because we didn't even ask about it in a fucking *interview*—we lose all credibility. Because of *you*."

My heart was racing. "I understand. I'll fix it."

She refused to look at me. "What you'll do is go through every single document on this chronology. Tonight. And you will compare the documents we already tagged for the interview and make sure there aren't other key documents missing. And then you'll redraft the interview outline, and you will explain to the partner why he needs to spend another day billing time on someone he already interviewed."

I nodded. "I'll get started right now."

"I'm sure your girlfriend will understand."

"I'm sorry?"

"I said, I'm sure your girlfriend will understand why you can't make it to her holiday party tonight."

The idea that Elinor had interpreted my request to take off for a significant other's holiday party made the penalty sting even more. Not to mention Emilie was going to murder me.

Elinor resumed furiously typing, and I stood there for a minute trying to gather my thoughts. I sat down in front of my laptop and silently debated whether it was worth risking a bathroom break so soon. I couldn't text Emilie from the conference room because Elinor had banned cell phones. I chickened out and started typing the most apologetic email I could muster, angling my computer so the screen protector would make it impossible for Elinor to see I was on Gmail.

I tried to explain what happened and apologized for letting her down, for not even being able to call her and explain ("I might get fired if I leave this room again"), re-apologizing for having been such a terrible friend since we got to the city. I reread before I hit send, my face burning hot. I knew exactly how she was going to read this, and I couldn't even blame her.

Elinor dismissed Angela at midnight. Then she sat there, presumably to punish me, until 2:30 a.m. I wondered what her personal life was like. I knew from social media that her husband was an academic researcher at Columbia, and they didn't have kids. I also knew they had a full-time housekeeper Elinor called and dictated tasks to throughout the day.

I waited until I was safely in the Uber to pull out my phone. Emilie hadn't responded to my email, but there was a string of angry 2 a.m. texts to our group chat with Connor, accusing me of making her look even more pathetic than she thought possible. I winced and pushed my head against the headrest.

She texted me a final message separately. Just so you know, I'm looking for jobs back in London.

I watched the dots as she continued typing.

Don't bother responding. I'm done with your chronic narcissism.

Chapter Thirty-Eight

Over the next week, each day was more miserable than the next. We worked sixteen-hour days in total silence. My lower back was in a permanent spasm. I had fantasies about developing sciatica severe enough to go to the hospital.

Because of Elinor's cell phone ban, I could only respond to texts on my way into the office or during a bathroom break. I hated how lame I sounded to the outside world.

Christmas came and went. Angela and I ordered Chinese food and spent the two hours Elinor was gone commiserating about the turn our lives had taken. It was like a shot of dopamine straight to the arm. Charlie texted Merry Christmas with a picture of a lit menorah.

A few days before New Year's Eve, I was in the middle of another three-hour witness interview when I missed a call from Charlie. He followed up with a text saying he wasn't going to be back in the city for New Year's after all; he was staying in Boston for the week and would fly directly to Montana for the retreat. His words felt cryptic and cold. Even if the chances of getting out of the office had been a hundred to one, I still felt crestfallen.

I wanted to hear his voice. I couldn't get a sense of whether he was betting on me not being able to get out of work, or if something else made him second-guess coming back. I couldn't shake the thought he regretted everything.

~

I was still in the conference room when Charlie texted at midnight to wish me Happy New Year.

We'd only texted once since he told me he was staying in Boston until the retreat. He had watched one of Andre's interviews on MSNBC and texted to say he "almost" believed the firm wasn't full of shit.

I tried not to be offended. I'd spent nearly every waking hour working on an investigation that I knew was aboveboard in every possible way. But for the media, it was just a political story, and to hear someone like Charlie all but siding with our opponents was infuriating. I was tired and sensitive, averaging four hours of sleep a night with a disappearing appetite. I wished the firm would decide we couldn't go to the retreat. I just wanted to stay on autopilot so I could finish the job and get my life back.

Elinor let us go at 10 p.m. the night before the retreat to pack. I spent the time schlepping loads of laundry down to the basement.

I worked the whole flight there, anxiously closing my laptop as we bumpily descended into Bozeman's snow-covered airport. Forty-five minutes and two conference calls later, the driver pulled up to a sprawling lodge surrounded by the Gallatin National Forest.

I checked in and wondered if Charlie's room was close to mine.

My phone buzzed as the concierge waved me over. My heart sank when I saw Leo's name instead of Charlie's.

Welcome to the wild west. Which building are you in?

A second text immediately followed.

How about an early, pre-happy hour drink? I'll drop a pin so you can find my outdoor bar. This place is literally a military base.

So much had happened since I'd had dinner with Leo a month earlier. Without thinking, I responded that a drink sounded great.

I worked from my room for the rest of the afternoon. I still hadn't heard anything from Charlie, but like clockwork, Leo dropped a pin at 4:30 p.m. with a message to meet him at five o'clock and to check the shuttle schedule.

The shuttle dropped me off at 4:58. I walked through the lobby to the heated outdoor bar, counting three hot tubs. I scanned the patio, finally spotting him behind a giant heat lamp.

He held up a chilled copper mug. "As I live and breathe. Samantha DeFiore, in the flesh. Welcome to Montana."

He gave a warm hug and a subtle kiss on the cheek. I already knew I was blushing.

"This place is wild," I said. It felt more après-ski and less lawyer retreat.

"The wild part hasn't even started. This is like the firm's version of Vegas."

"Now I'm scared," I said, only half joking.

"Andre tells me you're killing it on the investigation."

I relaxed slightly. "Really? He said that?"

"Another real feather in your first-year cap. Personally, I couldn't be prouder."

He couldn't have looked prouder.

"Try this, it's amazing." He took my hand and wrapped it around his drink. I felt my face flush again. It felt too familiar to take a sip from his drink, but too awkward not to.

I took a micro sip as the back of my throat burned.

"Montana's version of a Moscow mule. There's habanero."

"If it's not going to offend Montana, I might just order a regular Moscow mule," I said, my throat raspy.

"Suit yourself." He turned to the bartender. "Classic Moscow mule for the lady."

He asked me about the investigation as we waited for my drink. I felt my phone buzz in my blazer but didn't want to look rude.

The drink arrived as Leo raised his mug to mine. "To your first firm-wide retreat. I'm honored to kick it off with you."

His eyes locked with mine as we said "Cheers."

I *really* wanted to check my phone.

"Okay, tell me everything. You've gone quiet on me since our dinner." I read a touch of sincerity.

"Well, there really isn't much to tell . . . I've been glued to the office for the last few weeks, but I'm sure you already know that from Andre. We're all in the same boat. It's intense but going well."

"And what about Andie Reese? I heard she pleaded guilty?"

I nodded. "Did Eddie tell you about George Brenner?"

"Only that he's writing the screenplay for the movie. I'm such a fan. That dude is a fucking legend."

"It's incredible. It's the ending she deserves, at least in one way. It makes for great storytelling."

"Have you met him?"

"I've actually been consulting for him here and there," I said cautiously. "Well, before the investigation started."

His eyes widened. "*That* is incredible. I hope you'll remember me when."

I laughed. "It's been a lot of fun. He mostly asks questions I already know the answer to, so it's worked out well for me."

"I hope you know this isn't the typical first-year experience. But I knew there was something different the second I met you."

I looked down and ran my finger along the frosted mug. "I really appreciate that."

He grinned. "Now the pressure's on for me to find some way to steal you back from Eddie and Andre. I can't be sharing you too often."

My phone buzzed again. The altitude and vodka were like rapid waves conspiring against me. I wanted to see if Charlie had reached out, but it felt like I was under a microscope.

He pointed to the drinks. "So this is where the night starts off. I hope you know where it ends."

I looked at him nervously and shook my head. "Where?"

I followed his eyes in the direction of a hot tub.

"Every year, a group of us close down the night in *that* hot tub. You're part of that group now."

I didn't feel like it was the right time to share that I really hated hot tubs.

"Shoot. I packed in such a rush, I didn't even bring a swimsuit."

"Doesn't matter. This place sells whatever you need. You can pick one up before dinner." He checked his watch. "I should give you some time to do that. Firm cocktails start in thirty minutes."

"Hey, Sam."

My whole body felt the sound of his voice saying my name.

I turned to see Charlie a few feet behind Leo's right shoulder.

I jumped up, feeling an immediate head rush. There was steam pouring from the space heater next to us. One side of Charlie's glasses was fogged over.

"Leo, this is Charlie Bronstein. My officemate."

Leo extended his hand. "Great to meet you, man. We don't make the LA associates share an office, but as busy as this one is, I imagine you have it to yourself a fair amount anyway."

"The officemate jackpot, as we first-years say," he responded with a polite handshake. I noticed he was about four inches taller than Leo.

Charlie feigned a hammer curl with his luggage. "Apologies—my flight was delayed, so I just got here. Saw you on the way up and figured I'd say hello," he said, looking directly at me.

"Hope they didn't give your room away," Leo said cheerfully.

"See you later, then," he said to me.

Leo watched Charlie walk away as he finished his drink.

"Seems like you two get along at least." He winked as he grabbed his sport coat. "Don't forget to pick up a swimsuit."

Chapter Thirty-Nine

Charlie had sent two text messages while I was at drinks with Leo, one letting me know his flight was delayed, and another asking if I could let the front desk know he was checking in late, because his cell reception was bad.

Hey, so sorry—just seeing these now, I hurriedly responded on my way back to the room.

I changed quickly and headed to the cocktail hour downstairs. The music was deafeningly loud. I scanned a welcome table with a thousand name tags to find mine. The ambience was thick with lawyers drinking away the social anxiety. Charlie hadn't responded.

Two proseccos and several stiff conversations later, I found my way to the formal dinner with assigned seating. Waiters passed by with bottles of red and white. I was starving, tipsy, and exhausted at the idea of spending at least another hour chatting with colleagues I didn't know.

"White, please," I answered with a polite smile. On these few hours of sleep, red would have been a sedative.

I looked up to see a woman awkwardly leaning in from a few seats over, noticeably trying to read my name tag.

"They should really make the letters bigger," she said uncomfortably.

“I’m Samantha, from the New York office,” I said, trying to sound approachable.

“Cathy, from Dallas.” She had the odd combination of a pleasant voice and an unfriendly expression.

“This is my first firm retreat.”

She screwed up her face. “This is my twelfth, if you can believe it.”

“Any tips?”

She held up her glass of wine. “Don’t be the drunkest, and don’t be the soberest.”

I leaned over and clinked my glass to hers. “I’ll try to remember that.”

I pretended to busy myself with carefully buttering my dinner roll as the rest of the table seemed to have rounded out with varying versions of Cathy. To my left was a retired partner who had trouble hearing but was still invited to the retreats.

It felt like there were over a hundred tables. I was envious of whoever was seated next to Charlie. The head partners for each office took turns addressing the room. I didn’t notice that my wine glass was never less than two-thirds full until I noticed the room was spinning.

“After-party, then hot tub. In that order.”

Leo’s arm was suddenly wrapped tightly around my shoulder, his face so close I could feel his breath on my skin.

“How did you find me in this labyrinth?” I asked nervously.

Don’t be the drunkest, don’t be the soberest.

Cathy had disappeared. Something told me she probably wasn’t ending the night in a hot tub with Leo Hirschman.

“When there’s a will, there’s a way. I figured I’d save you when I saw you were next to Anderson Salamander.”

“That was only rough because he couldn’t understand a word I said. Otherwise, he was surprisingly sweet.”

“There’s always a way to salvage the night. Follow me.”

I needed to find Charlie. And a bottle of water.

The "after-party" was a big room with makeshift bars, a strobe light, and a DJ. I was planted next to Leo, sipping water as he introduced me to other attorneys and made endless small talk. I promised myself I wouldn't get another drink.

"You look amazing in that dress, Sam. Hope it's okay for me to say that." He leaned over, turning to face me directly.

"Oh, thanks . . . It's just a dress. I've worn it to the office lots of times."

He looked amused by my discomfort.

"Listen, there's something big coming down the pipe. I think you'd be perfect for it. I'll be representing the biggest names in the business to acquire a specialty theater chain. They're gonna totally revamp the way people go to the movies. If I can hold out until the investigation is over, would you be up for it?"

I perked up. "You wouldn't joke about that, right?"

He laughed. "Thought you'd say yes."

I paused. "I just can't take on anything until the end of the month."

"Totally get it. I can do the ramp-up. We're still finalizing the engagement." He smiled and looked at me intently. "I'll wait for you."

I felt dizzy from the flashing lights. His attention somehow felt bolder. Was it just his marriage that had been holding him back? I wondered if they had separated and if I actually wanted to know.

"Be right back," I said quickly.

Before he could respond, I swung open a door to the patio, cold air hitting me like an IV. I'd left my coat inside.

"Wondered if I'd find you out here," Charlie said so quietly, I thought it was in my head.

"I've been looking for you," I said, hoping Leo hadn't followed me outside.

"Can we talk?" he asked.

"Yes."

"Are you upset with me?"

"Why would I be upset?"

"Because I bailed on New Year's."

I watched the air form smoke as I shivered.

"We didn't have to spend New Year's together. And I had to work anyway."

"You never even asked why I wasn't coming back."

"It wasn't my business."

I turned to face him. "Look, if you freaked out, that's okay. I get it. We both knew this was going to be impossible. You were just mature enough to do something about it."

His glasses were fogging up again. He took them off and shook his head impatiently. "Like I said, you *don't* know—"

"We meet again! Charlie, right?"

I watched Charlie watch Leo drape his arm around my shoulder.

Charlie nodded. "Hey, man. Good night?"

"Great night. Hate having this one all the way on the other coast though. Trying to get her to make a move out to LA," he said, his words slurring slightly.

"How's that going?" Charlie asked.

"Brought you a beer," Leo said to me cheerfully. I peered at Charlie.

Leo stepped back. "Holy shit, I'm a jackass. I totally interrupted something here, didn't I? My bad. I'll let you two get back to it."

Neither of us said anything.

He looked down at his watch. "Hot tub's at midnight. Feel free to come by too," he added unconvincingly, looking at Charlie.

"Sure thing."

Charlie looked at me sideways once Leo was inside.

"That's the partner you had a crush on?"

I took a sip of the beer. "He's important, professionally. But any crush is long gone. Totally evaporated."

"Doesn't look like he knows that."

"What do you mean?"

"Well, he put his arm around you, and you just stood there."

"What else was I supposed to do? Jump back and yell 'cooties'?"

"If you're not comfortable, you shouldn't just let it happen."

My eyes narrowed. "Well, next time you're a first-year associate in that position, let me know how you decide to handle it."

He looked hurt. "Look, I'm not trying to sound judgmental. I've been watching him cozy up to you for the last hour, and it's not a good look. I know how important your career is to you."

"You've been 'watching' me?"

"I mean, not like from a dark corner—but yeah, I was around enough to notice."

"I haven't asked for your opinion on any of this, you know."

"I'm only saying anything because I care. I fucking care a lot. Things have definitely felt weird over these last couple of weeks, and I hate that. I don't really know what to do."

I felt embarrassed about Charlie noticing Leo's attention. Was I *that* girl?

I wanted to tell him how much I'd missed him, how it was *his* attention I wanted. It was him. Not anyone else. Instead, I bit my lip. I didn't want to have this conversation when Leo could walk back out any second. "I can't do this. Not here," I said helplessly.

"We don't even know what 'this' is yet."

"Whatever it is, I'm not good for you." I took another sip of the beer, my lips almost sticking to the frozen glass bottle.

He looked exasperated. "Jesus, Sam. You're just so hell-bent on convincing yourself that you're not good for anyone that you're going to miss out on something you'll regret. I'm not even saying that's me. But I know all the arguments you make in your head. And I don't buy any of them. You can do all the things you want to do without getting hamstrung by some schmo. I'm not here to hold you back."

I took another sip against my better judgment. I couldn't find any words that seemed right. I could feel my eyes filling up.

"I think I'm falling in love with you," he said quietly.

My emotions had gone full tilt.

I stared at Charlie. Behind him, Leo was hovering inside.

I took a shaky breath. "Charlie. We can't do this here. Please understand that."

Charlie reached into his pocket and handed me a room key. "Will you come by later so we can talk?"

I nodded and slid the key into my pocket as I watched him go inside.

"Clock's ticking, little lady." Leo reappeared, holding my coat. I felt like I was being hunted.

"I just need to find the restroom."

I locked myself in the last stall and pulled out my phone.

Building B, Room 1601. I'll wait up.

I leaned my head against the tile wall, fighting the urge to lie down on the floor. All I needed was for Elinor to find me passed out the next morning.

I begrudgingly put on the one-piece swimsuit I'd bought earlier without trying on, pulling my dress over it.

I squeezed my eyes shut and felt hot tears soak my eyelashes. I splashed cold water on my face, trying to put on more concealer. The altitude had sucked all the moisture from my skin, making it impossible to blend. I looked like a member of Cirque du Soleil.

I wondered if Charlie had gone back to his room. The idea of him seeing me in a hot tub with Leo made my stomach hurt.

I just needed to participate and be done with it.

Minutes later, I planted myself awkwardly on the edge of the hot tub. It looked like Leo was holding court, and for a split second I wondered if he'd forgotten about me.

I turned around to grab the water bottle behind me.

"It's a bad idea," Leo said, hoisting himself up next to me.

"What is?"

"Getting involved with the person you share an office with."

I laughed nervously. "Not sure what you mean. We're just friends."

He traced figure eights in the bubbling water. "I've been around a long time. I know an office romance when I see one. And it's just not a good idea. People always find out, and somehow you get taken less seriously."

I wished I was drunk enough not to read between the lines.

"It's not what you think," I repeated halfheartedly.

There was no way he believed me.

"Look. You have a bright future here, Sam. Sky's-the-limit type of future. Just trust me. It's not worth it."

I took another sip of water to stall. I hated thinking he was partly right. Had I really gone scorched earth on my entire life just to throw it all away on an office romance?

We were interrupted by a fratty senior associate parading around a bucket of Bud Lights. Water splashed everywhere. Leo took a towel and delicately wiped water off my face. He passed me a Bud Light.

I was finally recreating the college experience I never had, stuck at a frat party with no exit in sight. I felt asphyxiated by the steam and drunker by the second. If I didn't focus on breathing in and out, I was going to pass out.

I tried thinking of coherent excuses to call it a night. All I kept thinking was if I left, he would know I was going to Charlie.

"Bar's closed," someone announced. A lifeline. I realized people were getting out of the hot tub, toweling off, trickling out.

"I should get some sleep," I mumbled to Leo, putting my dress on without bothering to dry my legs or feet. I scanned the ground for my heels, nearly falling backward into the hot tub as I tried putting them on.

"Whoa there, you okay?" Leo steadied me, his arm cradling my waist.

"I'll be fine."

He smiled. "C'mon, I'll help you back to your room. Elevator's this way."

I gripped my bag. Charlie's room was in the same building as mine. Once Leo dropped me off, I could wait a few minutes and then find Charlie.

We reached the elevator, and I untangled myself from Leo's arm, leaning against the wall to steady myself.

Before the doors closed, I looked up and saw Charlie.

Chapter Forty

"This isn't my building," I said as the elevator doors closed, a hint of panic in my voice.

Even drunk, I knew Leo was standing too close.

"You're not in any shape to find your way back. This place is a maze. You can post up in my room for a bit."

I felt Leo's hand firmly on my lower back as we walked the empty hallway to his room. I watched in slow motion as he opened the door to a spacious suite with a working fireplace and full bar. He sat me down on a couch and brought over a Gatorade. It still felt like a strobe light was spinning.

He placed the bottle in my hand. "Drink this, you'll feel better."

"Thank you. But I should get back . . . I have an early start tomorrow."

He turned to look at me. "Sam. We're the same. We get each other. I know you feel it too."

Before I could respond, his hands cupped both sides of my face and I felt his mouth on my mouth.

I sat very still, willing myself to react. The words *I shouldn't be here* kept repeating in my head.

He pulled back slightly, the wetness from his mouth turning into hot breath on my cheek. "Your husband was a real schmuck to let you go," he whispered.

His flippancy hit like a cold plunge. An electric shock pulsed across my brain as my whole body tensed.

I'd shared so much of my personal experience leaving Ben. There was no way Leo could have forgotten how emotionally devastating it had been. I had an overpowering desire to come to Ben's defense. Instead, I pulled my bag from the corner of the couch and tried to catch my breath.

"I have to go."

He looked confused. "I don't understand."

"You don't have to."

He went and stood in front of the door. "Do you even know where you're going?"

I nodded and squeezed past him, fumbling with the door handle. I felt myself begin to cry as soon as I got in the elevator.

"Are the shuttles still running?" I asked the concierge, slowly articulating each word.

He pointed outside. "There's the last one. You know which building you're in?"

"Building B."

"I'd hurry."

I walked as fast as I could without tripping. I just needed to get back to my room, change, and find Charlie.

~

The curtains were wide open when I woke up, and I was blinded by the sun's reflection against the wet, white snow. For a second, I forgot where I was.

I opened a blurry eye, sensorily disoriented. My leg was asleep. My throat was so dry I could barely swallow.

My hearing came back first. There was a dull vibration coming from the rug. I leaned over and saw the contents of my bag dumped on the floor next to the bed.

I sat up and awkwardly massaged my calf to get the blood flowing.

The rug buzzed again.

I was still in the swimsuit.

I rolled myself off the bed, nausea hitting immediately. I found my phone under my makeup bag. I had twenty-seven text messages and eleven missed calls, all from Elinor except for one from Leo.

I stared at the screen, wishing my brain was playing tricks on me. Another text message.

I unlocked my phone, an immediate rush of panic setting in as I scrolled up and read Elinor's messages, which went from bad to worse, ending with a threat I knew she would relish making good on.

Get back to me within the next five minutes or you're off the investigation.

She picked up on the first ring. "Meet me in the conference room on the third floor in fifteen minutes."

I dropped the phone and scrambled to get dressed. I'd never looked worse. My eyes were puffy, and mascara had reached my chin.

Fuck, fuck, fuck.

I moved at superhuman speed, walking into an empty conference room ten minutes later.

In the rush to make Elinor's deadline, I hadn't read Leo's message.

You get back OK? We were both pretty fucked up, huh?

I squinted as I tried to interpret the text. Was he giving *me* a pass, or himself?

Elinor walked in with an indecipherable expression. She sat down and silently set up her laptop and her notepad, arranging a pen neatly at the top of the pad. She was terrifying.

"Did you go back to Leo Hirschman's room last night?"

The blood drained from my face. "It's not what you think," I said, my heart pounding so loudly I was sure she could hear it.

Her eyes narrowed. "No? Because it looked exactly like what I thought."

"Nothing happened. I made the right choice."

She gave me an unsympathetic smile. "The right *choice*, Sam, would have been not to oversleep. I've been trying to reach you since eight a.m. You were made aware from the beginning that I needed to be able to reach you *at all times*. Retreat or no retreat." She paused to read something on her laptop. "I don't think you need me to tell you that going back to a partner's hotel room is not a good look."

"I know," I said faintly.

"You should probably think long and hard about the damage you've just done to yourself here. And you should also know that I'm considering making a report to the management committee."

A thousand tiny beads of sweat covered my face.

She pushed her chair back abruptly and folded her laptop. "I need the Wylie memo by three p.m. If you can't make that deadline, don't bother showing up to the office when we get back."

I took a deep breath and dropped my head on the table. I wanted to take a cold shower and grind 800 mg of Advil into a gallon of coconut water.

I wanted to find Charlie and explain everything.

I made the deadline for the Wylie memo, but my nerves were shot. I felt ashamed and regretful, angry at Leo for kissing me, angry at myself for letting it happen, for drinking too much, for being spineless and too weak to go after what I really wanted.

I kept seeing Charlie's face when I got into the elevator with Leo.

I needed to explain.

Can we talk? It's not what you think.

I moved miserably through the mandatory retreat sessions, willing Charlie to text me back. My phone was silent. No one texted or called for the rest of the day.

~

I landed at JFK Monday morning and went straight to the office. Charlie never responded.

Elinor assigned us two major sections of the report on an impossible deadline. I needed total focus and concentration, and I was incapable of either. I couldn't get back on autopilot.

I stopped at Hale & Hearty for a cup of soup when Andie called.

"Hey, busy lady. Are you as excited as me for Thursday? Do you know what you're wearing yet? Don't forget you have a plus-one."

All I could hear was LA traffic. "Thursday?"

"Okay, I guess you're not as excited as me for the *book launch*."

"Shit. I'm sorry . . . This investigation has taken over my life, and I'm not being hyperbolic. I barely even sleep."

"They better let you out for a couple hours on Thursday. You're a huge part of this."

"I'm cleared to go. Eddie sent the partner an email."

"Good. Did you get a dress?"

"Not yet. Maybe I can hide in a corner, order a few options to be overnighted."

"You'll pull it off. So who are you bringing?"

I tucked a water bottle under my arm. "Is it too late to give away my plus-one?"

"You do you. I'll let the PR person know, because there's definitely a waiting list. Oh, and I cannot *wait* for you to see the book cover. You're going to die."

"Me neither. I'm gonna lose you in the elevator."

I froze. I had one new email from Susan Klein in HR. The subject line was just "Meeting."

I stared at the phone as my chest started to pound. Elinor must have said something.

Was I about to be fired?

She wanted to know if I was free that afternoon. I got back to the conference room, sweating with dread. How the fuck had I allowed myself to get here?

At 4 p.m., I chucked the untouched soup and made my way down to the forty-fifth floor, trying to tell myself my life wasn't over, even if my career was.

I knocked lightly on Susan Klein's door, and she waved me in.

"Samantha, come in. I don't think we've seen each other since your first day last fall."

"That has to be a good thing, right?" I said with a nervous laugh.

"Please, sit. How have your first few months been?"

I cleared my throat. The small talk was physically painful. I just wanted a swift execution.

"They've been great. A few missteps here and there, but—"

I lost my train of thought as her assistant appeared in the doorway and handed her a folder. I felt lightheaded as she opened it.

"This is just a bit of housekeeping. We wanted to let you know that we'll be assigning you another officemate, now that Charlie Bronstein has taken a leave of absence."

I stared blankly, trying to force my brain to keep up. "A leave of absence?"

She looked surprised. "I assumed you knew, I'm sorry."

"I've been away . . . I mean, I've been working from a conference room with the team handling the senatorial investigation. We haven't seen much of each other."

"Right, of course. He's taken a formal leave of absence to deal with a family matter in Boston. We're hopeful he'll be back in short order, but in the meantime, we're sorting through the logistics."

My stomach hurt. "Do you know why?"

"His mother's cancer unfortunately relapsed. I'm sorry. I thought you knew."

I swallowed the lump in my throat. I had no idea his mother was sick.

I stood up and smoothed my skirt, willing myself not to cry. "I should probably head back to the conference room now," I said numbly.

I took solace in our empty office, staring at Charlie's empty desk. This must have been what he wanted to tell me in Montana. I wished I had taken his room key and crept into his bed that night instead of letting my insecurity ruin everything. We'd disintegrated so completely that I didn't even have the right to be there for him as he was going through something as awful as his mom being sick. Part of me hadn't really believed Montana was the last word until now.

The office still smelled like him.

A text popped up from Angela. Elinor's looking for you.

I blew my nose. Coming.

I switched off the light and locked the door.

Chapter Forty-One

The three dresses I had overnighted from Bloomingdale's for the book launch still hadn't arrived by Thursday.

"I'm so screwed," I whispered to Angela. "I have that thing tonight, and I have no idea where the shipment of dresses went."

"Check the tracking info," she suggested.

"Right," I said, rubbing my left eye with my knuckle. All this work was making me suck at real life. I should have just gone back to Rent the Runway.

"FedEx says it was delivered two days ago."

"Did you check your office?" she asked.

My eyes widened. I grabbed my lanyard and darted up the interior stairwell. If they weren't there, I was going to the book launch in a gray suit.

"You idiot," I muttered to myself as I opened the door to three packages stacked on top of my desk chair. I carried the plastic garment bags to the restroom, trying each one as quickly as I could. They were all too big, even though I had subsisted on the no-exercise, pizza-and-Chinese-food diet for the last month.

My phone buzzed with a calendar reminder. We had a scheduled meeting with the partners about the report in fifteen minutes. I folded up a black Helmut Lang dress with a subtle cinch in the waistline, dropped the others back in my office, and grabbed a pair of heels from under my desk.

Three hours later, I walked up Fifth Avenue to MoMA. Andie was greeting everyone as they arrived.

"You made it!" she squealed as I walked in and tried to hide my laptop bag under my coat.

"Oh my god, *check* those," she said, giving me a five-second hug.

She stood back and looked at me. "You're lucky you have that naturally fresh-faced look, Sam. Only I can tell how tired you are."

"I have all the energy I need," I said, genuinely excited for her.

"Okay, go mingle without your plus-one, you power woman."

I checked my coat and held onto my bag just in case I needed to crouch in a corner with my laptop. My world was two stark realities.

There were blowups of the book cover everywhere. She looked amazing. Not airbrushed in the slightest, just her vibrant, sharpest self. I felt a strong sense of pride.

I spotted George Brenner holding court with journalists and a *Vanity Fair* photographer. He caught my eye and waved me over.

"Everyone, this is Andie's defense lawyer and my script consultant for the movie," he said warmly as the photographer motioned for us to move closer so he could snap a photo.

I politely excused myself as more journalists gathered around George. I grabbed a glass of prosecco and walked past the cocktail tables, each one topped with a placard displaying a short excerpt from the book.

"Do we know each other?" a voice asked from behind my shoulder.

I turned around. Something about him was familiar.

"I don't think so," I said slowly. His face was friendly but striking, with high cheekbones and ever-so-slightly tinted designer glasses.

"Frank Trustman. Are you based in New York?" he asked.

I nodded. "Sam DeFiore. What about you?"

"Originally LA, but I live here now. Maybe we've seen each other around town. What do you do?"

"I'm a lawyer."

"Ah. And how do you know the author?"

"I'm her lawyer."

He scoffed. "No way."

"Why no way?"

"Like, her lawyer for the book deal? Or . . . the other stuff?"

I laughed. "The other stuff. My firm represented her in the indictment."

He smiled. "Wow, that's impressive. You guys must love that the book's going to be a movie."

I smiled. "As long as she's happy, I'm happy. Are you in publishing?"

"Film and television. I'm a director."

"Would I have seen any of your work?"

"I've done a few small films. But I just finished a big HBO limited series that's coming out next month. Good reviews so far."

I suddenly realized I *had* seen him before.

"Did you go to the opening for that new gallery on Melrose a few months ago?" I asked.

He grinned. "*That's* where I know you from. You were there with Leo Hirschman. That guy is fire. I have friends who've used him for things here and there. A real shark."

"He's definitely got that reputation going for him."

I wondered if my world and Leo's world would ever coexist again.

Just then, Andie's literary agent, a striking blond woman with a warmth that contrasted her reputation for being the bloodiest negotiator in publishing, tapped her champagne glass behind a podium to quiet the room. After saying a few words about Andie's commitment to telling her story honestly and how proud she was to represent a book filled with grit and high stakes ("pun intended") and all the things good stories are made of, she motioned for Andie to come up.

"The first signed copy will be on your desk," Andie assured her as the room laughed.

Andie cleared her throat, and I could tell she was nervous. "I'm not used to being the center of attention for a positive reason," she started. "But the truth is that much of this story is a sad story. I talk a lot about addiction, not just to substance, but to power and money. I wanted to be the best, but more than anything, I wanted to be more powerful than every man sitting at those tables. That was the addiction that led to my downfall. I climbed my way back in many ways, and much of it is because of four people, three of whom are in this room today."

She looked at George and then over to me.

"One of my defense attorneys, Eddie Kaufman, couldn't be here tonight. He's busy saving another lost soul. But my other attorney, Samantha, is here. When I met Sam, I quickly realized how smart she was, but what I didn't know at the time was that she would become a true friend. Someone I trust implicitly, and not just as a lawyer. The kind of person who proves that you can be successful and still have integrity."

Frank leaned over and touched the back of my arm. "I'd love to hear more about what it was like working with her sometime."

The touch of his hand made me miss Charlie.

"I'll give you my card," I whispered back.

He looked amused. "Just in case I ever need your services?"

"You never know."

"All right then, I'll take a card."

When Andie finished her speech, Frank held out his hand. "Really nice chatting, Samantha."

"Sam."

He held up the card. "Hope to do it again soon."

~

The launch party was the last moment of respite from the investigation for the next two weeks. I woke up every morning with a dull headache, exhausted from pushing aside everything except what was necessary to stay afloat. We were working fifteen-hour days to finish the report on time. I got home after 2 a.m. and still couldn't fall asleep. If I wasn't working, my mind was on Charlie, wondering how he was and how his mom was.

By the last day of the investigation, I felt like a shell of a human. I sat motionless in the conference room until five o'clock when the last IT person carted away my monitor and keyboard.

I didn't know where to go or what to do. Emilie was presumably still in London and hadn't responded to any of my texts. Caroline's head would explode if I told her what had happened with Leo in Montana. Connor was spending the month working remotely from Edinburgh.

I'd never felt more alone.

I stuffed my laptop in my bag, swapped my heels for flats, and just started walking.

Half an hour later, I wandered into a small wine bar in Hell's Kitchen, a neighborhood too far west to run into anyone I knew from work.

I settled onto a stool at the back corner of the bar, hooking my bag underneath.

"Happy Friday! You looking for wines by the glass? Maybe a menu?"

The bartender's chipper demeanor clashed with his black nail polish, heavily tattooed arms, and spacer earrings.

"What kind of bottles do you have on special?"

"I've got this great French blend. Want to try it first?"

"That's okay. I'll just take a bottle of that."

He set down two wine glasses.

"It's just me," I said, sounding as miserable as I felt.

He poured a sip into the glass in front of me.

"I don't need to taste it. I trust you."

"Understood." He gave a generous pour. "I'm Pete. If you need anything, just holler."

Something about him made me miss Virginia in a way I never had.

For the first time in over a month, no one cared where I was. I could let myself spiral. I could become one of those first-year associates who crumbles under the stress of the job. Maybe they'd write about me on the soapy legal-gossip blog *Above the Law*.

"Sparkling or tap? Maybe something to eat? We make a mean romesco and mozzarella panini," Pete offered, momentarily rescuing me from my internal free fall.

"Can I stay if I don't order food?"

"Of course. Just figured you might need a little sustenance."

"That would be the mature thing to do."

"What type of reading you got there?"

I'd set an old issue of *The Hollywood Reporter* next to me. My casual companion whenever I was falling apart. "Just a trade publication. Movie stuff."

He looked interested. "Do you work in movies?"

"Not really. Kind of. I'm a lawyer."

"Movie lawyer?"

"Sort of."

"No way. You ever meet anyone famous?"

I shook my head. "Where are you from? Your accent reminds me of where I grew up."

"Just outside of New Orleans. How about you?"

"Virginia."

"A Southern gal in the city! I dig it."

"How'd you end up in New York?" I asked. I genuinely missed the art of conversation. Especially without Charlie.

"I'm a playwright. Well, I'm trying to be. I studied theater at Tulane, then worked as a bartender in the French Quarter. I became something of a local celebrity there, and the owner of this bar poached me. Convinced me I'd make more money in Manhattan and be closer to the theater action."

"How'd you become a local celebrity?"

"You'll laugh."

"I promise not to."

"I got pretty famous for my pisco sour, and the Food Network did a segment on me for *Bartender Battles*."

"That's amazing. Can you make one here?"

"We're mostly a wine bar, but I keep all the ingredients handy in case anyone recognizes me." He winked.

"Now I can say I've met someone famous. Can you make me one?"

"If you let me put in a panini. Not to overstep, but you're a wispy little thing."

I laughed. "Okay. One panini, please."

I learned that Pete was working on a revival of *The Three Musketeers*, only with two women and a transgender D'Artagnan. It was up for a slot at the prestigious St. Ann's Warehouse in Brooklyn, a feeder for shows that eventually swept the Tonys.

"Now you know everything there is to know about me. How come you're here talking to me on a blustery Friday afternoon?"

"Isn't that what New York is all about? Popping into a bar by yourself and meeting a celebrity bartender on his way to becoming the next big playwright?"

"Sure. You just seemed on a mission there with that bottle of wine."

"You're not wrong."

I watched him chop lemon wedges as I mentally replayed everything that had brought me to Pete's bar.

Reliving the last time I'd seen Charlie made my chest hurt.

"I hurt someone," I said quietly.

"Did they deserve it?"

"No. Not even a little bit."

"Did you apologize?"

"I didn't get a chance to. He moved to help take care of his mom. Who has cancer."

Pete winced. "You hurt the guy who moved home to take care of his sick mom?"

"Yeah. It's unforgivable."

"Can you make some sort of grand gesture to make things right? Maybe show up with flowers?"

"I had a chance to make things right, and I blew it. I'm pretty sure the last thing he wants is me showing up with flowers."

"Bet you're wrong about that."

"I don't think so."

I told Pete about Ben and Charlie and Leo, and all the alcohol in between.

"You know—I've been sober three years this March. The sauce can really mess things up. I don't know if that's the path you need to be on, but I've yet to meet someone who can say alcohol makes their relationships stronger."

"A sober bartender?"

"There's more of us than you think." He pulled up the sleeve of his black V-neck T-shirt. "Serenity prayer. I got it after my wife left me."

I turned to look at his face more closely. "How old are you?"

"Thirty-five. Why?"

"You just look young to have been married."

He chuckled. "Not by Louisiana standards. Or Virginia, I'm guessing."

"Touché."

He nodded to the empty cocktail glass. "I feel like I was doing a pretty good job getting you back on track, but . . . do you want one more?"

I smiled sadly. "Actually, I think I'll stop while I'm ahead. And I don't think that's the way the night would have ended if it wasn't for you." I slid my credit card across the bar. "Thank you. Really."

"Was it the tattoo?"

I laughed. "Maybe? My arms aren't as muscular. I'd look ridiculous."

He grinned. "Whatever it takes."

I sighed. "I was hoping this dull pain in my chest would've gone away by now."

"Sometimes alcohol helps. When it doesn't—that's worth paying attention to." He nodded encouragingly. "If you two figure things out, bring him by sometime. I'd love to meet him."

Chapter Forty-Two

I went home and stayed in bed for two days, watching old episodes of *The West Wing* on my laptop. I felt empty.

I spent February as close to a hermit as someone living in New York could be. Emilie had texted that she was staying in London, "maybe for just a month, maybe forever," but she finally promised to FaceTime me when she was ready to talk. Connor and Gillian were spending weekends at a rental upstate. Caroline was the only person I saw consistently. She knocked on my door every Saturday morning and faithfully dragged me out for a frigid walk through the farmers market.

It was late February when I reached the episode where Josh throws snowballs at Donna's window. When she finally comes down, he gives her his jacket and tells her with the sincerest look on his face, "You look amazing."

It was snowing. I'd left the window open, and the prewar radiator was working overtime. My unmade bed was the only reasonably warm spot. There were unwashed mugs with old tea bags everywhere and used Kleenexes next to dying plants. I was unapologetically leaning into the cliché fog of heartbreak. I hadn't allowed myself to drink since the night I met Pete, the sober bartender.

I paused the episode and stared at Bradley Whitford's earnest face. Without thinking, I pulled my phone out from under the pillows.

I wish I'd had the guts to send this so much sooner, but I didn't know if you wanted to hear from me. I still don't know if you do. But I need you to know that I am sorry. For everything. I wonder constantly how your mom is doing, and if you're okay.

I sent it and waited for my heart rate to slow back to normal. I knew there was a chance he would never respond, and the idea of "us" would keep fading. There would be other people in our lives. But I needed him to know, even if it was just this once.

I was falling in love with you too.

~

I was in bed reading when Andie called. We hadn't seen each other since the sentencing hearing last month, the week after the book launch. The sentencing had gone off with much less fanfare than when she pleaded guilty. She stood bravely between us as the judge delivered the sentence, grabbing my hand tightly at the very last minute. In what felt like a storybook ending to the first case of my legal career, the judge sentenced her to one thousand hours of community service. Eddie let out an uncharacteristic whoop. She wasn't going to prison.

"*They. Green-lit. The. Movie,*" she punctuated breathlessly through the phone the second I picked up.

I sat up straighter, propping the pillows behind me. "You're kidding. He finished the script?"

"Yes. And it's brilliant. The dialogue he wrote for Eddie's character is pure magic. I couldn't put it down."

I smiled into the phone. "What happens now?"

"We're making a movie!" I could hear her jumping up and down.

"Holy shit. You wrote the book that's becoming George Brenner's next movie."

"*We* did it. I'm able to be in New York this weekend to celebrate because of you and Eddie. You better be free tomorrow night."

"You're here this weekend?"

"I'm at the Soho House. Leah got me a room."

"Wow. Where's dinner?"

"Right here. I'm afraid if I leave, they won't let me back in."

"Ha. That's like ten minutes from my apartment, so that works for me. I don't travel well these days."

"Dinner tomorrow at seven then," she said and hung up.

I sank back down under the covers, uneasy at the idea of being out in the world.

But by morning, something had shifted. For the first time since the investigation began, I woke up feeling a spark of energy. I had plans.

Before heading downstairs to meet Caroline, I flipped through my closet, hunting for something that seemed appropriate for dinner at the Soho House.

I was searching for my keys under a pile of unread mail when Caroline texted to say she'd gone on a "pretty good" date the night before and wasn't going to be back in time for our farmers market run.

I sighed. I was out of coffee, and while I was finally giving my liver a break, my caffeine addiction had me in a death grip.

I walked to the coffee shop on Jane Street and ordered my usual latte to go, unbuttoning the top few buttons of my coat and loosening my scarf. When had it started to feel like spring?

While waiting for my latte, I checked my emails and was surprised to see an email from Frank Trustman, asking if we could have lunch that week to discuss a thought he had.

"Dinner and a lunch, *who are you*," I muttered to myself.

I walked down to Sandro on Bleecker and found a simple black jumpsuit with lightly ruffled sleeves and lace across the front.

I emailed Frank back as I waited to check out. Are you free Wednesday?

~

Later that night, I walked up Ninth Avenue, passing the door to the Soho House twice before my eye finally caught the covert placard.

"Name," a woman with a blond bob said flatly.

"Samantha DeFiore. I'm a guest of Andie Reese," I added, my neck immediately taxed from trying to make eye contact. She barely glanced at the list as she waved me into the tiny elevator behind her.

The doors opened to a dimly lit restaurant. I spotted Andie right away, reading something on her phone. She looked relaxed, as if we were two old friends just meeting up for dinner.

"I know you," she said, pitching her readers onto the table and giving me a tight hug. "You're the woman from that *New York Post* headline."

"Most cringeworthy headline ever. Even for the *Post*."

"You gave me my freedom, and I made you an indicted celebrity."

"Something like that." I grinned. "It's really good to see you. You look happy," I said honestly.

"No joke, I'm living the most vanilla chapter of my life, and I've never been happier."

I laughed. "Vanilla. With every actress in Hollywood trying to play you."

She sighed. "Exactly. I'm getting a second chance. Thanks to you and Eddie. And George."

"Did you tell Eddie about the movie getting green-lit?"

"Oh yeah. It was like telling my dad I invested in some annuity bonds that performed well. 'Andie, well done. You've been making excellent choices lately.'"

"That's a scary good impression."

"I know. Should I play myself?"

She handed me the wine list. "I don't want to be a buzzkill, but I'm not drinking. You, however, should order the most expensive Bordeaux in Eddie's honor."

I smiled. "He loves a good Bordeaux." I set the wine list down. The room felt unexpectedly private, with plush sofas and coffee tables separating dining tables. "I haven't had a drink since January. Seems we're in for a reasonable tab."

"There's a forty-five-dollar burger on the menu."

"Very reasonable. Why aren't you drinking? Did you have a bad bottle of 1942?"

"There are no bad bottles of 1942." She stretched the linen napkin across her lap. "I just wanted a little clarity. After the come-down of it all."

"I'm right there with you. We're living oddly parallel lives."

It was what I'd felt from the beginning.

She smiled. "Except you were the one saving me instead of needing to be saved. Saint Samantha."

I sank back into the velvet chair. "There's nothing saintly about what I do. It's not like I gave up everything to work for Legal Aid or become a public defender."

Andie shot me a sideways glance. "I never had a safety net until I met you and Eddie. You guys made me feel like there was more to me than just some person accused of breaking the law. Maybe you don't see yourself the way that I do, but I'm so grateful Eddie chose you out of every other associate who would have killed to work on this."

I pursed my lips. "You know he called me the 'deadpan' girl?"

"What does that even mean?"

"He said I struck him as someone who could deadpan salacious details."

"I weirdly know exactly what he meant."

She poured Pellegrino into my glass. "You're not just a good lawyer, Sam. You have layers. And believe me, they're going to trip you up sometimes. But they're also going to keep moving you forward."

I smiled faintly at the memory of waking up to Eddie's call the night after the Lincoln Center gala, tired and hungover, but happy. All my dreams coming true.

"Could you tell I was hungover the first morning we met?"

"Nope. I just remember how focused and eager you seemed."

"I didn't even know about the meeting until that morning. I'd gone to this charity gala the night before. My officemate, Charlie, came with me. We had a blast. I went to bed feeling like I was walking on air. And then I woke up to Eddie calling me at 7:30, and I had to pull it together." I chuckled. "And here we are."

"I always had a feeling there was something with Charlie. Just from the way you talked about him."

My eyes landed on the wine list, and I wished for something to take the edge off. "There was. Not anymore, but yeah."

I told her everything, starting with the gala and ending with Charlie leaving New York. My messages to him that had gone unanswered.

"I've basically been a recluse for the last month with nothing but time to think about how much I fucked things up. I don't even feel like I love my job anymore."

She looked at me squarely. "I'm sure it's gotten you this far, but have you ever thought about not being so hard on yourself?"

"Nope."

She sighed and rested the tip of her tongue against her upper lip.

"Look—I know how important your career is to you, but you're putting the same unrealistic expectations on a job as other people put on a relationship. There are going to be ups and downs. It's the commitment to it being more good than bad that makes it worthwhile."

"I know. But I can't stop thinking that I'm doing it all out of order. I'm out there in the ocean, but I never learned how to swim."

"That's the flaw in your solution. Progress doesn't have to be linear. There's no order of life experience to check off."

She squeezed my hand. "I know you think it's easier to cut off everything except your ambition. But you should stop that. Now that you're here, *doing this*, it's time to own your life—including your excuses—and cut yourself some slack. Figure out what balance looks like. You're a human being. Lean into it. Your own personal soft launch."

She sat back proudly. "I nailed it, didn't I?"

I smiled self-consciously. "They should really teach more practical attorney-client boundaries in law school. Rule number one: Your client is not your therapist."

"I'm not your client anymore."

"Thank God."

She handed me a glass of water. "So. What's it been like without my frantic calls?"

Chapter Forty-Three

"Do you like oysters?" Frank asked.

I nodded as he signaled to the waiter. "We'll do a dozen oysters. Preferably East Coast."

He winked at me. "Less salty."

When Frank suggested we meet for lunch at Jeffrey's Grocery, a restaurant known for oysters and Bloody Marys, I wasn't sure if it was supposed to be a business lunch or something else. Whatever his agenda, I was hoping to flex my client-development muscles.

He smiled. "My girlfriend loves this spot. She turned me onto it."

"What does your girlfriend do?" I asked.

"She does marketing for wellness companies."

"Ah. So you're dating outside the industry."

He smirked. "My last girlfriend was an actress. She was gunpowder in human form. Broke my heart into a million pieces."

"I'm sorry. But it sounds like you rebounded?"

"Eventually. It took three years. I couldn't sit still. Spent a year in India. Six months in Dubai. Then São Paolo, Santiago, and Mexico City before I felt like I was whole enough to come back."

"Holy shit. That's an amazing lineup, though."

"I met Sarah the first weekend I was back in the city. She was standing outside of Equinox pushing some hot yoga/mind meld thing. That was almost a year ago."

"I always wondered how real people meet other real people."

"I have a no-actress rule now." He glanced down at the menu. "Was this place out of the way for you? I didn't think to ask where you live."

"I'm on Perry Street, so very convenient."

"Nice. I'm in Tribeca."

The waiter returned with a platter of oysters.

"Your email mentioned you had a 'thought' after we met at the book launch," I said, my curiosity getting the best of me. Especially after he mentioned his girlfriend almost as soon as we sat down.

"Right."

He pulled a stack of papers out of a messenger bag on the floor. "This is my contract for a movie I was supposed to direct until I had a disagreement with the producers over casting, and the studio kicked me off the project."

I looked at the first page of the director's agreement.

"They were going to pay you $5 million to direct?" I asked.

"It's a big-budget movie."

"And they fired you?"

"And now I want to sue for wrongful termination."

"What was the disagreement about?"

"I wanted to rewrite the male lead as a woman. They didn't."

"Yikes. I'm assuming that's not something they'd want out there."

"That's why I'm bringing this to you."

I chuckled. "You know I'm just an associate, right? It's still my first year at the firm."

He grinned. "Yeah, but you work with Leo Hirschman."

"I have in the past."

"Anyway, I liked what Andie Reese said about you at the book thing. You seem smart. I'm not asking for any favors. I can afford you guys—I just thought maybe this could be a win-win type of thing. You bring me in as a client, get Leo to work with you on it, and we scare the shit out of these motherfuckers."

I hadn't heard from Leo since the retreat. He never followed up about the big transactional matter he'd teased in Montana.

I wondered if bringing in Frank as a client could level the playing field. I still wanted to work with Leo, but I was long past wanting more than a professional relationship.

I handed him back the director's agreement. "I probably shouldn't look at that until the firm clears conflicts. But this does feel right up Leo's alley. I can reach out to him."

"Terrific."

I felt a spark for work that had been missing since the investigation broke me down, and the retreat left a bitter taste in my mouth. I was pretty sure Elinor hadn't talked to anyone about what happened, but I needed to find a way to mentally move on.

Frank headed back to Tribeca, and I took the subway to Forty-Second Street. HR still hadn't replaced Charlie, and I felt his presence every time I walked into our empty office. I put on a Bob Dylan playlist while I looked up a federal statute Eddie had asked me to research.

My phone lit up with a FaceTime call.

I melted down as soon as his face appeared.

~

"Wow, wow—you okay?"

After how badly Ben and I had left things, his expression reflected genuine concern. I cried harder. I propped the phone against the monitor and covered my eyes with a Kleenex.

I took a shaky breath. "You just caught me off guard, I guess."

He gave a sympathetic smile. "Well, whatever's going on, I promise I'm not here to make you feel worse. I'm buying a car, and your name's still on the title for the old one. I just need you to notarize the bill of sale so I can trade it in."

The idea of Ben FaceTiming for such a mundane reason almost made me laugh.

"Sure. Just email me whatever you need . . . I can print it and scan the signed copy back to you," I said, wiping my nose and wishing I kept a box of tissues in the office.

"Cool, thanks." He hesitated. "Seriously, though—are you okay?"

I ducked. "What kind of car are you trading the Honda in for?"

"Mercedes. Convertible."

"Oh, wow. Trading up."

"Well, I sold *Baby Divorce* for six figures."

"You're joking."

"Yes, I'm joking."

"Not that there isn't a market for it," I added.

"I'm sure there is. But it won't be me writing it. I burned all the chapters. My therapist's two-hundred-and-fifty-dollar advice."

"That sounds . . . cathartic."

"It was. Although I did it on the balcony of my apartment, and my neighbor called the fire department, which was awkward. And I got a pretty hefty fine."

"Shit. That sucks. I guess I should feel partially responsible."

"Nah, it's okay. Turns out my neighbor is a cute girl who's also going through a divorce. And we're kind of dating now. So not the worst outcome."

"Oh, wow."

Was I lucid dreaming?

"Are you really seeing a therapist?" I asked.

He nodded. "And I know what you're gonna say."

"You never believed in therapy."

"I didn't used to. Then my wife left me and stomped on my heart. Twice."

I never realized how impossible it is *not* to make eye contact on FaceTime.

"I deserve that."

He paused, looking deep in thought. "Honestly Sam, before I saw you in New York last year, I would've done anything to get you back. I couldn't understand why you left. It didn't feel real. Maybe my head was up my ass the whole time, but I just didn't see it coming."

"And then I saw you in New York, and you were so confident . . . You'd blossomed right into that woman sitting across from me at that restaurant. And even though I really wanted to go home with you that night, I finally started to get why you left. New York, and this career you went after—it all looked good on you. But it also hurt because I finally realized you were never coming back. And it was like losing you all over again."

I felt a tear roll down my cheek. Maybe this new life *looked* good on me, but I didn't know if I'd ever feel like I really deserved it.

"I never wanted to hurt you. And this new life might look like it fits . . . but I don't think I know how to be happy. Or if I even deserve happiness after everything I put you through."

He shook his head. "It still fucking hurts. Especially after that night in New York. I needed space. But I'm trying to be happy."

I stared down at Park Avenue. "I didn't deserve you."

He smiled grimly. "Well—maybe that's true."

I felt the muscles in my face relax slightly. "I know it doesn't look like it, but I feel happier than before you FaceTime-bombed me."

He laughed. "I'm glad you picked up. Now sign that thing so I can lock down the Benz."

Chapter Forty-Four

I hung up with Ben and walked dazedly toward the elevator to the lobby, then down the escalator of the MetLife Building to Grand Central Terminal. For the first time since I started working at Abramson & Klein, I took a second to look up at the constellations magnificently etched in the ceiling.

I walked slowly down to Joe's. I paid for my coffee and ambled back through Grand Central. I climbed halfway up the stairs to the East Balcony and sat down on the side rail.

I stared down at the incoming FaceTime in my call history. Six minutes and twenty-two seconds.

I didn't feel like Sam the divorcée or Sam the aspiring lawyer. I was just me.

I stood up and put in my right earbud as I called Leo's office from my cell phone.

"Hi, Adele. It's Samantha DeFiore. Is Leo available?"

"Let me see if I have him."

I jogged down the stairs back to the concourse and spiritedly tossed the empty cup of coffee into a bin.

"Sam. How the hell are you?"

I raised my voice over the hubbub of Grand Central. "Never better. How've you been?"

I thought I heard the sound of kids playing in the background. "Uh, you know. Just okay, actually. One of our twins was diagnosed with a pretty severe learning disability, so I've been working from home quite a bit."

I paused. "I'm sorry to hear that."

He said he and Jessica were working on their marriage. He asked how life was, post-investigation. I admitted to only billing two weeks of work in February.

"I'm calling because I want to bring in a new client, and I'd like you to be the partner on the matter." I gave him the rundown. Who he was, why he wanted us to represent him.

He chuckled. "Sounds like the firm is going to have to let your low February billables slide now that you're a rainmaker."

"And I billed almost four hundred hours since December. Is that a yes?"

"It sounds like the kind of thing we should be involved in. I'm not shy when it comes to taking down studios. And I'm vaguely familiar with Frank's work. It seems like he's got a great career ahead of him. Is he based in New York or LA?"

"New York."

"Great. You can handle client relations then."

"There's just one more thing." I paused, taking a deep breath. "After Montana, I was scared that you would never staff me on another case. I felt like *I* had done something wrong."

I could hear him start to say something, so I spoke louder. "Please, let me finish. I don't want to revisit what happened, and I'm sure you don't either. I still want to work together, because there's a lot I can learn from you, and I have a lot of respect for you as a lawyer. But I need to know that you have respect for me as a colleague."

"Sam. I overstepped. Big time." His voice sounded small. "I was going through a lot of personal turmoil. You know that. But it's not an excuse for putting you in that position."

I physically bit my tongue, not allowing myself to say anything that would give him an out. I knew he was intelligent enough to read between the lines.

"It won't happen again."

"Thank you," I said graciously. "Then I'll run a conflicts check today and prep the engagement letter."

~

I slept in on Saturday and woke up just in time to meet Caroline after her morning spin class. As I walked to the farmers market, I remembered a podcast episode that Eddie asked me to listen to as background for a potential new client. I reached into my bag and dug around for my earbuds.

"*Excuse* me," I heard as someone impatiently passed by me.

"Sorry," I muttered, absentmindedly leaning my shoulder against the window of Cafe Cluny. I swore I'd thrown earbuds in my bag earlier that week.

That's when I saw him.

I stood there without moving, like the window was a one-way mirror, as if I was just as invisible as he was suddenly physically *there*, in my universe, back in the city. Having brunch down the street.

He was sitting with a woman. Her back was to the window, and all I could see was long brown hair and a red turtleneck sweater.

He was back in New York. He didn't need to let me know, because I wasn't in his life. Not in the way that he'd tell me when he was back in town. Not in any way.

I felt like someone had punched me.

I probably would have stood there forever, staring at his face, watching him sip coffee from a cappuccino cup with small red letters, spreading butter and too much jam on a croissant—if he hadn't seen me. I could see his lips moving as the woman turned around and looked straight at me.

I realized it was Perry.

I don't know what I expected either of them to do, but she suddenly began waving excitedly in my direction. I dropped the earbuds on the sidewalk and bent down to pick them up. When I stood up again, I could tell she was waving me into the restaurant.

I stiffened as I tried to figure out what to do. *Maybe she'll soften the blow of seeing each other for the first time.* I didn't have any idea if Perry even knew what had happened between us.

The doorknob jingled as I slowly opened the door.

"I'm just saying hello to some friends," I said to the hostess as I walked toward them.

Perry jumped up, wrapping me in a hug before she was fully upright. "Sam! I can't believe it. I convinced Charlie to meet me in the West Village, and he joked that we might run into you. And here you are!"

"It's a small neighborhood," I said nervously. "Hey, Charlie."

"Hey, Sam," he said coolly. His face gave nothing away.

Perry took a sip of coffee. "We're celebrating his new job at the Urban Justice Center. Every time I say the name, I feel like a better person."

I tried to look like my heart wasn't pounding. "You're finally doing it," I said.

He nodded. "I couldn't just keep putting in time. Life's too short."

Perry looked at her watch and jumped up. "I was *just* saying how guilty I feel, because I'm supposed to meet the girls at Five Iron—you remember the golf girls, Sam—and Charlie can't come because it's ladies only. I'm already super late."

She looked at him triumphantly. He shrugged and gave her a big brother smile.

"I'll get this. Have fun. Maybe I'll meet up with you guys later tonight."

"You better."

She grinned as she put on her coat, then looked directly at me. "We'll be at Scallywag's."

He carefully folded his napkin as I floated hesitantly next to the table for what felt like minutes, unsure if I should stay or go.

He looked up at me. His eyes held mine as I watched them change colors. I held my breath for as long as I could stand it.

"I was gonna have one more cup of coffee. Do you want to sit down?" he finally asked.

"Yes."

I let myself breathe out as I melted into the chair.

About the Author

Sarah Vacchiano is an entertainment lawyer based in Los Angeles. A graduate of Duke Law School, she began her legal career as a litigator representing Molly Bloom—the subject of the Oscar-nominated biopic *Molly's Game*, written and directed by Aaron Sorkin—and other high-profile clients in the media and entertainment space.

Sarah has served as an adjunct professor of entertainment law at Duke and is a frequent guest lecturer for NYU's Tisch School of the Arts and Stern School of Business. She lives in Los Angeles with her husband Matt, their son Gus, and pup Josephine (JoJo). *Soft Launch* is her first novel.